THE TIME WARRIORS

FIRST FOOTSTEPS

Owen Quinn

Copyright © 2010 Owen Quinn

All rights reserved.

DEDICATION

For my Dad, out there among the stars.

CONTENTS

Acknowledgments	I
First Footsteps	1
Return To Eden	12
Tombs Of Ether Part 1	46
Tombs Of Ether Part 2	70
Experiment Four Part 1	91
Experiment Four Part 2	123
The Infinity Web Part 1	153
The Infinity Web Part 2	191
Legacy	225

ACKNOWLEDGMENTS

Welcome to my dream come true, the culmination of a hard, long road with plenty of bumps along the way.
This is also my chance to thank everyone who has supported me along the way.
Bradley Wind for the brilliant cover and wait until you see the next three he's done. Find him on Facebook or Authonomy and throw some business his way.
Bill Jeffrey, my agent, who saw the potential right away and signed me to his books. Also Gerry McCullough, Mark McCann, Wayne Simmons and Frank Quigley for their support, good luck with your endeavours.
My father in law, John for designing the covers you'll never see and my mother in law Margaret for her good taste.
My Time Warriors groupies, Elaine, Freda, Mary, Patricia, Suzie, Chrissi, Joyce, Jay, Darragh, Bernie, Claire, Kylie, Barbara, Ann, Eilish and all the others including Sean Leargy who have been waiting for this for a while.
Followingthenerd for their support, Marc and Paddy, find them on Facebook.
My cousins who are too numerous to mention but hello, Louise, Adele, Catherine, Eddie and Liz. My family tree would make a book on its own.

My late grandmothers, Maisie and Elizabeth, for their love and wisdom growing up. Hugh Kennedy for his printers when times were hard. My English teacher Pat Mooney, who saw in me what I didn't and my primary school teacher Mrs McGuinness who was as insightful as Pat.

My family, my mum Josie who has always been there for me, my brothers and sisters, sister in law Tracey, who just wants a holiday in St. Tropez and my nieces and nephews who think Uncle Owen's famous. (Not yet kids!)

Barry Grant for his computer genius, without whom this would not have been possible and Jacqui for her feedback and good taste.

And last but not least, my beautiful wife Christine for her patience and honesty. She is my rock and my star. My son, Eoin, who wants to write stories about Bigfoot, in between wanting to be a doctor and birdwatching.

Thank you all for your belief and conviction. Welcome aboard.

FOREWORD

Welcome to my dream come true, the very first book about the Time Warriors.

So, what can you expect from this? What are my intentions?

Well, the Time Warriors actually began back when I was 16 when I hand wrote their debut adventure, Wail of the Banshee.

So where is that book, you may wonder. Well, to be honest, the 16 year old me's version of the Time Warriors is slightly different to the version you are holding in your hands now, and was put on hold by life until my Dad died of a brain tumour 6 years ago when I decided the book, which had been burning away in the back of my head for all those years, had to be written and fulfil a few dreams.

The problem was, I began the Wail of the Banshee, the first chapter of which can be read in the news section of my website www.thetimewarriors.co.uk, I suddenly found that although I knew Jacke, Varran, Michael and Tyran, I didn't KNOW them and couldn't go any further.

Who were they really? What paths was I going to send them on? How would they react to what I was going to throw them into?

OWEN QUINN

So, I began to devise what was essentially their first year of adventures. Following the examples of Doctor Who, Buffy and most series these days, I set them in a series of adventures, each separate but building on the previous one where their actions would force them to grow as people and characters and aliens would return from time to time. Threads would run through all the stories, all edging towards the series climax Tempest.

The Xereban belief system is everything happens for a reason and that is the structure these 4 books have been written to.

16 adventures, separate but connected, all heading towards a series finale in book 4.

This is the Time Warriors as their first TV series would be.

And do you know what? I knew them all by the end of it. And the journey was as much a learning curve for me as I found they all took themselves into new directions, places I hadn't envisioned for them as each story unfolded.

Now I know where they begin in Banshee so that story can be finished- their true origin story. Well, it worked for Wolverine didn't it?

In the meantime, enjoy the first set of adventures. Seeds will be planted that you won't see until the next book when they face the might of the Voalox Horror and the real danger begins. And even then, you haven't seen anything yet.

All I will say is, the most dangerous enemy is the one you know nothing about, everything happens for a reason and don't forget the bigger picture.

Please visit www.thetimewarriors.co.uk and let me know what you think or post on the Time Warriors fanpage on Facebook. See you soon!

PROLOGUE: FIRST FOOTSTEPS

Space was ablaze with hellish brilliance as the death throes of a billion voices choked in flame.

Orange, blue, red and green lightning danced like a kaleidoscope opera across the land as the planet's atmosphere began to evaporate. Time held its breath as within minutes an eternity of evolution died in the molten oceans that surged up from beneath the surface in great unfeeling geysers, devouring everything.

The planet was breaking up, black infernos blasting glacial chunks into space in halos of fire, whole continents shimmering into ash beneath the onslaught.

The stars were trembling in horror as already, bubbling wreaths of red hot asteroids were forming, tumbling end over end in brimstone flame that shot through space, a tapestry of tombstones marking the end for Xereba.

Amid the cacophony of destruction a lone vehicle hung limply in space like a frightened puppy, too shocked to move. Shards of planetary debris bounced across its shields in little spots of colour like oil on water, the mere tip of the iceberg.

This was the Juggernaught: the Xereban military's greatest achievement.

It was the first of a fleet that would never be built, created to stave off any potential invaders. Xereba had faced an invasion once before but the quick thinking of one military leader had averted the disaster, saving the people from being reduced to a life of slavery from a reptilian race called the Swarchek.

Like a bulldog, the Juggernaught defiantly faced the devastation head on, its hull laden with sensors and weapons, most of which were implanted in its shape, hidden from the naked eye; its manta shape reinforced with a self-sustaining skin that gave it an organic look.

Inside the vast curved craft was a stunned silence to match deepest space. The moment the energy waves had begun rippling across the planet, every alarm had triggered, sending the technicians and soldiers to their battle stations.

They had been trained well by General Solos and had acted swiftly. The energies killing their world disrupted the teleport system and so, praying to the winds of hopeful fate, they focused the beams on the surface and randomly scooped up whoever they could, from wherever they could. They could not control it, their hope futilely urging the beams to bring some of their loved ones aboard.

Tears burned their eyes as person after person materialized on board, shaken, nervous and lost. Others screamed like their very souls had been ripped from them, desperate hands reaching for loved ones that were no longer there.

Out of eight billion citizens only 1,243 were saved. The Juggernaught, once the first best defense of all Xereba, was now the last cradle of hope for the Xereban people.

Survivors were materializing all over the station but Solos, in his devious military brilliance, had cleverly made the vehicle two fold. He had stood in its command centre, six months before, beaming proudly as his image was projected across the planet.

"The Juggernaught not only acts as a multipurpose station to house over four thousand troops but it is capable of space flight. After all, what use is a space station that can't move when

attacked or indeed needed to manoeuver in order to fight back?" he boasted.

Some said paranoia made Solos think of every possible outcome regardless of the expense. They were right.

Too traumatized to think, the survivors could only stare about them at strangers' faces, desperate for a family member or a friendly face. But all they could see was their own grief reflected in each other's features.

One woman, Neera, had been teaching a class of thirty children, all bright and eager for the future. She had felt the ground tremble, the air gasp in a pinprick of complete silence before the fires came; unable to move, she watched as tornados of flame consumed her class as she was carried off by the teleport beams, useless hands reaching desperately at ash.

She sat weeping, cradling her head in her hands as the looks on the children's faces played before her; those innocent wide eyed babies who never even understood what was happening.

The shaken crew could only mumble empty words of comfort to the distressed. It was as if the universe had opened its dark side and smashed their planet from under them for no good reason.

Even the Xereban philosophy of everything happens for a reason seemed a sad excuse now under this mind wrenching loss.

Aftershocks rocked the Juggernaught as Xereba's agony intensified, vomiting its innards up as the waves shredded it mercilessly. The teleport was failing, its beams scattered by the planetary explosions as the deck began to buck unsteadily.

"That's it! We're out of time!" bellowed a thick set man.

The inertial dampers were straining to keep them upright as the explosions carried bigger chunks of rubble towards them. Bracing his stocky frame, he leaped forward and ignited the Juggernaught's mammoth engines.

They roared defiantly at the dying world as it swung left, shuddering as it moved, riding out the plumes of fire like a frenzied phoenix. The survivors clung desperately to anything to keep them safe against the shaking, terrified screams lost in the shrieking air as the engines fought to gain momentum.

Dargan gripped the flight controls as he willed the engines to full power, trying not to look at the disaster before him as a hundred faces of friends now lost screamed in his mind. Choking back tears, he narrowed his eyes and tightened his mouth as he made a silent vow never to forget them.

"I know these engines like the back of my hand!" he shouted over the crescendo, trying to look confident as sweat soaked his body.

Where they were heading he didn't know nor care; as long as they put distance between themselves and the inferno that was once their home. He'd been the chief engineer on the Juggernaught since its very conception so he knew what these engines could take.

There were days they almost talked to him in a language only he and they understood. He had no family, been married to his work, a loner most of his life but his heart was hurting at the thought of all those who never stood a chance; of all the lost tomorrows and promises never kept.

Today was a day where everyone hurt.

He glanced about him at the fearful sweaty faces looking to him for salvation. He could see they fully expected that any moment the Juggernaught would split apart and merciless fire would consume them all.

But he refused to let that happen; something or someone had to survive to tell the tale and find justice for everyone.

The Juggernaught's manta ray hull glowed red and orange under hungry flame that licked at it like wolves as it carried away the survivors, whose futures were as black as the space that bore them. Lost in their souls as well as life, they could only see solitude and death; destined to waste away in this metal tomb.

Except for one man.

He lay immobile on the floor, being attended to by a nurse called Vela, a broad woman who jumped right in to help the wounded to avoid watching her home burn. Somehow that kept her focused, being able to do something rather than stand by helplessly.

She had been on duty in the Tancara medical centre before an explosion tore it in two. Gently, she wiped the sweat from her blond fringe and sat back on her hunkers, putting her blackened jacket under the man's head. She tried to block out the buffeting as she stared at him, slightly unnerved.

His skin was like ancient parchment and his veins bulged out of his face. His hair, white as fear, mounted a strong face with sapphire eyes that stared widely but not moving. She could see broken veins on his nose and cheeks almost like the after effects of decompression. Trauma, she knew but from what? And what was he staring at? Vela shivered as she felt him look through her to focus on somewhere else.

He seemed very young to have such white hair. What has he lost compared to us to be in this state? she wondered, smoothing his hair.

Whatever it was, she hoped she would never see it.

He was alone.

No sound echoed here. No movement. Even his own heart was silent to him. Tar blackness stuck his feet to the ground that did not exist.

Like the first actor on in a play, Varran gradually became aware of faint shimmering lights in front of a black curtain. The curtain rose and reality shot through him in a myriad of colour that swayed and twirled and formed planets, suns, solar systems, even entire galaxies.

The universe exploded all around him, running like oil in the rain, solar winds shrieking in his mind like over excited children. He held his hands over his ears until the wind settled into a sound almost like a choir whose voices were so beautiful and moving it made the universe's heart beat faster.

Reality spread out before him in vivid shades, solidifying where he was standing on the heavens, far above time and space.

The universe in all its gregarious glory was a tapestry, with everything connected together in thought and mind. It was imbued with waterfall colors and nova wonder mixed with towers of elegance. Varran could barely contain his delight.

He laughed, stars trickling through his tingling fingers, light playing every fibre of his being.

Never had he felt such tranquility, such clarity of mind. He could feel other races talking to him, beings he'd never imagined. He could see reality interacting with time and thought; dimensions existing alongside others in some fragile ballet.

Suns bellowed merrily as they nurtured worlds teeming with all kinds of life that moons mothered in rest, sharing their dreams, pulling the blankets over them while they slumbered. Varran could see one being's dreams become another's reality, minds touching across the wastes of space.

From such things music and verse were born, lifted from a universal harmony that myriads sang but none could ever fully comprehend.

The universe was an ocean of ideas, vibrant with life that sang a song that ran for eternity. It touched Varran in a way he had never thought possible, reaching to his very core, opening his mind to limitless possibilities. His work became clear, the temporal equations and quirks in quantum mechanics rushing to him like long lost friends and the universe opened to him like some great honeycomb where each galaxy, each planet, each creature connected and functioned as a whole entity. He chuckled at how simple life was.

He gasped, buckling over, the stars falling from his hands.

A deep chill ripped at him, resonating through the universe, causing beings to look to the skies for answers. It gripped his soul, twisting it, forcing Varran to his knees. The stars shimmered where he fell, his eyes glancing heavenward.

A shiver on the horizon caught his attention. It was like watching heat bounce off a desert road. It rippled and swarmed toward Varran with frightening speed. A deathly stillness consumed him as time froze.

The shimmer expanded and moved, rolling onward faster and faster. He saw Xereba crumble as entire worlds shook to dust in the dark cloud's wake, lost in a red swell.

Dark, brooding, determined, it clawed light from the stars, sucked life from a thousand worlds and still it came ever closer. It ripped souls like paper, devoured the slightest whisper of butterfly wings, the laughter of children everywhere.

Like the firewalls that took Xereba, so this thing was relentless. Not caring what it destroyed; no room for compassion. It seethed up and around Varran like a demon wind, his heart turning to ice, his blood to flames. He saw its void face as it surged around and through him, tearing his flesh from his bones, hope from his heart. Life fell like melting fat on a fire.

Varran had heard of pure evil but here it was now facing him hatefully, consuming everything, bending it to its will. It wanted to devour all life, dominate and control, allowing for no survivors. It wouldn't stop until it had crushed love, hope and compassion. Reality itself turned to ash, fluttering down to be cruelly stomped on. This was the future, Varran realized, this was what was coming. Xereba had only been the first to fall. It saw him, knew him and charged right at him.

With a cry he shot upright, sweat sticking his body to the sheets. Vela jumped back with a scream. Varran saw her grey blue eyes, wide and alarmed. He felt strange, hot yet cold. Glancing round at the unfamiliar room, he stared at Vela, recognizing the jade nurse's uniform. His mind threw a hundred thoughts around at once. He knew it wasn't a hospital but he also knew exactly where he was, having been involved in the initial construction of the Juggernaught. It brought back only bitter memories.

With a wail of anguish, he realized what had happened as the memory of his vision came flooding back like a bad nightmare. Tears welled in his eyes as he wished desperately it really had been all a nightmare but every fibre of his being knew what had happened before anyone had even told him. He could see the fear in Vela's round face as she fretted over what to do.

She gently placed a comforting hand on his shoulder as she sat on the edge of the bed.

"It's alright," she said softly. "We brought you to one of the soldier's quarters. There's nobody here that hasn't lost somebody."

Her tone calmed him somewhat even though his heart was pounding in his chest. Varran wiped his eyes and looked at her. Sitting up, he saw his reflection in the mirror on the wall behind the nurse, his jaw dropping at the sight of his skin and shock of white hair.

The horror in his face gave Vela a chill down her spine. She felt her scalp crawl. His eyes were those of a man who had stared into his worst nightmare and survived.

"You don't understand," he croaked, his left hand shaking slightly as he touched his hair disbelievingly. "I know what happened."

Vela stared at him, suddenly frightened. Her voice dropped to an almost inaudible whisper. Her low level empathic abilities echoed like a distance church bell in her mind, a bell tolling for the dead.

"What do you mean?" Her question hid a hundred others that sprang into her mind but was afraid to articulate. Varran glared at the nurse, tears forming again in sapphire eyes. He suddenly seemed so frail.

"It was me. My name is Varran and I am...was a scientist for the government. My field was temporal mechanics, quantum physics, chiefly among other fields. Time travel." He caught the ripple of surprise. "Xereba aged to death, literally, as a result of my work."

Varran recalled his vision.

That was his only word for it. Maybe calling it that made a terrifying future like that less concrete, suggesting there may be a chance to change it. He wasn't sure himself but like all Xerebans, he believed that everything happened for a reason, no matter how tragic, and that the path would not become clear until events had played themselves out, either within months or maybe even until your twilight years. Only then could you connect the dots and see why certain things happened and how they shaped one's life and circumstances, no matter how harrowing things had been at the time.

As the universe fell, he saw one planet that stood like a beacon in chaos; the third planet in a system of nine.

Blue green swathed in white. It stood majestically against the darkness, defiance boiling from it and Varran knew this was where they had to find.

As the months and years dragged by and no sign of the blue planet, Varran was beginning to doubt himself. Others doubted too he knew and within the first months there had been three suicides. They had simply walked through an airlock and thrown themselves into space. And that weighed upon Varran even more. Hope was a ghost in the night and he was beginning to think they should settle on the first uninhabited world they came across and take things from there.

He must finally admit defeat and let everyone be free from the leash of his vision. If there was a path here, he couldn't see it but he was ready to step off it.

Suddenly the Juggernaught gave a gut wrenching lurch as something took control. It flailed wildly as if hit by a massive shockwave.

A blazing light filled the room. Shrieking tore the air. The holoscreen dissolved into a billion particles as the Juggernaught was moving too fast for the computers to process any information.

Suddenly all was still. The Juggernaught straightened out.

Varran gingerly got to his feet and stared at the holoscreen. It was a mishmash of colours and shapes. Gradually the image solidified.

Varran blinked, chewing his lower lip. His breathing became shallow as he checked the data in front of him and rechecked it.

It was a system of nine planets; the third a blue, green world swathed in white. The hologram reflected in his tears.

"It's real!"

The excited Xerebans had mounted several surveys of the planet they had discovered was called Earth inhabited by humans who looked very like Xerebans; this only served to reinforce Varran's belief in their path. They would have no trouble blending in.

It was the year 1894.

Varran saw potential. Humans were on a tightrope; one step would plunge them back into a dark age, the other, enlightenment to the possibilities of the wonders of the universe.

They had religions, differently practiced depending on what part of the world you were in but all contained a similar theme of one creator which Varran found delightful.

It was primitive yet potent.

"Think of them as an unopened flower," Varran argued. They decided that their only safe course was to assimilate into human culture (it was after all at a point where public records were hardly detailed).

Many cities had outlying villages while others had miles of wilderness. The Xerebans would live on as many different countries as possible.

Language would not be a problem as Xerebans had the ability to translate and speak any language they encountered with hours of hearing it spoken.

Certain Xerebans matched the diverse human coloring and they would get by, by easily bartering their skills both intellectual and physical. They could not interfere with human development or rise to positions of power in the governments which were as splintered as the cultures.

They had to keep their origins secret for fear of causing massive damage to humankind. Mankind would have to discover the universe for themselves and that there were other creatures out there both good and bad. When they had reached that level of maturity, only then could the Xerebans tell their story.

Varran would stay behind as the keeper of the Juggernaught, continuing with his work and preparing for what may come, which he was now sure was coming. He had much to do.

First he would travel Earth, learning about the peoples there and embracing all they had to offer. His love of life burst forth and he travelled alone for over nine years.

The Juggernaught lay hidden in the asteroid fields that littered Earth's system while the others integrated into their new lives.

He found much to love and much to fear but as he saw more, Varran knew this was the way things were meant to be.

The scientist lived alone, continuing his work and becoming more and more isolated.

Of course, the others contacted him regularly for advice or to update him on human cultures and traditions and he visited as many as he could when he could, but life gradually got in the way and the contact lessened.

Meanwhile, the first of the Xereban children were born on Earth and were to grow up knowing of their heritage at 18, the age of understanding. This process had been refined with the help of a geneticist on board who injected every survivor with a gene that would trigger in every future child born.

On their eighteenth birthdays ancestral memories would trigger and show them of their past, of Xereba's destruction and the journey their ancestors took.

As the years passed, he discovered he wasn't aging. His white hair was a constant reminder of tragedy and he hated it. Hope was all he cared about as he walked the Australian outback or stood on the Giant's Causeway gazing out to sea or simply leaning on a fence watching a herd of cows grazing, their low mooing strangely calming. Earth certainly had some bizarre creatures living on it. With his non aging he couldn't form lasting relationships or take a lover as he didn't know if he was just aging at a miniscule rate or if his experiment had left him permanently this age, frozen in one moment in time, a prisoner of time itself.

Time would tell. It always did.

Over a hundred years later, fate set in to bring three new people into his life, Michael, Jacke and Tyran.

He watched them, knowing they were Xereban but so human in nature and ideas, there was no difference between the two.

They are the Time Warriors and these are their stories.

RETURN TO EDEN

The great shape ploughed through the canvas of space in silent beauty.

It was as if multicoloured stars had come together and solidified in one expansive gesture. It was jade and azure, golden molten spires and towers criss-crossing its form to give it an intricate behemoth stature. Surrounded by a red hue, it sliced impassively through the twinkling stars and blankets of icy nebula gases.

Its pyramid form stood miles high, like an old giant sailing ship, majestically crossing the unknown expanses of the oceans of the universe.

Regal glaciers of pulsating crystal flowed across its hull, forming a solid exterior for its occupants. Pulses of blue light danced between the towers, like choirs of angels celebrating the joy of life itself, giving the crystalline vessel an almost inviting glow.

But none had been invited here for a long time. It had sailed for centuries, eager, determined and wilful. Its journey had been epic; a chapter in the book of the history of the universe where much had been seen and been discovered in the quest for knowledge.

They were nearly home.

Many believed the journey had been too long and eagerly anticipated the moment when they would welcome the feel of the sun on their faces, the wind kissing their skin, rain trickling like nectar from the heavens. They longed to walk the valleys they'd left behind so long ago, gaze upon their monuments with the grass beneath their feet as their sheep bowed respectfully all around them, leaving them to look contentedly upon the night sky with its plethora of constellations and say, "We have travelled there." When that happened it would be accomplishment enough.

As it came to a swirling planet encompassed by a series of coloured rings, the ship seemed to give a sigh. Saturn spun in space as a silent witness.

Nearly home. Nearly there.

Just beyond the swarm of asteroids that laced the outer rim of our own solar system sat a shape; dark and motionless against the starry backdrop.

Over three miles across, it perched in space like a giant black and red manta ray, its armoured curved hull marked like an ancient warrior with strong red lines.

Its skin was almost whale like, secreted with thousands of miniature scanners, alarm systems and weapons. Shuttered hatches and windows dotted the rims but allowed no view in.

Its front section tapered to a bull like head, its sides curving back and around to house two sections flanking either side, giving it the impression of a strongman charging forward, head down, with a barrel under each tautly muscled arm.

It had been built to make any aggressor think twice about attacking its titan curves. It gave the impression it could explode any moment with a furious storm of hell fire and its broad girth would smash any opposition in its path into insignificant shards.

This was the Juggernaught, military pride of the once flourishing world of Xereba. It had been the planet's first and best defence against alien incursion, a statement of one man's mind.

But Xereba was dead, destroyed in a surge of energy that had literally aged it to death.

Now the Juggernaught was the last refuge of the survivors of the catastrophe, arriving in Earth's solar system decades ago. It was now a sleeping giant, most of the survivors locating to Earth and assimilating into human society.

Now it was the home of a scientist named Varran who had been caught up in the accident that had destroyed his world. He had been discovered a way to travel in time but his breakthrough had been placed under military jurisdiction.

Seeing they intended to turn it into a weapon, Varran and a few sympathetic friends had gone on the run, continuing the work in secret and all the while, he had been pursued by a government faction under General Solos' orders who was eager to meld his work with the Juggernaught to create the ultimate weapon.

But in a blaze of soldiers' gunfire, his world had shuddered to ash. He had survived but at a terrible cost.

He had not aged a single day in over one hundred and twenty years so he had isolated himself aboard the Juggernaught. He would outlive them and he had lost enough loved ones already. His curse was he had no idea if he was ageing too slowly to register or was locked in a single moment of time forever.

However, circumstances had brought new people to his life, three young people, Xereban descendants who had been caught up in an alien attack on time and space, threatening the Earth.

They had joined him in his vow to fight injustice and prevent the coming of a vision he'd had as Xereba died. A vision where evil had walked the whole of creation and consumed it. Something dark and unfeeling was out there and he knew the battle would be fought here, on a shimmering blue green world called Earth. He didn't know when or how, just that Earth was pivotal in the battle ahead.

Over the years he had perfected his work and, having discovered his project had already been partially integrated into the Juggernaught's systems, had persevered to finish it. After all, he had the time. The battle station would be a force for good and he would use it more wisely than the military had ever intended.

At the moment, he was seated in the main command centre of the station. It curved around him in lines of softly chattering consoles and computers, all streamlined by chrome and leather backings. An oval command table dominated the room, its charcoal black design tempered by the various brightly lit screens and monitors set into it. Large screens were placed above various stations which in battle, would link directly with the tactical and engineering and provide automatic updates on whatever was happening. Its ceiling curved into a central port above the command table, thick girders leaning to form the nexus of the main computer.

All information was fed straight to the central table which could generate a solid hologram in mid-air of whatever he needed to see. Varran, under Jacke's suggestion, had placed various plants about the centre to give it a less militaristic feel and make it more homely.

At certain points along the walls hung three tapestries from an Indian American reservation he had visited years before, a gift from the tribe from whom he'd learnt a great deal. They were hand stitched and portrayed great battles in the tribe's history and how they saw the universe. He had been astounded at their knowledge of aliens and one tribe, the Anasazi, were a particular fascination for Varron.

He had learned of their mysterious disappearance from a Native American he had befriended shortly after his arrival on Earth. Were they taken by beings from another world?

He had never encountered a culture like it with their connections to nature. Their knowledge outweighed accepted science so Varran had stayed for a while and discovered a hidden regal tranquillity within these people.

They were proud of their traditions and he had adored their artistic abilities. They had shared everything they had with him freely and asked nothing in return and sometimes he got the feeling, they had been expecting his arrival all along. His origins were no great surprise to them at all.

The wall to his left held a medium silver bookcase with books on several periods of Earth's history. Of course, the advantage Varran had was he could travel back and witness it first-hand. He had often read something which made him smile and shake his head as if listening to a child getting his words muddled. But there was still so much history he hadn't seen.

Perfecting his work on the Juggernaught kept him focussed and the years had flown by.

But his attention now was focused on the news report playing before him in mid-air on a holographic screen. Varran's thick white hair gave him the look of an old man in his sixties at first glance but the youthful face and shining sapphire eyes betrayed his age.

Dressed in a dark navy shirt with black trousers and scuffed dark boots, he sat arms folded across his chest. His brow was troubled as he watched the scenes of devastation unfold before him.

Pakistan had been hit by a massive earthquake in which thousands had died. Whole cities crumbled into rubble as people's lives were ripped apart.

Many had been children and his mind flew back to Xereba's destruction.

Over a century had passed but the memories were as fresh as a winter morning. His eyes closed briefly as little bodies wrapped in white sheets were brought out from the collapsed buildings. He saw mothers screaming as they cradled their dead youngsters, fathers on their knees in the streets, screaming for lost ones.

One minute they had years of watching their families growing up, the next, mourning their deaths.

Wiping his eyes, Varran felt guilty. He could help but could not reveal the presence of the Juggernaught. Mankind wasn't ready for that revelation. He could only stand by and weep with the rest of the world at the tragic scenes.

One day he would make good on all his inactions but not today. Someday, he knew, someone would ask why, if he had been around all this time, why he not helped in these types of disasters.

All he would say that day would be because I couldn't.

He would arrange for some of his fellows on Earth make hefty donations to help these people, go in with the relief crews and help rebuild the devastation. But it wasn't enough, he knew. Moist eyes glanced to his right where a large concave alcove was inset into the wall.

Lined with silver and gold back panels, four columns of light ran up its length and met in the ceiling above where a hexagonal panel lined with what seemed like glittering gems hung down over the floor panel which was split in four sections. It hummed with dormant power and he could feel tiny static charges occasionally leaping from it. He had the power to go back and change things, warn them of the oncoming cloud and evacuate but he couldn't. He had made the rule they could not interfere in events no matter what and it gave him small comfort to know they could at least, give a helping hand in the aftermath.

Everything happened for a reason.

That was the Xereban belief, one that was ingrained in Varran's mind.

It had guided them here to Earth and he could not deviate from it. He had to trust he would see the path after the events had passed. Even in the blackest pit, there is a path, although it was hard to believe when the image of the woman clutching her dead child refused to leave his thoughts.

He spoke, his voice quelled by the pain of what he had seen. "Computer, continue monitoring and instruct our companies to help with whatever relief is necessary. Varran; priority one; code black." Allowing himself a deep breath, his head flicked as the command table began whistling an alarm.

He was at it in a second. The door swished open and a young ebony woman of about twenty five swept in, her face lighting up in a beam of white teeth on seeing him. It disappeared as quickly when she noticed his sallow frown.

"Computer, focus sensors on that area and transfer visual and tactical report to holoscreen!"

Jacke knew by his tone something was wrong. Throwing him an inquisitive look, Jacke felt a chill as he looked stonily at her. "Call the others."

You could feel the tension in the air.

It felt to Jacke that the very computers around them had quietened as if holding their collective breaths. The colours from the holoscreen before them played on all their faces. Tyran and Michael had rushed up as soon as Jacke had called them on the intercom. They had all been present on the Juggernaught on and off for the last few months in order to learn its systems and learn how to fly the Dagger fighter craft in the hangar bays.

The air was still as all eyes were focused on the picture before them. Michael's brown eyes drank in the cathedral vessel with its flickering crystalline bulk.

Of average height and build, his slightly pudgy face was still, his brown hair still damp from a shower. His quarters were two decks away, near to Jacke and Tyrans'. He had become instinctively slightly over protective of the two girls ever since they'd been thrown together.

His only living relative was his feisty grandmother, Maisy, his parents having been killed in a car crash years ago and as an only child had been brought up by his grandmother in a quiet suburb of London. His family were everything to him and the girls fell under that category now, with Varran the father figure.

He'd never admit it but he had a crush on Jacke but he didn't think she'd noticed. He couldn't help but notice the outline of her bra beneath her red jumper. He returned his eyes to the holoscreen.

Besides, he knew she'd never think of him like that, girls never did think of nerds like that. He was like a brother, apparently, or he was too good a friend, a phrase he had grown to hate years ago. He and Tyran bickered constantly, each trying to get the last word on each other. To an outsider it seemed as if they hated each other but not so. Their sense of humour was very similar and they had that comfort zone where you could put each other down but be safe in the knowledge the other knew you were joking.

Tyran wore black jeans and a white T shirt with a splurge of orange on the front. She always looked well even when she hadn't dressed up, he thought comparing his own blue jeans which never seemed to fit him round the behind and always felt slightly too tight around the waist. He stood one leg behind the other.

Scratching his right armpit, the material of his brown short sleeved canvas shirt was making him itch, he cocked his head slightly.

"Big, isn't it," he mused, almost to himself. Throwing him an impish grin, Tyran saw an opportunity.

"Size not being one of your strong points," she quipped. Recognising the implication, he gave her a wry smile fixing her with a sympathetic look.

"Told you many times, if you want me just say so. I hate to see someone suffering," he said with a mock compassion. She just glared back. Folding her arms she looked back at the image.

"The only one who'll suffer is the poor next girl who sees you naked." She raised a warning finger. "Brad Pitt, not Brad Tit." She smiled to herself as she saw him frown, desperately trying to fire a comeback.

Smiling softly at her new friend's banter, Jacke jumped in.

"Ever seen anything like it?" Her question was directed at Varran who was watching a scroll of data run across a monitor to his right. Shaking his head, he drew himself up, folded his arms and stroked his bristly chin thoughtfully.

"It's amazing, quite amazing," he breathed. Interested as she was, Tyran rolled her eyes as she recognised the lecture stance. Here we go, she thought glibly.

Noticing her expression, the Xereban scientist suppressed a chuckle. Her facial expressions always made him laugh and the best of it was, she didn't realise it.

"For those interested," he started pointedly, (Tyran pouted innocently), "that shouldn't exist. It's an engineering impossibility. We tried to do it back on Xereba but the molecular cohesion never took." His mind drifted far across the galaxy to another time, old faces appearing before him; "It was very disappointing," he recalled. "Although it sprouted a photonic rainbow as it collapsed; very beautiful."

"A chocolate saucepan," said Jacke, her Irish accent sounding melodic to Varran. He frowned at her, unsure of the reference. She grinned. "You can make a saucepan from chocolate but as soon as it hits the heat, splat, it melts." Varran nodded seeing what the black girl was getting at.

"Like framing a snowflake," he enthused, "I see what you mean. Chocolate pots; like it, must remember that." He made a mental note, filing it under Earth metaphors.

"Glad to see a hundred years of isolation hasn't done you any harm," smirked Michael, "much." Tyran gave him a playful slap on the arm. Ignoring them, Varran went on.

"I never thought it was possible but obviously someone managed it and to quite a degree, unbelievable piece of engineering. See here," he pointed to the rear of the vessel, "no engines." The others leaned closer, puzzled. Anticipating their next question, he burbled. "It absorbs fuel directly from space. These spires draw in energy of all sorts while the smaller dome nodules suck in matter and convert directly into the main structure."

"You mean like a whale swimming through a shoal of fish," reasoned Michael, "it just opens its mouth, so to speak, and swallows. No effort required." Varron jabbed his finger pointedly.

"Exactly!" he beamed. He was almost jumping up and down with excitement. "Oh I'd love to meet the people who built it, or rather grew it." Jacke's eyebrows shot up.

"Must have been a big tank," she said.

Lost in thought on the engineering principles, Varran could only nod, while chewing his bottom lip.

Tyran was sitting casually watching the numbers on screen. To her surprise, she found she actually understood what they meant. Shifting slightly in the black leather seat with chrome back rest, she looked again to be sure she wasn't going to look stupid.

"Why is it heading for Earth?" Snapping his head round, Varran studied the data, fingers dancing across the console, rereading what was in front of him. A concerned look crossed his thin features.

"You're right," he agreed. "Coincidence maybe," he suggested.

Michael chimed in. "Something that big could do serious damage if it was hostile; any weapons?" Shaking his head, Varran shrugged uncertainly. "I'm not reading any but it is storing an enormous amount of energy. Whether that's for propulsion, life support or weaponry, I'm not sure. Its layout is totally unknown to me; for all I know those spires could be weapons of some kind." He brought a new section of screen. "Carbon dating makes it….undetermined."

"It's old then. Is there anyone aboard?" asked Tyran, running a hand though her short blond spiky hair.

"Can't tell from these readings," answered Jacke, reading off figures. Varran watched her silently; secretly elated she had been studying the Juggernaught's systems as well as studying for her psychology degree.

With everything that had happened in recent months, it was a wonder she had had the time for anything. "It seems to be surrounded by a shield or is that glow just for effect?" Michael joined her and pressed another control. Good, urged Varran, keep going. The young man's head rocked slightly as he read the data on screen.

"No, you're right. It's a shield of some sort. See these spikes in the output frequency, dead giveaway."

"Three months ago you couldn't even work the telly remote," chipped Tyran.

"And three months ago you were interesting," he pricked. Jacke grinned.

"Touché," Tyran grimaced. "He's getting better."

"Computer, hail that ship." There was silence for a moment. Varran didn't look surprised when it told him there was no answer to its call. He told it to repeat but again nothing.

"Scan shield frequency specifically for pin pricks, speed and locations along the ship's spatial wake," he instructed, arms spread across the command table, narrowed eyes fixed on the holoscreen.

A rush of data appeared beside the ship's image in tiny white lettering and numbers. He made a satisfied sound in his throat and noticing the three expectant stares as if for the first time, breathed out.

"No shield is perfect especially encompassing such a large area," he explained. "The strain creates microscopic holes in the lower ranges which all forms of beams can slip through."

Michael caught where he was going. "If they won't answer us, we go to them."

"I don't like bad manners," said Varran icily.

"What if they're all dead and it's just a Marie Celeste?" Tyran wondered. The look on Varran's face was coldly dispassionate.

"Then we'll not have to worry about manners." There was something in his tone, a steely determination that unnerved her slightly but she reminded herself of how much he had given up for this way of life.

Somewhere in the depths of the great crystalline ship, something stirred as it became aware of the Juggernaught's hails. It was surprised. Something was there, intelligence? Here? It could not be a threat if they could not pierce the shields despite their primitive attempts.

Nearly home; nearly there.

The trio stood in the coral lit hexagonal chamber watching an annoyed Varran fussing over the command table. They threw each other a bemused look.

Jacke cleared her throat causing him to briefly glance up, his face puffed crossly.

"If anything goes wrong, we need you here to get us out," she soothed, seeing his grumpy face. "Besides if there really is no one there you can come over and I'll stay here; fair enough?"

Varran humped but grunted a suppose so. Michael had given each of them a hand unit, a slender mobile phone like device, silver in colour with black indents, that slid apart and acted as a multi-functional machine allowing them to scan, record, communicate and analyse amongst other things. He looked decidedly uncomfortable, eyeing the chamber uncertainly.

"Are you sure you'll get us through the holes ok? I mean this used to go wrong on Star Trek all the time. I could rematerialize inside out!" he fretted. Jacke shook her head disparagingly.

"That's The Fly you're thinking of," she chided. "Baboon."

Pulling a face, Michael muttered it was of little help. Varran straightened up and rubbed his hands together before crossing his fingers on both hands for them all to see. If he couldn't go might as well play on their nerves.

"Be alert," he warned steely as he activated a sequence on the console.

The Stepping Stone, the teleport system he'd built lit up with a growl of power as a double helix of sky blue light swirled around each of the three young people. They became transparent and faded, Michael's eyes shut tight. The glows faded and Varran shoulders slumped worriedly.

His stomach was churning as he turned back to the image before him. He leaned closer, his eyes narrowing. His instincts were gnawing at him but he didn't understand why.

It was like the world had melted around them as the blue haze faded to be replaced by shades of white and ice green. Jacke was the first to react as Michael opened his eyes and felt himself.

"You're still in one piece," said Tyran, "though I'd swear you're a couple of inches shorter."

"Really?" gasped Michael, patting his head and checking the length of his jeans. Tyran smiled craftily. "I didn't mean height." Stifling a smile, Jacke did a full turn as she looked about her curiously.

"Switch to scan and record mode," she told the hand unit. The others did the same. Zipping his dark navy jacket up, Michael commented on the chill in the air. Sniffing, Tyran noticed a tang of sulphur in the air, like the smell from freshly fired cannons.

They had reappeared in a circular corridor, similar to an old Victorian sewer in height and width but it was made entirely of some sort of crystal. Its walls were smooth to the touch but beneath the surface were millions of black and light green nodules that seemed to move and collide, forming larger nodules with a spark of jade light. It was like a firework display compressed into a bubble.

Jacke closed her eyes as she ran her slender hand along it. Her skin tingled softly in a not unpleasant sensation which rippled across her body.

Despite the chill in the air, it was warm to the touch. The light seemed to come from all around them though there was no discernible light source. As she looked, it was as if the surface of the walls were shifting almost when they weren't looking.

Tyran had ventured further ahead, her unit held before her, watching the small screen as it took in everything she did and probably more.

"Wonder what part we're in?" wondered Michael as he examined a box like indent that had appeared from nowhere. It had no circuits or components as far as he could tell. It was simply there and had no obvious function.

"Communications mode," he said more softly than he realized. "Varran can you hear me?" He waited a second before trying again but there was no reply. "We're on our own," he breathed uneasily.

"He'll find a way through," Jacke said encouragingly. Nodding in agreement, Tyran insisted Varran wouldn't have sent them and leave them stranded. If the shield had one weakness which had closed up, then the Xereban scientist would find another.

"Is anyone picking up any life signs?" Jacke asked, screwing up her face as the sulphur smell became stronger. She brushed her dark hair tinted with chestnut from her eyes as she looked back the way they had come.

"Jesus!" she started, causing the others to spin round. They instinctively took a step back. The corridor was gone, a solid wall of crackling crystal in its place.

"How the hell did that happen?" cried Michael as he pocketed his unit and pushed both girls forward. "GO!"

Jacke and Tyran bolted but Michael crashed to the floor as part of the wall shot out a tentacle and wrapped round his leg. He kicked at it, hands clawing but it held fast. Blood traced the crystal as it cut his fists, dragging him away.

The floor heaved and shot straight up in front of the girls cutting off their escape. Michael's cries made them retreat, moving to help him but with a hiss the ceiling sagged and more tentacles spewed forward and coiled round them. The floor was bubbling like lava, the surging crystal throwing them off balance. The ceiling was collapsing like melting toffee as it closed in on them, sucking at every part of their bodies, slowly smothering them.

Jacke couldn't hear Michael anymore and she had lost sight of Tyran. Her almond eyes widened in terror as a scream died in her throat as everything went black.

She awoke with a desperate gasp, drawing in a deep lungful of precious air.

It was dark and she blinked, little blue and yellow lights flickering in front of her eyes in the haze. She had felt like she was drowning and she instinctively looked round for the others.

As her eyes adjusted to the darkness, she could just about make out a figure to her left. Jacke reached out but couldn't move. No matter how hard she tried she couldn't get her arms or legs to move.

Grunting in frustration, she yelled out to be released. Someone had to be out in the darkness watching them. She could feel it as her mind itched as something brushed the surface of her thoughts. Had the others been seriously hurt?

< It has a temper. Very different to what we are used to.>

< The genetic structure is virtually human yet there is a minute difference, virtually nothing but an interesting point all the same. Most unusual.> Jacke craned her neck to see who was speaking but it felt like the words were echoing in her mind and not in her ears.

<An evolutionary leap like that would be impossible without alien interference.> argued a female, the quality of her voice like ice crystals spilling across metal.

"Excuse me, it's rude to speak about someone while they're present," Jacke said trying to sound as insulted as possible. "Why don't you show yourselves and we can talk. We mean you no harm." She caught a soft chorus of startled whispers which seemed to come from all around her. "You can obviously see into my mind."

She made sure she emphasised the last sentence, just so they knew she was well aware of their intrusion. "Well?"

< It speaks to us like equals. How insolent!> A male voice this time, Jacke thought, making a mental note of the different voices.

< We should terminate them immediately.> Jacke relaxed momentarily. Michael and Tyran had to be alive.

"Terminate us for what? For coming in peace?" she barked. "Surely we can talk face to face? Please release us so we can communicate. Again, we mean you no harm!" Another chorus like a shoal of ghosts swept all around her, giving her goose bumps. She could still smell sulphur but the atmosphere seemed warmer despite the darkness. There was a stone silence and Jacke shivered involuntarily as the dark seemed to press in on her.

In an instant the darkness evaporated as a blinding light flooded the room causing her to close her startled eyes from the sudden pain. Gingerly she opened them again. Before her were seven beings. They looked like gods from old hieroglyphics found in many civilisations.

Seven foot tall and swathed in luxuriant robes that looked like silk, they regarded her. Each wore a different colour robe, some with exotic patterns gilded with gold or silver, others with none but still the material shone regally. They were humanoid with pasty complexions. Their eyes were black dots which shone malevolently from angular faces topped by a mane of golden hair. Their thin lips and stares made her think of an old school mistress she once had, Mrs Carson, who gave her that stare before dishing out detention.

They were stood on a platform made from the same crystal as in the corridor flanked on either side by two enormous sculptures of some sort of animal that looked like a cross between a dragon and a horse, its great claws slashing the air for eternity. The cathedral like room curved upwards lined with rows upon rows of balconies all alive with the fiery crystal.

Hundreds of similar humanoids filled the balconies watching the scenario below. Tapestries hung from every balcony of the amphitheatre, shifting slightly in the air, each adorned with complex designs and images.

The silence for such a large gathering was thunderous and Jacke realised a green light was playing over her body, locking her in place. A rush of electricity shot through her and she could move her arms. Her feet however were stuck to the one spot.

A groan made her look right and with a wash of relief she saw Michael and Tyran coming round, wakened by the sudden light. You were captain of the debate team in school, she told herself, so make this good. She steeled herself and stared confidently at the gathered crowd. I'm pissing myself, she thought ruefully.

Jacke smiled, her teeth a ray of white against her dark skin, lighting up her face.

"Either I'm dead or we're in an episode of the X Files. Which is it?"

Jacke's heart was pounding and a sick feeling rose in the pit of her stomach as she stared at the beings intently. She was quaking inside but hid it well.

Years of facing bullies and tormentors about the colour of her skin had perfected her poker face. She was afraid of no one.

Frowning slightly she shivered as a curious sensation rippled over her as if she could hear faint voices through a wall.

All eyes were on her, a fact she was very well aware of but she held herself steady, waiting for them to say something. Trying to ignore the beautiful plumes of light that shimmered up around the jade crystal translucent walls, she focused on the lead being in the saffron robes. He was scowling at her intensely but it was more than that, she realised.

Was he trying to probe her mind, see what was in there? Had her defiance been interpreted as a challenge of some sort in their eyes? Conjuring up a rather rude image she grinned before chiding herself. This wasn't the behaviour Varran had taught them. Their aim was to make peaceful contact but Jacke wasn't feeling the love right now.

< Who are you? Why have you invaded our home?>

Glancing at Jacke, Michael wondered if she had heard that too? He knew from her expression she had. Hearing voices is all I need, he thought, glad he wasn't losing it.

The creature had referred to their vessel as home rather than ship. Bit strange, he mused, his eyes darting all around to try and gauge as much as possible. He heard Jacke answer in a loud voice.

"This isn't an invasion!" she cried out in her best debate voice. "We tried contacting you but never received a reply."

<So do you believe silence is an excuse to trespass on our property? Did it not occur to you that we were aware of your message?> Its tone was surly with more than a hint of arrogance, the words almost hissing at them. Whether or not it was intentional, it irked Tyran who was already annoyed by her being frozen to one spot.

"Then why not answer? It's common courtesy to speak when spoken to," she pointed irritably. "Besides, we thought you might have been hurt or the ship abandoned." The domed head swung in her direction, fixing her with a look of pure unfeeling malevolence.

It was silhouetted by a dark blue arc of light that stretched the pillar behind it, spreading its shadow out and darkening its face as the thin lips peeled back in a smirk.

<We do not afford courtesy to lower species. They are meat.> A chill of fear threaded Tyran's spine as it held her contemptuously.

"Lovely," she quipped, mentally urging Jacke to pitch in. Before any of them could speak, it swept down closer to them like a burst of smoke.

<Why have you come here? Have you invaded our home, taken our keepers as cattle?> it breathed. <What damage have you inflicted upon our legacy?>

Holding her panic in check, Jacke held her features steady. She could almost see her reflection in those piercing eyes. They were so black it was like a living void threatening to suck her soul from her.

"We have invaded nothing and I don't eat beef," she answered slowly and forcefully. "We already told you we thought there was no one aboard your home…." It cut her off viciously.

<Not this home, insect. This home!> The air shimmered before them allowing a globe to form. As the shapes and colours settled, the warriors failed to hide their shock.

Before them was Earth.

"That can't be your home. It's mine! See the second cloud on the left, house with the double glazing, red door. Can't miss it!" shot Michael. Jacke hissed at him to shut up. Being a smart alec would get them nowhere; heading for Earth was no accident because these beings were going home.

"With respect, are you sure you're correct? This is home to billions of humans. There is no record of your ever having been there," explained Jacke, her Irish accent at odds with the pristine tones of the creatures.

< Do our temples not stand on Mount Tegra defiant as the burning sun rises in the east? Have you not seen our works shape the lower species as they worship our likenesses? Do they not stand in awe as their tiny minds are pricked by the voice of gods? The voice that tells them that we would return one day> Jacke felt the raw indignation which swarmed all around her like an angry hive. Not sure of what to say, Jacke recalled Varran's advice to always be honest.

"I'm afraid not." Her words were like a hammer against glass as a chorus of voices swept through her mind like a hurricane breeze. She felt their outrage and anger towards them for their defiance.

The image of Earth changed into a lush tropical valley with screeching colourful birds wheeling before a blood red dawn beneath a majestic mountain range upon which rose a fabulous building made of granite.

It stood like a medieval castle, strong and sturdy but with subtle differences. Carvings in the walls made from some crystalline material, seemed to grab the sun and absorb it, making the energy its own.

Pulsating from its perch, the building looked out across the dense vegetation and seemed to cry out defiantly to challenge nature itself with its ornate spiral stairs and geometric shapes that contained pattern within pattern.

Another structure appeared amid a vast desert where humans and their beasts of burden trudged to bring tribute to the beings that reared above them, their faces as cold as ice. The being whirled round on them.

<This is not how we left it? Humans you called them.> It glanced back at the hordes watching who seemed agitated. <They took our name and twisted it to suit themselves. Such arrogance! Such betrayal!> It spun back to the three young people helpless before them.

<We are Numaran! They took our name and made it to fit themselves.> Michael nodded to himself.

"It's like Chinese whispers," he said. "The more a word is passed along the more it moves away from the original but retains elements of the first word." Tyran looked at him puzzled

"But there is nothing like them in the history books."

Jacke joined in, her voice low but her frown deep. "There might be. Those buildings reminded me of Mayan or Aztec, something along that road."

"And the Mayans disappeared or were wiped out or something." He glanced at the Numarans. "Could it have been them? Are they Mayans?" Shaking her head doubtfully, Jacke disagreed. "Basis for the ancient Gods maybe," she wondered aloud. She paused, considering.

"If I may be so bold but if this is your home, then why have we no record of you or this technology? A ship like this made from crystal is beyond human bounds. Surely there would be some trace, some record of your existence?" She kept her voice calm but loud so the Numarans didn't sense her fear. The energy running through the ship seemed to increase as if the Numaran collective anger was spurring it on.

<We raised them from the mud. We walked the earth while humans crawled on their bellies, scraping for food. We taught them how to make fire, make clothing from the elements around them and the basics of all civilisations. Reading and writing from which sprang their ability for art and sculpture. They were willing subjects who revered their gods and constructed the citadels for us to dwell in. They sacrificed and paid homage for all we had done for them. They lived fruitful lives under our guidance and for the first time they looked to the heavens and saw….possibilities. We culled those with those thoughts. They were getting above their station.>

The Numaran paused, remembering the past. It looked at them, its pasty features impassive.

< We grew bored so we looked to the stars. As to how this ship was constructed? The answer lays hundreds of miles beneath the planet surface. We tapped this material, an intelligent form of life which once freed from the depths, shared our lust for travel. It yearned to go forth into the heavens and see all there was to see. It shaped itself to this form in which we would be sustained indefinitely. We live such long lives…>

"No shit Sherlock," butted in Tyran, earning her a sharp glare from Jacke. She pulled an apologetic face sarcastically.

<The humans were to take care of our temples until we returned, safeguard our way of life. They knew no other life, dared not think any other thoughts. They owed us everything.> Its arrogance sang in their minds like a shiver.

"You mean you never let them forget it. You kept them in a slave mentality." Michael stared at them, not the slightest whisper of emotion flickering across their pale faces.

"And it never occurred to you that they would explore your cities and learn for themselves how things worked?" continued Jacke, incredulous at their arrogance.

"Life is all about evolving and changing. To think a world would stop just because you left is beyond belief." Her words brought that buzz in her thoughts again. "You killed anyone who had a spark of imagination or dared to ask what lay beyond. Don't you see, you tried to frame a snowflake, couldn't be done."

Almost trembling with anger the lead Numaran swept right up to her.

<And we will do it again. It is our home.>

Worried he was going to attack Jacke, Michael shouted at him. "Not any more. It's like leaving your home empty for a year and thinking it'll be the same when you come back. Something will change. Cobwebs will be spun and nature creeps in," he said angrily. "Insects gather while mice scurry about the attic."

<Cobwebs can be swept away.> it retorted. <But you claim Earth as your own. What gives you the right?>

"We were born there," stated Tyran.

<As were we.> cut in the Numaran, his face melting into a smug look. Jacke realized what they meant as she pieced together what they had told them.

"There's no record of you in the history books because you existed before a single word was written," she breathed in awe.

<Without us there would have been no history to write,> it said. The look in its eyes was frightening.

"Millions of years ago maybe, but like the dinosaurs, you have no place there anymore. Life is too different, mankind is too different. Try to quell them and they will retaliate. It is their world now, not yours." Jacke words brought a reaction because as they watched, the lighting seemed to dim as a deathly silence fell over the masses. The Numaran turned slowly on his heel, surveying the others, the chorus silent in the warriors' minds.

Almost like dead tumbleweed blown across a street in an old western, the mood shifted, almost imperceptibly, but a shift nonetheless. Anger had subsided, arguments falling to the wayside and a calm like the eye of a hurricane settled over them all.

One voice.

<If the humans have truly evolved as you say, shall we see what they have done to our Eden?> It swept forward and seized Tyran by the head, fixing her with those soulless black eyes that betrayed nothing.

In that second Tyran was suspended in mid-air with a million aliens piercing her mind, ripping back the layers like bargain hunters in the sales. They saw everything about her from her beginnings in the womb, her ancestral memories of the Xereban flight into deep space up to the second before the Numarans had taken her. They saw the world as she saw it and a trillion more she had forgotten.

Michael and Jacke struggled against their restraints desperately trying to get to her. Their cries were ignored as the hordes around them seemed to fall into a collective trance.

The air shattered like a video on fast forward as images of life on Earth tumbled around them. The images expanded, spreading to encapsulate the Numaran and the three Time Warriors. Smells and sounds crashed their senses as the Numarans began to eat into all their minds. Life became a crescendo of screams and explosions as images formed all round them, dragging them all into the Numaran psyche.

Desperate screams as planes are smashed into buildings, a mother allows herself to be used by perverts just to feed her children, a man lies dead in the street, his chest soaked in blood for a few clattering coins, people battered and burned for the colour of their skin, children becoming addicts, babies born with a death sentence for being the wrong gender, the beautiful blue oceans awash with the blood of a hundred whales, their gullets sliced open, a kitten screaming as it burns alive, an old woman freezing to death because the government fails to give her enough to live, bombs falling and people burning in the name of oil, proud ancient trees falling so a second rate pulp book can be published, hulking machines bulldozing rain forests, not even aware they are wiping out hundreds of species all in the name of progress, whispers in dark alleys, hope lost in the roar of a gun, disabled children locked in cages while the sun shines on happy parades, happy slapping, the homeless wasting to death on heartless streets while people laugh at videos of accidents on telly, a boy hides in a playground terrified of the bullies, a little girl hides from her abusive father, a wife walks into a door for the millionth time, families murdered in feuds, oceans choking on pollution as drugs make the young old, thousands disappearing without a trace while perverts wear titles to stalk their victims, pain, tears, death, so much death at their own hands, so much hate, so much despair......!

With a jerk the Numaran screamed, a shriek so profound it brought tears to its eyes as it stumbled away, hands over its head in despair.

Tyran fell to the ground, her restraints gone. Jacke and Michael stumbled as their minds cleared from the mental attack. The amphitheatre dimmed, red arcs of light slashing overhead as he air crackled with emotion. They're connected to the ship itself, jumped through Michael's mind as he steadied the shaken Tyran.

<What have they done? What have they become?> bellowed the Numaran, falling to his knees. His expression was desperate, the face of a witness to a great tragedy. <This is not the Eden we knew> it breathed sadly. <They have wiped us from history, from their very minds!> it wailed. <They have become a threat to nature itself and must be dealt with. We will have our home again and stand proud over our realm, return it to its former glory!> The images it had seen in the Warrior's minds burned like a branding iron. <And you call that progress,> it hissed hatefully at the warriors. Jacke jumped to her feet, Michael by her side.

"You're only seeing one side. There is so much goodness as well, people that strive to stop events like you have seen, who die to do it. Humans have walked on the moon and look to the stars to better understand themselves!" she declared, arms open in a hopeful gesture. Rising to his full height again, the Numaran gave her a disgusted stare.

<They will never reach the stars.>

"Aren't you willing to listen? Can't you see you could teach them so much? Help them reach a better way," Michael added. "We chose this life to protect them because for every bad person I know there are so many more good ones. You cannot stand here and judge everyone for the sins of a few."

<But no matter how hard they struggle, no one can stand against one individual's goals. It only takes one to corrupt the rest of them and they all slide towards destruction. The bad outweighs the good.>

"And how good were you when you murdered people for thinking for themselves?" gasped Tyran as Michael helped her to her feet. She was white; her brow beaded with sweat and looked like she had been crying for a fortnight. Her eyes were shadowed as they burned towards the Numarans. She drew a deep breath and pulled herself upright.

"I hate bullies," she growled.

<You are vermin.> He moved his head slightly as if listening to a voice. <You will all be exterminated, your blasphemy razed to the ground and a new Eden will be born from the ashes. This time it will be different!>

With that, the ground beneath the warriors opened and they were sucked down a shaft; straight into the icy wastes of space.

As their lungs burned for air, the familiar sight of the Juggernaught command centre solidified all around them, Varran's concerned face almost bursting with relief at seeing them.

"You couldn't have done that earlier?" snapped Tyran as she rolled over onto her back almost crying. Almost embarrassedly,

Varran garbled that they were trapped inside the ship's force field but when they were expelled into space, he grabbed them with the teleport beams. He had been more concerned than he let on and was relieved they were safe.

"I take it they have no manners," he said rhetorically. Michael's face flushed with temper.

"Blow them out of the sky!" he cried. "Shower of bastards," he growled.

"Who are they?" asked Varran as he watched the vessel power up and surge forward determinedly. Jacke joined him, arms crossed. She watched the ship hatefully, her heart still beating fearfully.

"The Numarans, originally from Earth, acted like gods, don't like what man has done to their Eden so they going to wipe all of us out and restore Numaran rule."

Varran grimaced.

He paused, remembering the woman on the news earlier, cradling her dead child. She probably wished she had the power to turn back time and

bring her child back. His heart broke when he thought of her. She would go on mourning, wishing things could be different; probably wishing someone would help her.

But if the Numarans reached Earth, no one would survive. Millions would scream for someone to help them as the skies darkened. Varran glared at the holoscreen before him. He wouldn't allow it. That nameless woman would have help; let her live and find some comfort.

"Well?" demanded Michael. "Let's use this station for what it was built for!"

Varran fixed him with a look so determined, so cold, it took Michael's breath away.

In a second, Varran darted into action. Rushing round the command table, he shouted instructions to the computer, smacking controls as he went. Systems hummed into action as weapon systems lit up all around them.

With an air they hadn't seen before, the warriors watched Varran as he turned and looked at them.

"I swore to use this technology for good and to defend this planet from whatever's coming. If this is to be the evil I foresaw, then well and good. But I have to send you home, now. If I have to, I'll ram the Numaran ship and set off the self-destruct." He ran his hand along the lit up table. "There's more than enough power to do it. But I want you all safe to carry on just in case."

"Not a chance," protested Tyran. "We all have families down there." Michael nodded.

"And I am not going to sit and wait to see if the death rays fall from the sky," he said determinedly, "to hell with that." Jacke stood by the others in agreement, her expression tautly determined.

"You taught us too well. We're staying. They had condemned everyone on the basis of one rotten apple. Maybe we can show them different."

For a second, tears burned Varran's eyes. They had known each other for such a short space of time, yet here they were ready to die to protect strangers who would never know what they had done. Fate had chosen well. Begrudgingly, he nodded.

"In that case, you know what to do."

If you listen carefully, even space has a voice, a subtle harmonic of solar winds that croon softly in celebration of an ever expanding universe that teems with millions of life forms.

Draped against the heavenly vista of sparkling stars and planets, cloaked in swirls of colourful nebulae and gas clouds was a slow moving cloud of asteroids of invariable shapes and sizes. Some said it was the remains of a tenth planet, others the leftovers of our solar system forming.

With a determined roar of engines, a great shape rose from within, asteroids falling from its hull like water from a rising kraken. It sailed upwards with grim determination, veering like a Goliath in the direction of the Numaran ship.

Varran sat upright, his body tense in the raised black leather command chair, his eyes locked on the image of the crystalline vessel that threatened their entire existence. He hadn't survived the loss of his home world just to lose his adopted one to a bunch of false gods with delusions of grandeur. The wailing mother fleeted across his mind again along with a thousand others. He had travelled the Earth extensively and had met many good people, enough to strengthen his faith in the human race.

His expression grim, he glanced at a read out on the left arm panel of his chair. With a light nod of satisfaction, he breathed deeply.

"We are clear of the asteroid field. Operation Trident will begin in three minutes. Everybody ready?" he addressed thin air. One by one, Jacke, Michael and Tyran answered him in nervous but brave tones that they were.

"Let's do it!" yelled Tyran heart pounding in fear.

"Computer, initiate Dagger waves one to five in fifteen second bursts, all systems tied to main computer with full autopilot control. Launch in 5, 4, 3, 2, 1," Varran paused giving the vessel one last look.

If the Numarans had detected them, they obviously didn't see them as a threat. It was after all five times larger than the Juggernaught. No matter. A bee sting can kill in minutes.

"Launch Daggers!"

On either side of the Juggernaught's forward bulk, two black hangar doors rimmed with red, peeled back.

Like smashing a bee hive, dozens of spear head shapes shot forward and spread out in attack patterns, all sensors aboard focusing on the retreating Numarans.

Seconds later they shot forward, weapons bristling. Fifteen seconds after that another wave flew out, fifteen seconds after that another. Like a swarm of missiles they plunged forward, dozens of determined Daggers eager for battle.

Space lit up as they fired barrage after barrage of blue and green lasers at the Numaran ship. Its shields lit up like oil on water in an array of colours as the tiny attack fighters skimmed and twirled about it like dancers performing an epic ballet as the stars were obscured by the colossal blasts of energy upon energy.

The Numaran ship slowed but did not turn. Its surface rippled and crackled as sheets of energy gathered across its mass and shot upwards to the coral crystal spires.

With an imperceptible whisper, giant bolts of lightning shot from the spires in concentric waves. Registering the blast, the Daggers dived away sharply but some were too slow, shattered in millions of pieces as they blast dissolved them in mid-flight.

"Trident two, initiate!" Pressing a sequence of buttons, Varran braced himself as a roar built up within the Juggernaught, its systems crying out to each other as the ship shuddered.

Like a giant bracing himself against an enemy onslaught, the Juggernaught's surface began to change. Its forward bulkheads retracted and the mighty side arms lifted with a growl, allowing the left and right sections to drop away, their hulls contracting to form an armoured shell giving the impression of an armadillo with its layered overlapping arced shields.

With a blast of engines, they shot forward as the top layer of the remaining section lifted off and took the same shape of the others before following them. Varran smiled to himself proudly, watching the three sections of the Juggernaught roar across space, their powerful engines ablaze with angry power. Varran opened the communication link and gave the three youngsters a word of encouragement.

"Remember to get yourselves past the Numaran just in case I fail."

"Understood," they chorused, knowing full well they would not leave him alone to face this battle.

"And just in case something goes wrong, I just want to say how proud I am of you all. You brought me back to life when solitude had become all I knew." The emotion in his voice was clear but he held himself proudly, resolute in the task ahead.

"Okay drama queen," chided Jacke, her dulcet tones calming him. "Let's get this show on the road. Good luck!" Her section seethed forward.

"Christ, I'm bricking it," breathed Michael before realising the comm was still open. Tyran couldn't resist what may be her last chance.

"There's a lovely thought," she crowed, "going to my death with your dirty underwear. Hope to god it's not a thong." Michael grinned to himself, imagining her face but said nothing. Tyran found herself wishing he would strike back with a smart answer. She somehow had finally got the last word.

On the small monitor screens in their cockpits, the Numaran ship grew larger, the Daggers swooping around it like wasps in a crescendo of light.

"What sort of weapon is that?" asked Tyran before realising she was whispering. The great ring of fire passed overhead and she involuntarily ducked.

Glancing at her lucky rabbit figure stuck with blue tack on the half circle controls in front of her, she shook her head. He was her lucky charm because she found him in the street just before she bought a scratch card in Jefferson Newsmart and won £1, 500 on it. Not that she was superstitious or anything. She rarely bought scratch cards, thinking them a waste of money but not that time. She rolled her eyes at the little fawn and white figure.

The onboard computer flickered, announcing her distance from the target. She powered up the weapons and felt the cockpit shudder as the cannons on either side of her exterior folded out and sparked in readiness.

Jacke was the first to reach the battle as she banked upward and sideways and targeted the spires. With a blaze of fire, the cannons shot a stream of laser bolts like a machine gun on super speed. Parts of the Numaran shield was faltering under the onslaught as its resources were focused on powering their weapons. A halo of fire ripped a Dagger apart not ten metres away from her and Jacke jumped as she veered to the left and downwards, dodging the stream of Daggers zooming all around her.

Now I know how my brothers feel playing their Playstation, she thought wryly. She couldn't see the stars as space seemed to be filled with the Daggers and the sheer cliffs of the Numaran crystal ship that spat flame like a dragon. Sean Connery's a brilliant actor, she thought to herself for no good reason as she spun in a loop.

The logical part of her mind knew it was a mental defence to take her mind off the stress she was under. A damaged Dagger floated out of nowhere right in front of her. She pulled on the controls desperately as it filled her view screen but her attempt was too late as it smashed into her flank, taking out an engine.

The ship rattled and screeched as she spun helplessly towards the Numaran shield where she would vaporise as surely as the sun rose. The ship jerked again as the under wing of Michael's ship nudged her sideways away from the lethal shield, sending her tumbling end over end into open space. Great, I won't burn, she thought, as she read off the damage alert and silenced the red flashing lights and alarm shrill. Smoke filled the cockpit as fried systems sparked and sizzled. But I'm going to suffocate.

Tyran watched Jacke's ship fall away, a great chunk burning in her side. Her heart pounded fearfully as her initial euphoria died. I could die out here, she chilled. She closed her eyes and took a deep breath. But I won't go alone, she vowed.

Firing everything she could, she pounded the nearest spire, already weakened by the Dagger assault. She faced it head on pouring every ounce of fire power she could muster.

With a massive explosion the spire erupted and fell apart, great cracks running up its length. Glacial chunks collapsed into another which broke off with a shimmer of a billion crystal pieces, each lit up by the laser blasts. It looked like the stars were falling from the sky.

With a cry of triumph, Tyran shouted over the intercom.

"That's for you Jacke! See that Michael? Teach them to poke in my brain!"

"And they had such a small space to poke in." Tyran's face broke into a wide grin at the sound of Michael's voice.

"Glad you're still kicking; your turn." She could almost see his mischievous smile, those brown eyes sparkling. She leaned round to see where he was and waved despite the fact he wouldn't see her. Her joy turned to fear as she saw his ship smashed into by a ring of fire. She watched as its surface crackled with flowing energy like ants. It trembled and faltered before falling on its axis.

The Numaran ship reared up behind him as it surged forward before retreating under a relentless barrage of missiles that shook it to its very core. The Juggernaught swept in like an avenging angel, blotting out the stars under its attack.

The Numaran vessel visibly rocked under the force of the blasts and let rip with another blast from its spires. The Juggernaught spun as if in pain and fired a volley of laser cannons. But the Numaran held its ground as it spewed wave upon wave of energy on the Juggernaught. Like giants in hell fire they threw assault upon assault at each other lighting space as if the heavens themselves were opening up.

Varran gripped the arms of the command seat as the Juggernaught rocked under the pressure of the Numaran weapons. Consoles were exploding around him and the air filling with wraith-like black smoke.

<You cannot win. This is our home and we will reclaim it. You have failed.>

Gritting his teeth, Varran silently apologised for failing his friends and the Earth. Soon billions would die because he had not been strong enough. He saw Michael's dead ship floating while Tyran was firing at anything she could, desperately hoping for a last minute miracle, for that last minute rescue where they would all sit around and laugh about it later.

They were finished but the Xereban engineers had built this station well and even Varran had only a fair idea of its firepower when it exploded. But he knew it may be just enough to stop the Numaran ship and send it into oblivion.

"Computer," he said calmly. "Initiate self-destruct. Set for twenty seconds. Divert all power to shields including life support and set the Juggernaught on a collision course with the enemy ship. Code Varran 4902 mark 7 black. Initiate!"

With a last heave, the Juggernaught grumbled as it built up speed as the countdown began. He couldn't even see what had become of Jacke and the others as he gripped his chair and braced himself for the impact.

"Now I'll know if I can die or not," he muttered ruefully.

All around him fire roared, making the very stars retreat. The roar of the engines was deafening as the hull shuddered under the Numaran attack. Smoke filled his throat and his eyes watered from the heat and sorrow. "I'm sorry," he whispered to the weeping woman.

Suddenly there was silence.

The holoscreen showed the crystal ships bough almost within touching distance of the Juggernaught's hull but the fires were still, flames frozen in time, the noise quelled. Drifting wreckage hung in space like model planes suspended from a ceiling.

"THIS STOPS NOW!"

The voice boomed from all around them and for a second, Varran thought it was the Numarans pulling a last sick stunt.

"THEY WILL NOT DIE TODAY. NOR WILL THE PEOPLE OF EARTH!"

<Who are you to interfere?> seethed the Numaran. < We demand justice!>

"BE SILENT!" A vast curtain of golden light had surrounded both ships and everything in the immediate vicinity, frozen in time and utterly helpless.

"NUMARAN, YOUR TIME IS PASSED AS THEY SAID BUT YOUR OWN ARROGANCE BLINDS YOU. LEAVE HERE AT ONCE OR WE WILL DESTROY YOU. YOUR EDEN IS LONG GONE, IF THERE EVER WAS SUCH A PLACE. GO NOW!"

<This will not be forgotten,> warned the Numaran.

"DON'T LET IT BE; FOR YOUR OWN SAKE. AND BE WARNED; NEVER RETURN!"

Agonising seconds passed as the Numaran ship held its ground but slowly, the great crystal vessel lurched forward and retreated along its path, back out into deep space. The golden veil began to fade as it retreated.

"Wait!" pleaded Varran, reaching into the air out of pure instinct. "Who are you? Why did you do that?"

But there was silence as the light faded. He slumped down on the floor, putting his head in his hands. No one heard his relieved sobs.

Two days later, Jacke found Varran sitting on the observation deck, watching the endless trails of asteroids floating outside. It was large airy room decorated in cream with chrome sofas and seats. Various plants were dotted around the room and on the walls hung portraits of various landscapes from Xereba and Earth.

The Juggernaught was reassembled once more with the living skin healing itself while Varran had beamed teams of engineers and computer specialists from Earth to help repair the damage inflicted by the Numaran attack.

All were of Xereban ancestry and aware of their history and the scientist welled up when he saw their selflessness. He knew some of them would also help in the reconstruction of the earthquake ravaged region and it made the last couple of days more bearable. Sensing his sombre mood, Jacke sat beside him, slipped her arm in his and lay her head on his shoulder. His hand squeezed hers appreciatively. Neither spoke, they didn't need to.

The glass door slid open and Tyran and Michael's shadows fell across them. They looked at each other and Tyran quelled a comical quip at the sight of them. It wouldn't have been appropriate. They had been so close to losing it wasn't funny. Instead they sat on chairs on either side of their friends and stared out the window.

They knew how lucky they had been, how close the Numarans had come to retaking the Earth and yet thanks to the intervention of some unknown force, they had survived.

Any doubts Varran had had about how cruelly life had treated him had been crushed in that moment. Something had been watching over them, and he knew some would have called it

God: but he seriously doubted God would make Himself visible so readily even if the Earth was in peril and especially to non-believers like himself.

No, whatever had happened, whatever was still to come, Varran was more certain than ever, it was the right path.

The Juggernaught had carried the survivors to Earth for a reason, time would explain why eventually. But for now the scientist was comforted by a saying humans had, that life never handed you anything you couldn't handle. He knew somehow that woman cradling her child would survive and go on and so would he, side by side with his friends.

Life was full of wonder.

"I wonder what other Earth history has been forgotten," wondered Varran suddenly. "You know, for all our technology and so called knowledge, we still know so little."

Michael smiled softly. "I remember a joke someone once told me. They said that the first page of the bible had been found." He paused, trying to get the wording right. "It said, all characters herein are purely fictitious and any similarity to a person or event is purely coincidental." He breathed through his nose. "Makes you think."

Jacke nodded catching his meaning. "Only good thing is history is an open book to us thanks to his nibs here." Varran smiled and looked at them.

"Let's go see."

THE TOMBS OF ETHER PART 1

They didn't know these tunnels as well as he did or they would have known to look up as Sril's scaly athletic form slithered into an opening in the ceiling and vanished into a series of overhead conduits.

His elbows and knees were scraped from the stony white crystal surface but he ignored the pain as best he could. He had never experienced pain before and he didn't like it at all.

He pressed on, the shouts of the aliens fading behind him. He knew by their guttural tones his escape had not gone down well. It took a while to process their language in his brain but Sril knew enough syntax to know "He" would be furious. How could one man alone be responsible for this; if so, how?

His breathing shallow again, Sril paused at a junction, silvery veins allowing him to see.

A feeling of hope surged in him. It was quite a remarkable sensation.

No Etherian had ever had to fight like this and Sril had no idea what to do. But he knew who could help from the billions of life forms in the universe that he was aware of. They would be able to deal with the invaders once and for all.

Dropping on all fours, he froze as he surveyed the passage.

Beyond that door was his salvation. Listening intently for alien voices, he scampered along the crystalline walls and sniffed the air. So far, so good, he thought. He was doing it properly, as it should be.

Clinging to the wall, he shimmied across the ceiling and down into the large chamber. It was dimly lit by a pale blue aura that cast deep shadows.

Keeping to the shade, he crept to a rhomboid console lit by an organic looking growth of controls.

Slim clawed fingers skimmed the panel as a slight sigh of power filled the chamber. His hearts beat faster as he watched the mottled shape rise from the floor on the opposite side of the chamber and move silently upward towards the opening in the ceiling, the blue haze playing off its turtle like skin. A ray of daylight made Sril blink as he nodded to himself.

One last hope.

If it made it past the ships in the sky, it would be, as humans say, a message in a bottle.

Deactivating the console, Sril turned to hide in the overhead tunnels, desperate to stay hidden until help came. He failed to see the hulking figures in the gloom. He was cut down in a hail of fire.

"It's not Numaran then."

Peering over Varran's shoulder, Tyran tried to make sense of the hologram sensor reports that scrolled in midair before them. She squinted, her sky blue eyes rapidly failing to catch any of the data.

Resting her chin on Varran's shoulder, she pouted, patiently waiting for the Xereban scientist to explain everything.

She felt a chill of anticipation run through him as he tensed at the readings.

Next minute she stumbled forward as he dashed round the panels, snatching her perch from beneath her. Varran seemed to barely realize she was there.

Tyran watched Varran as he seemed to dance a little jig as more and more data came through.

Although she had a gift with computers, all this Xereban technology was a little lost on Tyran. She glanced at the oval hologram table with its rows of touch controls and the little multicolored lights that danced in rhythm with Varran.

She knew that all around her were millions of tiny sensors in the skin of the Juggernaught, recording and transmitting data right here. It seemed almost like a sleeping dragon.

Varran clicked his tongue and sucked his bottom lip as his fingers weaved the controls like a harpist. "Organic engineering," was all she heard him mutter as his left foot began to tap.

Tyran cleared her throat noisily and precisely to no effect. Not even her infamous glare moved the Xereban to acknowledge her presence. He always seemed so alone to her, but then he had been accustomed to his own company for a very long time, and besides, he relished his work and every bit of new information that came through on the sensors was like a Christmas present to him.

Work, she caught herself thinking, we actually get paid for this. She could scarcely believe it sometimes but it had her idea to get some sort of wage for this if they were giving up normal jobs etc to help Varran. Thanks Dad.

He had a daily routine where Varran would get up, exercise and eat a simple breakfast of one banana, two oranges, a piece of buttered toast and two mugs of tea. He had been drinking from a cup until Jacke showed him the joys of a mug of tea.

"Very few Irish take a cup of tea. They may call it a cup but only a mug of tea starts the day and keeps it going," she declared. Memories of her family flashed back when she told him that.

Tyran had warmed to the Irish girl quite quickly. Having no sisters of her own, it was nice that Jacke had taken Tyran under her wing and taught her kick boxing. As Jacke told her, you really didn't know when you were going to need it.

As Tyran knew only too well, there were too many weirdoes wandering about in the world not to have some form of self-defence. Her train of thought was interrupted by a cry from Varran.

"What?" she jumped.

The Xereban scientist held her with wide excited eyes and for a second Tyran was lost in the clarity of his sapphire look.

"Organic!" he breathed, clasping his hands across his mouth as if the sound of his voice would scare the object away. Tyran nodded blankly.

"I see," she acknowledged, "like veg you mean."

The look on Varran's face told her she had said the wrong thing. He looked like a man who had failed to teach a puppy a new trick. He crossed to stand beside her and pointed to the hologram display. "There."

Tyran looked at the numbers and letters and shrugged her shoulders dejectedly. Varran sighed and stretched his aching back.

"Organic as in grown," he explained, "as in our people never achieved it." He paused, his face seeming to see another time and place. "Tried it but didn't quite succeed." He flexed his shoulders and rolled his neck.

Oh no, thought Tyran, he's going into lecture mode and I'm the only one here. Brace yourself girl, this could get seriously boring.

Fortunately for her, Jacke and Michael entered the command centre at that very moment.

"Glad you're here," she beamed a little too quickly, earning her a reproachful glare from his majesty Varran. Tyran returned it with a disarming smile but it didn't deter him.

"Organic ships are virtually unheard of," he began. The others looked at Tyran who nodded to the hologram and the shape it was tracking.

"They are supposedly self-repairing and sentient. There was a race I heard about from a Meran trader called the Rodans. They travelled through space using a squid like creature." Varran paused trying to remember the details. His brow furrowed slightly. "It was, I think, a symbiotic arrangement wherein the Rodans secreted a fluid the squids fed on; quite amazing."

Jacke's face scrunched in disgust. "You mean they travelled in the belly of those things."

Varran nodded. "A fantastic opportunity for research and a perfect example of life forms living and working in harmony."

Michael nodded in agreement. "Look at those little birds that clean crocodile's teeth or the fish that attach themselves to sharks without getting their arse bitten off." The girls looked at him.

"OK Spock," muttered Tyran.

Michael raised his hands defensively. "I like wildlife programmes," he said.

One of his earliest memories was of him sitting with his father on a black leather sofa watching a documentary on deep sea life.

He had been fascinated by the different fish that looked nothing like the ones on the supermarket shelves. There were fish like angels, ones like ghosts and all manner of animals that looked like something off one of those science fiction shows.

And not only that but the stories from fishermen and divers about strange monsters that no one had ever catalogued made Michael wonder what else was down there, swimming about undiscovered- the unknown.

"There have been stories, well, more legends really," mused Varran, "about these sentient ships." He watched the tear drop shape with its turtle like hull on the hologram glide soundlessly before them, a great calm overcoming him. "It has been said that some organics committed suicide in the wake of their pilot's death such was the connection between the two."

"How sad," sighed Tyran.

Her comment brought her a rueful look from Michael.

"Shut it," she growled. Zipping his smirking lips, he turned to hear the rest of the story. Varran seemed to be almost in a trance.

"I know it's impossible but it is claimed the Lidara star constellation is in fact an organic ship that died of a broken heart." The girls were transfixed. "It took off into deep space after its pilot was killed in an accident but could not find another love. So, it flew to Lidara and became the cluster. The more fanciful idea is that the ship broke apart with grief, hoping somehow that its lost love's soul would be guided back to her in starlight." Jacke could feel herself welling up.

"That's beautiful," she breathed, her voice cracking slightly.

Bemused by their reactions, Michael chirped, "And who said romance was dead?"

"The lack of notches on your bedpost," cut Tyran smugly. Varran ignored them as the sight of the ship brought memories of Xereba. Memories that came like a honeysuckle scent on a warm summer breeze.

With its smooth mottled shell, the organic ship looked like some exotic tear drop with a blue green hull undulated with lemon streaks. Jacke stood up and crossed to the hologram image.

"Are you looking for a lost love?" she whispered. Her eyes stroked the image and the more she looked at it the more it gave her the impression of melancholy. "Can we go over?" she asked an equally entranced Varran. Nodding, he placed an arm round her shoulder. Jacke's caring and sensitive nature always inspired him but it underlay a fierce loyalty towards anything she cared about. It would not be wise to get on the wrong side of her.

"Why not?" Michael jumped to his feet and threw on his khaki jacket. "I've always wanted to meet a legend."

Jacke threw him a sideways glance. "Never met Tom Baker then," she quipped, face beaming.

Wondering who Tom Baker was, Varran began the startup sequence for the teleport. He locked the controls for normal space time, calculating the spatial latitude, drift and the organics' relative position to the Juggernaught.

"I'm not reading any life signs on board but the atmosphere is breathable. Be careful none the less."

He was almost bouncing on the balls of his feet as he waited for the three youngsters to get onto the teleport pads in the hexagonal chamber. Whipping on her tan suede jacket, Tyran tossed Jacke a hand unit from a locker in the wall next to the chamber before pocketing one herself.

These were small hand units that could carry out many functions, thus eliminating the need for an armful of cumbersome equipment. Varran and an engineer called Folon had designed them when he had travelled the Earth.

They could scan, analyze samples, determine medical problems, link with the Juggernaught's main computer and act as a communicator. It was neat, compact and flipped open to reveal a small screen.

It was much like a mobile phone shape and as human technology had progressed, it allowed Xerebans to function in the modern world without suspicion and if the units were stolen, they automatically melted on tampering.

Varran looked at them alert and eager for the adventure.

Despite their human ways and attitudes, Varran saw shades of his people's thirst for life in them and it was rubbing off on him. It felt at times like he was experiencing life for the first time through them.

Here they were ready to jump unquestioning into the unknown and had already shown great courage and resourcefulness in their new lives, fighting for the cause despite never having known Xereba bar what he had shown them on the historical records or seen in their ancestral memories.

Varran wished they could have seen his homeworld's sprawling quartz plains and rainbow waterfalls which rose miles above those that came to see them.

If only he could show them the multicolored skylights of the underwater colonies of N'ja where many lovers swept up in its majesty were bonded for life. Indeed, Varran's parents had married there.

He saw fiery trepidation in his friends' faces with each new challenge and this was no exception.

As he joined them on the teleport pads he ordered the computer to initiate automatic remote retrieval mode and to transport them.

As the wave of blue double helix energy swept over them, Varran took a deep breath. However when the wave faded he realized they were still on the Juggernaught!

He swiftly looked round only to see Jacke and Michael blinking blankly at him.

Tyran was nowhere to be seen.

Varran leapt off the pad and rushed to the central console. "Oh no," he breathed. Jacke and Michael were at his side in an instant. They stared at the image before them, dread creeping up their spines. The ship had gone. So had Tyran.

Her mother was humming.

Tyran snuggled into the soft pillows and pulled the pink Barbie quilt tighter round her. Her bedroom door was a column of light and her mother with her shiny brown hair and comforting blue eyes lay partly on the bed beside her. She was gently stroking Tyran's long blond hair in time to a lullaby, watching lovingly as her daughter fell into the arms of dreams.

Tyran had been ill with sinus trouble causing a faint wheeze whenever she breathed.

Mother's singing always gave onto good dreams; dreams where the sun shone at the right temperature and children played under a wraparound blue sky and cotton ball clouds.

There were no monsters as long as mother sang; no evil to scare small children.

But the dream seemed short tonight as Tyran stirred and realized the humming was not her mother but emanating from all around her.

Blinking confusedly, she stared at the salmon colored membrane walls that glowed slightly. The floor was smooth like marble but not cold to the touch.

The ceiling curved above her in spidery webs of membrane that quivered from time to time. Sitting up, the image of her old bedroom fresh in her mind, Tyran felt her scalp crawl as she realized neither her mother nor Jacke and the others were with her.

Tentatively, she called out for them. No one answered. Varran had been so excited at coming here; surely he wouldn't leave her here alone just to satisfy his own curiosity?

Could this be Michael's revenge for all those jibes she'd gotten him with? The ultimate in the last word.

Her heart quickened as she got to her feet, her boots making a squeaking noise against the floor.

Brushing down her ski pants, Tyran examined the weird structure in the centre of the arched room.

Several strands as thick as a person ran from ceiling to floor like sinew in a muscle. They vibrated on touch like a web trapping a fly. It was dry to the touch although the sinews looked slimy.

Running her hand across the mottled grey and white walls, it reminded her of the feel of moss.

An arch led out into a corridor with similar strands all over the place, widths and lengths connecting walls and ceilings. The glows in the walls varied too as if reacting to her.

Steadying herself, Tyran knew she had to be inside the organic ship but couldn't tell if they were moving.

Maybe the teleport had failed, a power surge maybe and the others were outside on the Juggernaught wildly jealous Tyran was here and they weren't.

Suddenly adventure didn't seem so exciting when you were alone. And Tyran hated to be alone. Reaching into her pocket, she pulled out her hand scanner.

"Activate visual scan and record mode and relay to the Juggernaught," she said quietly. Just because Varran hadn't detected anyone aboard, didn't mean there was no one. She did a 360 degree sweep and tried to focus on the screen.

Try to get all you can, girl, she ordered herself. Focus on getting something for your trouble. Trust me to end up like those three in the Blair Witch. Your life locked in a camera.

Gingerly, she moved ahead, scanning as she went, the humming reverberating all around her like a wind chime embracing a breath on a humid summer evening. There was no obvious mechanics or computer terminals, no machinery of any kind she could see. The scanner wasn't much help either.

The technology was too different for it to compare and analyze.

All there was, were these sinews and strange indents in the walls every few meters.

Tyran stopped, a thought occurring to her. If Varran was right and this was an organic ship, then there was every possibility it was alive and if so, did that mean she was now walking through its guts? My God, what if this was its stomach and she could be digested any minute?

Her mind raced through the notion, dismissing it on one hand but the very chance of it happening turning her own stomach.

The others had better be trying to get me out of here, she thought nervously. "Switch to comlink," she said. "Contact the Juggernaught." Silence. Tyran's heart skipped a beat.

"Retry comlink, maximum range, all bandwidths. Begin." Licking her dry lips, Tyran waited, willing the little piece of machinery to stretch out and give her a link home.

Her breathing shallow, Tyran blew through her lips and steadied her nerves.

Right, she thought, focus. What would Varran do? What would he expect me to do? He chose me to be part of this life, to fight the good fight, so let's think. This ship must have a brain or a bridge. Sensible, have to get there. But where's that?

Calling up the comlink's data on the layout so far, Tyran told the handset to extrapolate the most likely position of the bridge given the ship's dimensions as scanned by the Juggernaught.

It bleeped lightly and the blue screen swirled as it ran through the external design and created a three dimensional layout as per her instructions. It blinked almost triumphantly as the light played on Tyran's azure pupils, creating a mini starscape. Grinning, Tyran pressed forward, the coral like sinews brushing like web over her body.

General Tork stood gazing out over the Etherian citadel, its coral and white spires spread over miles in various shapes and designs.

Some were domed, others square or triangular, dotted with openings covered in opaque screens. The material of the buildings sparkled from the pale lilac light that sprayed the cloudless sky above them and even to a Vorg warrior, the beauty was not lost.

Snorting, Tork smelt the tinge of sweetness in the air but no smell he had ever sensed before. The vista filled him with memories of his homeland before the wars.

It too had been a sight to behold.

Battlements and towers everywhere challenged any being to invade them. It had not been as colorful as this but the passion was in the layout. The Vorg's cities had been a monument to strength and power. You could almost feel it at dawn; the seething of a behemoth rising from the depths.

Although, Vorg architecture had neither squares nor rectangles, for they believed once cornered, you were dead.

So, their cities were a mass of domes and amphitheatres with no corners, a belief that permeated every aspect of their society.

From the clothes to their warship designs, the Vorg sent out a message; they were defiant and would fight to the death for there was no one that could beat them into a corner, no one that could crush them in the inferno of battle.

Such a noble idea, Tork mused, so noble it effectually ended the Vorg species and its culture. Cursed in fighting over territory and dispute over victories, saw a massive civil war that launched countless missiles as one faction sought to wipe out the other and claim their spoils.

In the end everyone lost.

Tork recalled standing on a craggy hilltop watching his precious homeland burn in savage flame.

He could smell the burnt flesh of colleagues and allies spew through the black air, assaulting his senses as viciously as the screaming missiles that had carved their way to here, heralding the onslaught of cold death that ravaged the land.

The sky seemed to have melted with the carnage, clouds hanging like used candles against a blood red sky.

Where children had once stood learning the Vorg warrior code was ash, the great plumed domes shattered like glass in ruins so crumbled there was no telling where pride and foolishness ended.

Tork had cried for his fellows, his black booted feet dragging through the rubble, his tusks retracting in horror at what lay before him.

The shattered hulls of saucer warships crumpled and torn blended into the burning landscape; great harbingers of destruction that had been felled by a rain of torpedoes from the ground; a last desperate attempt to save millions as they ran for homes that were collapsing around them in molten explosions.

Tears evaporated as missiles detonated all around them, screams of disbelief as the end of the world came like a flood.

Tork stared around him, desperate for something recognizable, a remnant that he could hold in his four fingered hand and hold up to the devastation and cry, "You didn't take it all! We still survive!"

He threw his leathery head back and roared at the heavens where he knew the first warriors of the Vorg lineage watched in dumb silence at what had become of them from the next life, their tears falling from the skies to soothe the molten landscape; a final act of mercy.

Tork smashed at broken walls, his knuckles bleeding from the impact as he hurled boulders in frustration, his pain overwhelming. He sank to his knees, snorting hard as his chest filled with the ashen smog, small squalls of dust spraying where he fell, his ragged uniform covered in the bloodied ash of the dead.

He had lost his family and friends, their faces swimming before him in anguished swarms, the screams in his mind the only sound in the silent void.

He fell forward onto his hands, his fingers brushing against something delicate beneath them. It was blackened around the edges and shivered in the hot winds. Gently brushing the dirt from it, Tork stared at it.

It was a book.

Small, thin and very light, it sang to him, words shining like a beacon. The General held it like a new born, not sure what to do. A tear fell onto it and he gently wiped it off, afraid that even that could dissolve the last piece of normality.

Sitting back on the ground, he studied it, turning the pages.

Time seemed to stop and a feeling of hope began to stir within him as he read the words.

Fate had dealt a harsh lesson to the Vorg. All their pride and mighty war cries, all their battles against enemies that dared to face them had been to no avail.

Their greatest enemy had been themselves and their desperation to prove to each other that even the Vorg were superior to each other had brought about their own destruction and left themselves wide open to pillaging enemies.

Tork drank in the writings as his world burned around him.

It was from the old time, depicting the rise of the Vorg as a unified people whose greatness came from within. They had looked about them and saw the world as it was, an opportunity to make their stamp on creation.

In this spew of death, Tork realized that the Vorg had stopped being one race a long time ago and no one had even realized it.

Power, greed and personal gain had blighted their history. The Vorg were unstoppable as one race, one spearhead that ploughed through history. Now it was gone.

If there were other survivors, Tork knew he had to bring them together again and never more allow their race to fall to this.

They were the Vorg, fierce warriors whose very name had brought down worlds.

Now they teetered on the verge of extinction, the tongue of death snaking round their heels.

Tork read on and the words came in a torrent of prose that almost shone from the paper. Their strength lay within.

THE TIME WARRIORS – FIRST FOOTSTEPS

The pride of the Vorg was their unification against all others. There was no internal disputes and all lived together harmoniously.

This was how it should have been and if they had remembered that then this disaster would never have happened. Tork swore it would never be so again.

Rising his shining eyes to the world around him he swore to the first warriors their tears would not be in vain and he would raise the Vorg to the heights of greatness once more. They would be feared but not in the way they were.

Tork read the last sentence.

"Where there had been desert, there would be forest. A single flower defies the great fire that consumes the mighty trees. A newborn grabs the finger of its parent and holds fast. This child is saying I am here."

Looking at the pink grey sky, the Vorg leader allowed himself a small sigh of contentment as he took in the myriad of circular ships that he commanded.

Iron silver in color, they hung above the citadel like vast boots ready to stamp down on an insect. Perfectly spherical with no corners, they were trimmed with a shred of crimson, the Vorg battle color with each layer armed to the teeth.

It was a worthy armada, one that had risen from the ashes of the Vorg home world and was helping rebuild its future.

The Vorg no longer declared war unless the price was right.

Tork started as his communicator gave a shrill cry. Breathing deeply, the General drew his mottled leather cloak around him as he lifted the communicator and switched it on.

"Speak," he said gruffly, bristling at the thought of their contractor's attitude. The rough tones of his first in command Rell came through.

"General. The escaped ship is approaching."

Tyran kicked the organic wall in frustration and immediately bounced back as if she had dropped an ornament in Harrods.

"Sorry, sorry, sorry," she muttered. Bowing her head, she tried to think clearly, trying to find an option.

If this thing was indeed a living ship with a brain, then it should understand how she felt. After all, it only took her against her will and hadn't given any indication of its intent.

Placing her hand deftly on the wall, she felt it shudder softly. The thought of a doctor's cold hands fleeted through her mind.

"I'm sorry for kicking you but you're not being very helpful. You brought me here and you haven't said a thing. Maybe you haven't got a mouth so are you telepathic? I'm not that thick," she smiled encouragingly, "8 GCSES and a first aid certificate." She paused, eyeing the pale pink material for a response. It vibrated twice. Was that an answer, Tyran wondered. She sighed.

"If you could just give me a clue," she pleaded. "Every time I think I'm close to a bridge, you move the walls like some big muscle, keeping me in one place." Her tone was scolding now. "I mean, come on. Give me something to go on!" No response. "Fine!" She sat on the floor, the little contours fitting round her behind so she was comfortable. She glared at the wall. "I'm not moving."

With that, the ship tumbled end over end.

Gliding in across the sky, the organic ship slipped between the Vorg cruisers effortlessly, using the limited clouds as cover. It expected more resistance but none came. The ominous circles stood their ground, unmoving.

A central spire reared before them, a large oval gap forming in the top level, allowing the lithe ship to swoop in unharmed. It leveled out and silently drifted to the cavern floor. The walls dotted with tiny white crystals, pulsed in reaction to its arrival as the ship settled on the ground. There was an echo of boots as the wall parted and large shadows fell over the innocent looking hull.

Tyran was on her feet in seconds as the ship came to rest.

She knew they had landed and her mind raced with possibilities. Good or bad, she mused. She had no weapons, no means of defending herself if the worst came to the worst.

She hoped this ship had enough sense not to land her in danger with no forewarning. A breeze of warm air rushed over her, giving her the impression of a plane's engines coming to rest. There was no noise. Silence.

Tyran stood poised to run if need be. She pocketed her hand unit, ready to go. A portion of wall shivered and peeled back revealing two large shapes.

"Hello?" prompted Tyran. "Is this your ship?"

With savage grunts, the figures stepped forward into the light and Tyran's heart skipped a beat. She glimpsed a large chamber behind them housing other ships like the one that had kidnapped her.

Time seemed to slow as the tusked leathery faced monsters in black padded armor raised lethal looking rifles and pointed them straight at the frightened girl. They hissed gloatingly, slimy tongues licking yellow razor teeth.

With a defiant yell, Tyran charged straight at them. She fell beneath the thump of a fist.

Dazed, she was aware of being swept up in one of their muscular arms and carried off. She watched the door in the ship close quietly.

"Some bloody help you were!" she blasted before she passed out.

Tork took in the vast amphitheatre that reared up around him like a plume.

It spiraled like a vortex above him, thousands of coffin indents patterned in the blue and white crystalline surface, each sealed by a pale yellow covering like a mesh, housing darkened figures within. Steps snaked between the lower level housings.

It reminded him of a solidified smoke plume from a cobron energy bomb and tapered off high above him, wisps of pale grey mist circling watchfully almost like wraiths bewailing the great tragedy that had befallen their charges.

The walls of the chamber pulsed with restrained power as if the amphitheatre was breathing in time with its sleeping occupants.

In the centre of the corralled speckled floor was a wide hexagonal raised dais made of transparent lilac crystal, tiny shivers of energy shooting about inside.

A series of triangular crystals ran the length of it amid a spray of rectangles and circles. The technology was foreign to the Vorg and distasteful with the use of any shape but a circle. It was of little interest to him.

The job was the priority, not the spoils. His black eyes spotted the figure on the steps nearby and immediately he tensed. This man had provided the contract but Tork hated the contempt he had for the Vorg.

When initial contact had been made, he obviously knew Vorg history, yet his tone, his stance brimmed with nonchalance. The Vorg were as lower life forms to him, muscle to carry out a job. He had no appreciation for the skill and pride the Vorg took in a job nor, Tork suspected, did he care if any Vorg lost their lives in the process.

He knew of Rell's dislike of him as well as the troops who had had contact with him but the contract was binding. It was the way of the Vorg.

The figure was examining one of the sleeper chambers with a hand held device that emitted a series of sounds that sounded like a professor clucking over an experiment.

With a slight tilt of his white haired head, the figure rounded to look at the approaching general. Leaping from the stone steps, his landing raised small dusty clouds that gave off a smell like freshly cut grass.

Tork reached the central console and watched his associate come towards him. The more jobs the Vorg took on, the more Tork realized the galaxy was full of strange and bizarre creatures with their own agendas and ways of life no Vorg had ever imagined.

This one was different.

His stride was confident, his frame possessing an arrogance that matched his stature.

His shoulder length white hair swung proudly around the red skinned face which made the full mouth of teeth shine like the moon over the Katarsis Lakes on the Vorg home world.

The nose was slender but gave him a regal air. The perfect skin, the intense blue eyes, betrayed nothing but determination. The clothes were a rich fabric the General had not seen since the fall of his civilization. A gorgeous royal navy shirt clasped at the neck by a gold pin matched his fitted black trousers, tucked into shiny knee length boots was completed by a long cloak of a deep saffron color, its edges trimmed with gold lilt.

He called himself the Collector, his real name a mystery and his attire gave one the impression he only liked the richest, most luxurious things in life.

With a deft flick of his hand, he switched off the device and slipped it into a silk belt pouch attached to his side. He stood opposite Tork at the central console and gave him a wide smile, a smile that made the General bristle.

"Well, General, I trust you have captured whoever that ship brought back?" Tork's tusks retracted slightly in surprise and he chided himself for forgetting his first rule. Never underestimate anyone. His gruff tones gave no irritation away.

The Collector waved his wrist at the Vorg, still grinning.

"Handy little thing," he said brightly. "I acquired it from a Chandran on a backward little planet in the Chandra system. You know the Chandrans; old acquaintances of yours, I believe."

He left the words hanging, knowing full well that the Chandrans had been old enemies of the Vorg and had delighted in their downfall.

When Vorg fell they had scavenged as much as they could from the surface and orbital stations before engaging in a past time of hunting Vorg warriors for sport.

Ignoring him but battling his temper, Tork kept his voice steady.

"The Chandrans are well known for their spy technology which they stole from us but the occupant of the ship is being brought here as we speak. A female I believe." The Collector rubbed his hands together excitedly.

"I love mysteries, don't you General? Why did they send for her? What threat could she pose? Is she a god? I've never met a god before." He paused breathlessly before meeting Tork's harsh gaze. His eyes narrowed slightly and he smiled that smile. "Not for the want of trying." He spun on his heels laughing and flung his arm over the general's shoulder. "What a great day! Enjoying it General? Are you?"

Tork just glared at him and said nothing. Shaking his head, the Collector regarded him sympathetically.

"You're a part of history and you don't even realize it."

"As long as payment is made, history does not interest us," Tork replied coldly. Nodding the Collector pursed his lips.

"That's all you care about. Good. Rebuild the economy. Lift the Vorg to greatness again. Like the phoenix from the ashes." He frowned, his skin almost like living liquid. "I don't actually know what a phoenix is. I heard that phrase somewhere but I really must get two for my collection." Tork looked at him puzzled. The alien met his gaze as if reading his mind. "When possible always get two of something." He tapped the side of his nose and whispered, "You never know."

His behavior made Tork wary.

Outwardly it was an almost light attitude but his eyes betrayed a fire, a thirst.

What he wanted, he got.

And Tork knew how much the Vorg were being paid to secure this world. For one person to possess such wealth astonished Tork for he had never witnessed the like before but it had been too good a contract to turn down.

He watched as the man drew a palm sized machine from his hand, flick the edge with his well-manicured thumb and run it along the layout on the console.

It sighed like a spring breeze as the Collector studied the readings. Spindly spider like legs sprang from it and sank into the console, the energy pulses within increasing in strength.

His head sprang up at Tork.

"You mentioned payment. Only when this place is secure and it's not secure yet, is it my brave warhorse General?" Clenching his left fist, Tork held his accusing stare.

"He also is being brought here." The Collector snorted sarcastically, muttering to himself about how it took them long enough.

Turning at the sound of his name, Tork smiled as the last Etherian was carried in over the armored shoulder of one of his troops, Boraz. The light green frame swung in time to the heavy soldier's steps.

"I hope the payment's ready." The Collector caught the jibe in the General's voice and smiled slightly.

"Nice to see the warrior spirit alive and well," he breezed. The console clicked and buzzed as the top began to change into the outline of a body. Tork realized it was the same shape as the Etherian and watched warily.

"Place the body here," ordered the Collector, his face stern and determined. "Better be no marks on him. This is precious merchandise." More gently than he would have liked, Boraz laid the unconscious body into the shape and stood back, accepting a grateful nod from his General. Policy was not to ask questions but Tork's curiosity burned.

How could a species be merchandise?

He knew of slavery and lower classes but the orders had been no alien to be harmed in any way. All weapons set to stun and blood lust to be restrained.

As he looked around him, he wondered what these chambers were for and what would one man do with millions of beings like these.

Engrossed in his study the Collector was smiling as the energy levels rose and a vortex of power formed beneath the console.

His device extracted itself and moved to another section, implanting itself in the material.

Tiny wires snaked from the triangles and circles and pierced the Etherian's flesh. The chamber walls were alive with spears of energy which shot down and through the machinery into the central dais. The Collector's breathing quickened as his features froze his eyes alive with power.

"So that's what you're for," he breathed, nodding to himself.

His head jerked as Tyran shouted at her captors. Lizard like, he leaned forward, soaking in every detail about this newcomer. Tyran, held between two soldiers, was marched towards Tork.

"This is what was in the escaped ship." Tyran glared at the creature before her.

Its leathery brown face with its rows of tusks that ran up the face and across the ridge of the head was unnerving enough but its black studded body armor let her know these creatures were no pushover.

The barrel weapons looked like they could cut you in two so she stayed put, shaking but looking them straight in the eye. She was aware of the red skinned alien creeping round behind her.

At least he looked human, nearly.

"Did you bring me here?" she demanded. The General snorted to himself. "Any chance?" Still no answer. "Look, we can stand here all day and say nothing or you could just send me home, after all," she motioned to the Etherian, "you seem to be in the middle of an operation."

The Collector smiled cautiously at the stony silent Tork.

"Fiery little thing." He swooped round Tyran like an owl on a vole. "Tell me," he said, taking her hand and stroking it. "What's your name?"

"Tyran." Snatching her hand away, she cocked her head at him. "Love the skin." Chortling and almost blushing the Collector ran his hand across her short spiky blonde hair and gazed at her delightedly.

"And I love yours, a peachy pinky white, gorgeous. Is everyone like you where you come from or are you the only one?" She was surprised at the question but this charm reminded her of a saying her dad had when warning her off creeps. A shark always smiles before it bites you in half. That's the feeling she got here.

"There's only one of me," she smiled back. "Sorry." His eyes darted all over her, making her feel distinctly uncomfortable.

"What makes you special, I wonder?"

"Wit, charm and personality," she answered lightly.

"Oh, I can see that already," he purred. "But something else..." He regarded her like a Chinese puzzle box. "Why did he bring you here?" he asked pointing to the prone figure on the console. "Why now?"

Tyran looked at the Etherian and the hundreds of caskets around her. Was this an invasion? And why would the ship deliver her straight into its enemies' hands, or claws in this case, she mused.

"I don't know him. I don't know where I am and I don't care. I'd like to go home please." Her tones were clipped, precise and determined. It amused the Collector that she held his burning gaze. She was indeed fiery.

"No, you're staying," he said abruptly. "You were brought here for a reason and I'm going to find out what that is." He stepped back to the dais and looked at the Etherian thoughtfully. What's the connection he wondered? He took out an oval hand held device from his pouch and held it up for Tyran to see. The lack of reaction didn't surprise him.

"This is a marvel of technology. I obtained it from a dying hermit on a backwater world who found it on the streets of Devane. He never knew what it was but I tracked the readings, such readings. It sang to me across the stars." He beamed. "I love romance." He walked along the body. "Know anything about temporal mechanics, anyone? No? It focuses on a pocket of space and accelerates the passage of time within that point. I've had astounding results." Tyran shook her head and prodded the guard next to her.

"Loves to talk doesn't he?"

"Yes, I do," cut the Collector. "so, let's see what happens when I do this." He inserted the temporal accelerator into the console and stood back, arms widening dramatically as the air throbbed with power.

A blaze of red and grey light formed in midair and began to sizzle and swirl, undulating and playing over the Etherian. The hair on the back of Tyran's neck and arms stood on end as the atmosphere crackled with the swirling vortex that engulfed the alien.

His form faded from view, obscured by the vortex wherein billions of tiny particles expanded and collapsed in micro seconds.

The Collector was engrossed by the display and a wide smile spread across his face. The Vorg troops nervously stepped back bar Tork, who stood and looked into the inferno before him defiantly. It was as if the universe had been compacted and boiled alive in just these few meters, Tyran wondered if this was what Varran had witnessed when Xereba had shattered beneath the forces of accelerated time and had literally aged to death.

It was frightening her and she expected to see the Etherian's skeletal remains burn to dust any second.

Like a dancer, the Collector shot forward and turned the device off.

The vortex seemed to fold in on itself, fading and cascading into nothingness, allowing the Etherian to be seen again.

But he had not aged.

He had changed into a different creature.

Tyran watched the Collector fold his arms triumphantly and mutter, "So that's it."

The scrawny green alien had transformed into a being whose musculature and breadth matched any Vorg warrior and instead of scales was brown bristly fur. Its hands were talons with vicious looking claws and the head was panther like with folded back ears.

Tork had a bad feeling, a warrior's instinct and stepped back cautiously, weapon ready. The Collector laughed at him.

"No need to be afraid. He's perfectly safe."

A claw slashed upward, talons extended, catching the Collector across the chest.

Purple blood spurted out and he fell back screaming. Tork bellowed orders and the Vorg drew their weapons.

Tyran jumped back behind her captors, desperately looking for the nearest door and trying to remember where the hangar bay was.

The Etherian leapt to its feet and snarled, yellow eyes darting round. The Collector was crawling away, fiddling with his pouch as the Vorg formed ranks.

"Don't shoot or the deal's off!" cried the Collector. "Tork, I'm warning you!" Tork trembled as the battle lust gripped him and against his better judgment, ignored the warning. He ordered stun only and drew his weapon.

The Etherian shot off the dais and sailed over their heads. There was the sound of a weapon discharged but with one sweep, the transformed Sril grabbed Tyran and fled out the nearest door.

Once outside, he swung upwards and into the overhead shafts. Clinging to the huge arm for dear life, Tyran closed her eyes.

All she could think of was being swept to the top of the Empire State building in the arms of a great ape.

TOMBS OF ETHER PART 2

After what seemed like hours, Tyran opened her eyes as Sril stopped his rollercoaster of swinging and clambering and finally came to rest.

She felt massive arms gently pull her away from his stingy fur and she fearfully looked up at him. Her entire world was filled with this mountain of fur, muscle and claw from which two yellowy eyes glared down at her. Guessing since she was only five foot six, this creature had to be just over six and a half feet.

Okay, she thought, have to stop calling aliens creatures. Varran would say they were beings. Different but sentient all the same, no matter what they look like. There was a bellow of orders from a Vorg squad far below.

For a second, Tyran jumped as she thought the Collector or one of those warthog things, sorry, beings had found them and their flight had been all for nothing. But there was no one else with them. It must be the acoustics from the way the streets are laid out.

At first glance, they were in a room right on top of a tower because she could see right across the citadel from here. The vista was astounding and she stared at the beautiful colours the buildings gave off from the sun's rays. It was like a hundred rainbows performing a ballet through a prism exploding in a cascade of color that fell like snow. Squinting, she looked up at the sky and the dark circular ships that hovered above the city.

"I take it those are not yours," she stated rhetorically. Somehow she couldn't see this creature aboard those ships. Again, Varran's face popped into her mind scowling. Sorry, she thought, never judge a book by its cover. No matter how gruesome, she added with a wry smile.

"I think I look rather handsome." His feline features curled in admiration as he studied his reflection in the materials in the wall.

Her face froze as she fixed the bea...sorry, being, with a rabbit in the headlights look. He gave her the most melancholy face she had ever seen and she realized he had spoken to her about his looks. He tilted his head slightly, a wry smile showing white fangs. Squatting down to Tyran's level, he asked, "Well?"

She took a step back from the rotten breath and folded her arms across her chest. He chuckled in a wheezy deep growl that made Tyran smile. "You're not expecting me to scratch your belly are you? Because, well, you know, alien germs and the like or my germs, either way, could be bad for you."

"No, not at all." His puzzled expression showed her just because he looked feline, his habits weren't.

Tyran leaned against the window sill, tired and sore. Her arms and legs ached and she could feel the stiff ache of bruises where this being had held her tight. Like a great ape that resembled a killer panther/Bigfoot, he sat down exhaustedly, his massive hairy shoulders slumping forward as he let out a sigh.

"I am Sril; pleased to meet you Tyran of the Earth." She stared, her mouth forming to ask how he knew her name. Instead he held up a large claw, the bestial eyes suddenly full of wisdom and something else.

"It was I that sent for you."

Temper like a tornado, the Collector ran another of his little machines from his pouch over the wounds on his chest. The flesh was knitting together without even a scar and to Tork's astonishment so was the material of the shirt. His face must have betrayed his curiosity for flaming eyes locked on him.

"Damned primitives!" roared the red skinned humanoid, although to the General he seemed somewhat paler. He thrust the device into Tork's face, causing the Vorg to retract his tusks defensively and hiss threateningly. "What's wrong General? Scared? I have a million little tricks collected from all over the galaxy from a hundred and three different worlds, worlds where fungi and lichen are more reliable than the mighty Vorg war fleet!"

He spun angrily on his heels, his cloak like a great wraith in the wind. "Tell me, General weren't you questioning payment a while ago? Payment, payment, I wonder what for. The job isn't finished yet. The contract is incomplete!" Cheeks flared with frustration, he trembled angrily as he stared out Tork. The Collector came right up into his face, unafraid of the ridges of pointed tusks that lined either side of the dark weathered face. "I could wipe every Vorg from the sky in an instant with a single breath if it pleased me." Tork held his gaze concerned only that they would not get paid. He knew this was a dangerous man but he was not afraid of him in the slightest.

"If that were so, then why couldn't you steal this world and its people on your own?" He delighted at the curt realization in the red face. "You may have gadgets and toys that do miraculous things but two small aliens evade you like the wind through your fingers. No matter what you think of me or my race, at least we will honor the contract. If there is no honor among business, then the greater goals will never be achieved." Tork's heart swelled proudly as he felt his words lift his men above this distasteful creature's slurs.

"Slurs General?" goaded the Collector. This time Tork was taken aback; how had he known his thoughts? A hateful smirk gripped the Collector's face.

"Surprise you what I know General. More than you could possibly imagine. What a sad race you lead; self-appointed ruler from a cloud of ash who prostitute themselves for a few credits to build nice little shelters for the young and the old." Tork's chest rose proudly, pulling himself to his full height.

"We stand together as one race, proud we are rebuilding our world; proud to put ourselves above the petty disputes that brought us to ruin." He glanced sideways, making sure his men heard his words and drank them in. "We have stood again where many thought we never would." He was interrupted by a hearty round of applause and cheers.

"And yet it was you and others like you that burned children alive and cut down the elderly all in the name of conquest and power. All hail the mighty warriors that stood on the bones of the helpless," growled the Collector, his voice dripping with distaste. "Find me those escapees and our contract is complete." Tork glared at him. "Now, General!"

They had sat in silence staring at each other for a while, Tyran too angry to even speak. Sril had tried to break the silence a couple of times but Tyran stood resolute.

"You're not usually this quiet," he began. She snapped and stood upright her face a picture of fury.

"How the hell do you know? We met like two minutes ago and suddenly you're the expert on Tyran Scott. What is going on here? Why did you bring me here?" Sril smiled a silly chimp like grin and snorted. He shook his great head amusedly.

"You have no idea how right you are. I do know you very well, born 17th February 1988 by your calendar in St. Bartholomew's hospital at 3am to Lisa and James Scott after an 18 hour labor. Your father cried as your mother held you in her arms forgetting her pain as you became her world." He paused, regarding her softly.

"Should I go on?" A million thoughts rushed through the girl's head as she wrestled with the fact an alien was telling details of her birth. She couldn't speak as Sril nodded reassuringly. "It's alright. That's why the Collector has come here; for us, the Etherians."

"And the other aliens?" she ventured. Sril called them a means to an end. They had no idea why the Collector was doing all this. They were just doing a job and finding it all rather hard to control their fighting spirit.

"But what's so special about you?" asked Tyran. Sril bowed his head sadly. His eyes had clouded with grief.

"Haven't you guessed yet? With us the Collector has the greatest library in all creation. He can access every being, every planet, and every event as it happens through us. We know everything including the lost histories or the past that is rewritten by others hiding dark deeds. We know every secret there has ever been." Sril paused. "We are the library."

The Collector watched the remaining Vorg hatefully. Insects, he grimaced. He was so close to success and they had allowed two rogue elements to escape. Why had that Etherian brought the girl here? She obviously was a means to stopping him but how? She was attractive, so frail looking yet she possessed an air of knowing more than she should do.

The sight of the Vorg and himself hadn't fazed her at all as if alien species were an everyday thing to her. He leaned back wearily against the console and looked around at the chamber with all its sleeping occupants.

As long as they were secured and his little machine controlled their slumber, he could extract them at will and use their knowledge to discover the universe's hidden secrets and take its forgotten knowledge and power for himself.

Of all his collection, this was the greatest addition. Access to millions of years of history, parts of which long forgotten elsewhere but not here. Here, he would find the lost races antiquities and use their technologies to further his own. He would bring his entire collection here and use Ether as his power base.

Briefly, he wondered how long it would take him to move the contents from sixteen planets to here. He had collected so much over the years, collected being the polite term for some of the methods he'd used over the years to obtain it. What he wanted he got.

He touched his left temple and closed his eyes, the device under his skin amplifying his mind, letting it reach out and search for the girl. He got a sense of terrified whispers from the sleepers and ignored them. He felt the blood rush of the Vorg soldiers as they searched fruitlessly, eager for their next job which might bring them battle. Come on, he urged the machine. I paid enough for you before I killed the seller.

Tyran sat with her knees pulled to her chest as Sril explained their history. Millennia ago, a race of beings, so powerful and so enlightened, had seen their world destroyed, their civilization reduced to rubble. They had touched other worlds in other dimensions, seen the life blood of the universe and all its intricate connections. They had sailed the universe learning and teaching. They had stepped in chaos and soothed its troubled brow. Ether had been on the verge of dying from massive environmental changes brought on by a shift in the sun's orbit. The beings had arrived and were dismayed at the sight of yet another world dissolving into time forgotten like a pauper's grave.

So using their great knowledge of the infinite dimensions they had offered the Etherians a life line, one they were free to refuse. Someone had to live to remember the tides of time, not just the big historical events but everything. Every life form had a story, a thread to weave in the tapestry of time. The Etherians would receive perpetual regeneration. They could not die but every century would enter the sleeper cells and be reborn into another form. Each form would be shaped by the environment hence Sril's current form.

It had been shaped by the threat brought by the Collector and the Vorg. No one alive knew about Ether, yet the Collector somehow found their location, which constantly changed throughout the dimensions. The beings had determined it was the best way to keep the planet free from detection but somehow the Collector had found a way to track their next location. He knew exactly when to attack, just as the sleep began. Now every Etherian, all eight billion of them were trapped in the cells all under the planet's surface, unable to change to their next form. The Collector had forced Sril's change just because he wanted to know what the next physical form would be.

"But how does that make you a library?" asked Tyran, her mind reeling with organic ships and immortality. Sighing, Sril gave her those sad eyes again.

"Every Etherian is constantly absorbing every event in the universe and it is stored in their brains. I, for example, am the repository for Earth history. I know every being born, how they lived their lives. I see their part in shaping the world even when they didn't. The universe is alive, Tyran. Every creature is part of a symphony they can't comprehend but they feel it. Varran knows it; he has but glimpsed the heart of it. Even the lowliest tramp lying in the gutter hears it and calls it karma or luck. I could tell you things about Earth no one even realizes happened. I know of the Xereban coming and the role you are all to play. Such knowledge was never meant for one person and we will go on until the universe ends."

Tyran stared at Sril admiringly. "Amazing, so you know what is happening at every given moment and you store it like chapters in a book." Sril nodded. "Is Michael a virgin?" She grinned under the Etherian's withering scowl. "Alright, so why did you bring me here?"

Sril folded his claws, his brow furrowing. "It went perfectly. I told the ship to deliver you to the Vorg who would bring you to the Collector at the precise moment of my change."

"The organic ships are part of the process, like antennae," Tyran reasoned. "When I arrived, your change would give you the form strong enough to out run the Vorg, scoop me up and take me offside." It was a smart move but risky as well. Sril gave her a stern look, his bulky frame tense.

"You are the key to ridding us of the Vorg. Without them, the Collector will not be able to secure my world for his own. He cannot be allowed to trap us here!"

Frowning, Tyran threw a glance at the ships hanging in the sky outside. "Are you sure you didn't need Luke Skywalker?" He gave her a dour look.

"He's a fictional character from a mind very attuned to the universe, Tyran." Sril pointed out quite seriously. Tyran nodded as if she was hearing this for the first time.

"No," he continued, "you are the key to our salvation."

"How exactly am I supposed to get rid of the Vorg and the Collector? I didn't bring my Wonder Woman costume."

Sril straightened gravely. "You are going to kill every last Vorg on Ether."

Appalled by what she had just heard, Tyran got to her feet and gaped at Sril disbelievingly.

"The hell I will!" she shouted. Taken aback, Sril rose and looked at her in bewilderment and asked why not. "I won't commit mass murder just for you, I can't!"

Puzzled, Sril turned on his heel, thinking. This doesn't make sense, he thought. He turned and looked strangely at her. Could he be mistaken? Was his information inaccurate? No, it was not. Etherians saw events as they happen, there could be no error. Grabbing his arm, Tyran, visibly angry, demanded to know how he could get it so wrong, how he could think she was even capable of such an act. Varran would never have accepted her into his company if he thought she was remotely like that.

The thought repulsed her.

"I asked you a question."

Sril turned to her and looked at her with confused eyes. The air was suddenly clammy and her clothes stuck to her. His next words chilled her.

"Because, you've done it before."

In his mind, the Collector was suspended in midair as a myriad of faces and thoughts flew all around him in a kaleidoscope of colour and shapes. Thoughts took solid form, creatures, cities, infinite nebulas of green lightning, vistas he could not register nor process. These were like blinding lights making him wince involuntarily and he was hungry, eager to devour such knowledge but it shot past and through him like a bullet train. He found it hard to focus on the girl.

So many sleeping minds caused massive interference, silent screams caused by the interrupted changing. They were aware but locked in helpless forms from which their instincts screamed for release. Each mind was communicating with the other, cries of a gap, worry that precious history would be lost, that Earth's book would lose some chapters that may never be recovered. The Etherian reason for being was in jeopardy. Nothing like this had ever happened before and they didn't know how to deal with it.

Like a maelstrom, the voices and images swirled and combined into a rage of particles that shot at him, pulling the Collector in all directions. He felt his body being sucked apart molecule by molecule, as though the power was trying to cut the bonds between his atoms. He was in danger of being ripped apart and fired into the maelstrom, a memory lost in stifling sands of time. Focusing hard he reached out with his mind and with two hands, pulled an image towards his chest, hugging it like a greedy child. It reeled in his grip, bucking and baying for release. It burned at his skin, blistering it and peeling it from the flesh in ugly wounds.

With a scream, the Collector let it go and it sped off back to cover among the vortex of thoughts.

He fell to his knees in the sleeper chamber, his skin glistening with sweat, his breathing labored. Falling back on his haunches, the Collector pulled the device from his head and waited for the trembling in his body to subside. He could feel his hands aflame but was relieved to see they were unscathed, his skin as smooth as ever.

Burying his hands in his face, he shook as a chuckle grew within him, reaching a hearty and smug laugh.

"I think I would have remembered killing an entire race," shot Tyran sarcastically, her fierce glare fixed squarely on the hulking Sril. Despite his savage appearance he looked like a lost child whose mother had just scolded him.

"But...," he began.

"NO!" yelled the petite girl. "No buts! You have the wrong girl. Jesus. What sort of people are you?" Sril rose to his full height, his panther face suddenly decided and determined.

"We are the Etherians. We are the sum knowledge in the entire universe. I could change your entire being with one phrase but it is forbidden. We absorb and process and tell the stories that have fallen by the wayside and I know Tyran Scott of the planet Earth, that you are more than capable of wiping the Vorg from our skies!" Tyran shook her head squarely.

"I'm still lost on the whole genocide thing. Maybe someone wasn't absorbing properly," she spat harshly. "Let me contact Varran. The Juggernaught could probably..."

The viciousness in Sril's voice made her jump. Aware of the saucer ships outside, she suddenly knew where the rock and the hard place was.

"August the 23rd 2009. You willingly and cold bloodedly took the life of a feline that was strung up and murdered by you."

Tyran's face fell as she paled, her eyes dropping, unable to look the frustrated Etherian in the face. Her mouth opened to speak but Sril pressed on. "I know every step you've taken, every word uttered, every action taken. You have no secrets from me, no matter how much you cry otherwise. Right now, I am your conscience."

"Shut up!" she warned, fists clenching. "You weren't there. You don't know!"

Coming closer, Sril pressed on. "I didn't need to be. Let me remind you."

It was summer and the fifteen year old Tyran had outgrown the need to dress up as a blood sucking fiend or zombie with one eye hanging out. She had never wanted to dress as a witch or a fairy princess. Instead, she wanted to do what the boys did because their costumes were far cooler than hers. She loved football and was always hanging around to play a game. Her first kiss had been with Jason Cotton behind the local leisure centre after five a side night. It had tasted of chewing gum and beer and she recoiled from his slimy tongue. He had never picked her for his team after that and she never understood why his mates sniggered and shouted after her that she was a sliding door. Of course when she did find out what they meant she told everyone that Jason was hung like a door mouse which wasn't far from the truth.

But that was long after that night. The night she had tried to impress Jason on Halloween night as they drank cider and smoked cigarettes behind the leisure centre. Behind it was an overgrown copse that the locals used as a dumping ground. Wild cats lived there feeding on mice and rats and birds. The boys challenged each other to capture one of the cats without getting clawed to death. Tyran knew not to even attempt going after one of the cats which hissed and arched angrily to intruders.

But this night was different.

The boys were brave, smoking things they shouldn't be and laughing round the bonfire they'd made in the copse. Dance music throbbed through the night air which was heavy with the stench of burning tyres and rubbish; of beer and cigarettes, and body odour from some of the least hygienic crowd. The music throbbed rhythmically through Tyran, making her move to the beat, swaying like a tribal dancer. The cider had been sweet but strong and she felt muzzy but good. She was doing just what Jason did and she so wanted that kiss.

One of the gang, Farter Murray (farter by name, farter by nature) came whooping out of the undergrowth, holding something up. He behaved like he'd won a prize and was dancing around with joy, yelling for everyone to look. Tyran focused and realized he'd gotten the grand prize. The mewling form of a small ginger and white tabby cat clung to his nicotine stained fingers, its blue eyes wide with fear and crying softly. Its claws stuck into his skin but he failed to notice. He was so elated by catching a cat, he didn't care. The fact it should have been an adult cat was lost on everyone. It was a cat. And Jason knew what had to be done.

He tossed a rope over a low hanging branch and between them he and Farter tied the kitten's back legs together. Once secure, they let it swing. It's terrified cries amused everyone even Tyran. Jason could do no wrong and she fuzzily noticed him spray something over the little creature, its fur slick with beer, as she thought.

"Tyran, c'mere," he beckoned and she came unquestioningly. He took a deep drag of his Regal cigarette and grinned at her through the white mist.

"Here, see how quickly it goes up." She obligingly took the small object from him and groggily smiled at him. What was she to do again? Frowning she saw his green eyes fix her with a look of absolute power. He said two words, just two small words that would change everything.

"Flick it."

Unsure, she did so, sparking a yellow orange flame that caught the hanging kitten. It went up like a firework. It sobered Tyran instantly and she fell back screaming. The fur exploded with flame and the kitten's agonizing screams shattered the night air. Jason and his mates roared with laughter as the tiny creature fought to escape but its efforts made it jerk hopelessly.

Tyran covered her ears, having never heard such a scream before and she could only watch helplessly as the kitten blackened and twitch convulsively as it died a horrible death. It had only been a kitten, a baby which Tyran would have cuddled and fed a saucer of milk. But she had killed it. Her love for a boy and the desire for his lips on hers had let her get drunk and deliberately give another animal a horrible death. As she stared at the charring twitching remains of the kitten she remembered its beautiful blue eyes looking at her. She screamed over and over at what she had done as the crowd laughed at her.

"How can you refuse us when I know you can destroy an innocent life without a second thought?"

Rage consumed Tork's heavy frame as he strode determinedly through the glittering coral and white passages of these…these…tombs. Sleeper chambers indeed. That red skinned freak had an entire population on its knees, in a prison of their own making.

The perfect trap.

Resistance to the Vorg occupation had been virtually nonexistent because the aliens had all placed themselves in the chambers hours before the fleet arrived. Tork had stood on the bridge of his war carrier; arms behind his back watching his ships take formation in space and glide like death chariots to the orange pink world below them. The land masses grew revealing gigantic mountains, empty deserts and lush forests that stretched beyond his view. In the midst of all this was the citadels all built in concentric patterns around the continents. Several were constructed on stilts in the green oceans but none showed life signs bar the vast central citadel.

From orbit, it gave the general the impression of a massive receiver but he dismissed it as his warrior side was itching for spoils and spoils were forbidden by the new way. He had pulled the remnants of the warring factions together from his own world's burnt surface and showed them that the past was a grim warning. That the Vorg were not going to be remembered as a race whose own ambition became a cancer that ate them away. The giants had been reduced to newborns again and like the newborn Tork gripping the outstretched hand of a rival faction's leader was a statement-WE ARE NOT FINISHED. No Collector, not by any standard.

The air was electric with raw emotion as Tyran stared out the window, Sril hovering over her like an avenging angel.

"Well?" he said so softly it boomed in Tyran's burning ears. Sril winced as he glanced heavenward and closed his eyes. "Your friends are worried about you. They are desperately trying to find you but to no avail. Help us and you can return home."

He watched her back stiffen as she slowly raised her head. A rivulet of sweat trickled down the back of her neck, disappearing behind the collar of her jacket. When she spoke it was with muted tones that bore the strength of a victim fighting back.

"You know," she began without turning "I don't know who is worse, you or the Collector. As far as I can make out, the Vorg are being paid to do a job and the Collector is an asshole with lofty ambitions. You're just an asshole." Taken aback, Sril accessed his memory of human dialect in the sub context slang. His face was a mask of shock and surprise.

"You belittle me for daring to save my people from slavery?"

The small Earth girl turned to face him, her face hard and unforgiving. "No. You're an asshole and a coward. You expect me to fight your fight without question and when I refuse you fire a piece of my history at me like a torpedo." Her expression was hard, her voice like ice. "How dare you. I think your information system leaves a lot to be desired. What was I feeling?"

"What?"

"When I burned that cat alive." She shot back. "What was I feeling?" Sril's mouth twitched.

"Not sure? Don't know?" she bit. "Well I do." She took a couple of steps closer and Sril felt a real sense of uncertainty. Had he unleashed something in her? Had he sealed the Etherians' fate?

"You claim to know me, every thought, every feeling. It was over before I'd realized what Jason had sprayed on the cat. If I could play that moment back I would tell him to piss off and free the kitten. But I was in love, thought I was, and I would have done anything to keep on his good side. Anything just to know he still noticed me. You have no idea the nightmares I had over that kitten and it might seem strange to some people but not to me. I can still hear it scream as it burned alive and I did it. Me. Because I was drunk and wanted a tosser to say he would kiss me again."

She shook her head sadly, giving Sril a pitiful look. "You and your kind have never been teenagers. You live in perpetual adulthood. You've never been sick in your parent's garden after too much beer, never watched someone you fancy kiss another girl. Never sat in your bedroom and hugged a pillow watching a soppy movie because you feel so ugly and disgusted no one wants you. Ever been lonely Sril?" The Etherian shook his head.

Tyran gave a wry smile. "Maybe you lot are lucky in a way." She sighed.

"You know the story but you don't know it." She paused, her voice trembling.

"You're reciting the event with no understanding of the pain involved. You're mistaking mass murder for growing up. You make mistakes and stumble and fall but you get up again and take that with you forever. Everyone makes mistakes and I did. A big one, one that goes against everything I am but I went on despite the back stabbing and the pain. Can you say the same? I hate myself for killing that animal but I can admit that. It seems to me Etherians absorb other people's lives because they can't live their own." She held his look. Sril looked alarmed, almost tearful.

"Then we are lost. The Collector has won."

He saw Tyran stiffen as she stared behind him. He swung round. General Tork stood, black and crimson battle armor catching the light proudly through the window. He filled the doorway, poised for attack, the barrel of his vicious looking weapon pointed straight at them.

His face was a picture of triumph.

"Contract concluded," he sneered. "You never noticed the tracker I planted on the back of your clothing, girl."

I'm never getting home at this rate, Tyran thought ruefully.

God, she'd never find out if James would ever find out if Cindy had cheated on him and was carrying someone else's baby.

Did Sril know about soap operas? She glared defiantly at the Vorg, refusing to show she was afraid.

"If I'm going down, I'm going down fighting!" she bragged as Tork gave her an almost sympathetic look.

"I have no idea why he thought you would be their salvation but at least you've got guts. In the olden days you would have made a worthy opponent," he offered.

"I made a mistake General," jumped in Sril. "Let her return home." He threw her an apologetic glance. "I should never have involved her. We will cooperate if you spare her." Tork seemed to waver slightly but shook his head.

"I cannot. The contract was to secure this planet and its people. With your capture it is done and we can leave. Unfortunately the Collector appears to be obsessed with the girl and he will never let her leave. She is now part of the deal." Tyran crossed her arms and tilted her head slightly, fixing the Vorg with a curious stare.

"Tell me General. Why do you do this? You're obviously an army so why haven't you killed anyone? You let the Collector treat you like dirt but say nothing. Bit strange, don't you think?"

Her words had an effect as Tork's shoulders slumped slightly and snorted; his ridges of tusks tightening; must be their version of skin crawling mused Tyran. A haunted look crept over Tork's face, his eyes betraying a deep sadness.

"My race once stormed the stars before we almost wiped ourselves out. But in the depths of tragedy we found a new purpose and zest for life. We had lost our way years ago and have clawed back from extinction. War is pointless. Once it was full of glory and spectacle, endless victory parades and joy in the domination of other species. But now…" he paused, face awash with emotion. "We hire our forces out for jobs too big for the few. For a fee we render our services as warriors. We are not assassins nor do we kill for sport. We fight to rebuild our world, to give its economy life again. Everything we have done has rebuilt homes, hospitals; entire cities have crawled from the ash. It gives me no pleasure to leave your people in The Collector's hands but to save my world, I have no choice."

A sudden burst of laughter made Sril and Tork look strangely at Tyran. Her face was red a she took a fit of giggles. "Varran would love this. He's always on at us to find peaceful solutions," she nearly choked as her eyes watered. She slapped Sril encouragingly on the lower back.

"Sril, you were right after all. General, I'm going to get rid of every single Vorg on this planet." Tork raised his rifle, aiming squarely at the Tyran's head.

The Collector almost burst with delight as Tork and a squad of weary looking soldiers ushered in the tall hairy Etherian and his small blond haired companion.

"Glad to see you're not totally useless, my leathery friends. Took you long enough," he baited. "Where did you find them?" Tork glared hatefully at him.

"They were plotting against you."

The Collector pulled an amused face.

"It must have been a short plot. Now Tyran" he purred crossing to her, "shall we discuss where you're from?"

"My mother," Tyran mocked. But he wasn't deterred. "I bet she's as lovely as you. I'd love to meet her. Perhaps after my business is concluded here and I absorb it into my collection, we can visit your world and see what delights I can procure."

"Or not." She held his stare. General Tork spoke up, distracting the Collector's attention.

"Business is concluded, Collector. Our contract was to secure this world and its people. With their capture the contract is fulfilled." The Collector gave him a rather pained expression.

"I suppose it is. Very well." He took out one of his devices from his belt pouch and pressed his thumb against it. It gave a little electronic whine and the Collector showed it to the General. Nodding approvingly, the General grunted satisfied. "The payment has been transferred."

"Now," The Collector motioned to Sril, "time for you to join your fellow citizens in their sleeper chambers. Then we will have no more trouble out of you." Sril stood where he was and said nothing. Tork and Tyran stood saying nothing too, just staring at the lavish alien innocently. The Collector's instincts prickled and he slipped his hand into his pocket deftly. He was suddenly aware of Vorg soldiers positioning themselves almost in a circle around him, claws gripping their weapons too eagerly.

"General!" said Tyran dramatically, "Is your contract fulfilled and all monies paid as per your agreement with the Collector?"

Tork almost grinned. "Yes it is." She glanced at Sril and nodded agreeably.

She approached the uneasy Collector as he stepped further up on the central console. It was as if all the sleepers were aware something was happening, a sliver of hope in the blackness. The very air heaved with anticipation.

"Sril here brought me to rid his world of the Vorg and you. But for the life of me I couldn't figure how a slip of a thing like me was going to beat all these good soldiers. But I don't have to. You did it for me once you transferred that money. Sril, have you something to say to the nice General?" Beaming, Sril leaned down to Tork.

"General, we have no money like the Collector here but we do have a planet full of precious gems and minerals that could give your world a healthy boost; materials to build better cities and ships and accelerate your rebuilding programme. Since this job is over would you consider working for the Etherian race? You would be the first in history to do so but we can more than compensate you for your trouble." Tork's tusks relaxed as he considered.

"What will the contract consist of?"

"We would like to hire you to get the Collector off our world. Is that too much?" He could hear the relief from the Vorg soldiers as they itched to carry out this job. The Collector's face fell as Tork agreed and turned to look triumphantly at him.

"Oh very good, very well played; shouldn't have paid until you two were secured," he bleated.

No longer able to conceal her grin, Tyran laughed. "You live and learn!" Nodding his head slowly in agreement, the Collector chuckled, "Indeed you do, my young vixen. Indeed you do." In a second he leaped forward and grabbed her, gripping her tightly and planting a hard kiss on her lips. Before anyone could react, he whispered something in her ear and flicked one of his seemingly endless devices. He waved as a blue light formed around him and carried him away.

"I WILL be seeing you!" he declared, his voice echoing as Tyran fell back into Sril's arms. A crossfire of energy beams from the Vorg rifles split the air as their prey vanished.

Two days later, Sril, Tork and Tyran were walking down a plaza filled with exotic sculptures. Some twisted like angels dancing while others seemed to depict various figures from other times and places. Tyran admired the jade and azure quartz they seemed to be carved from. They caught the sunlight in a way to make them seem alive.

"Your people make these?" asked Tyran, as the streets became more crowded with the Etherians.

"We don't just listen to the universe all day you know. Have to keep busy. While away the hours," replied Sril lightly.

"Yeah, eternity must drag." She looked around at the buildings and the streets. They were teeming with Vorg and Etherians. Tyran felt a little unnerved by the two vicious looking species around her.

"Thank you for the payment," acknowledged the General.

"I hope it does some good," smiled Sril. The General shook his head disbelievingly.

"You have no idea how much. We do not intend to return to the old ways. This will give us a chance not to rely on other species for jobs. We can focus on other things for a while." He ran a claw along a sculpture like a lion but with horns and dinosaur wings. "I might even sculpt."

"General we have no need for such things. Take it all if you want." Tork blushed.

"I think they have," laughed Tyran. Tork took her hand and leaned forward so his forehead touched it.

"Thank you. The Vorg will never forget what you have done for us this day. May we take you home?" Tyran shook her head.

"General, I don't even know how far away my home is. Besides, Sril brought me here, he can send me back." She stood on tip toes and kissed Tork on the cheek, careful to avoid his tusks. He snorted shyly before bowing. As he walked off, his cloak vibrant in the warm breeze, they heard him ordering all personnel to return to their ships for departure.

"A new dawn begins!" he bellowed, waving at Tyran and Sril as he strode off, a definite spring in his step. Sril offered Tyran his arm. With a smile, she took it and they headed off towards the hangars.

"One question, how did you load the Vorg ships so quickly?" Sril winked and tapped his forehead knowingly.

"Knowledge of the universe," he quipped. They looked up as sonic booms heralded the departure of the Vorg saucer ships.

"I bet Tork's a very happy man," she grinned.

Everything looked the same and yet felt brand new, thought Tyran as they approached the same organic ship that brought her originally. Etherians, all in their new feline forms, waved at her, calling their thanks. She shyly waved back. The turtle shell blue and green hull rose before creating a doorway for her to enter. She wasn't very good at goodbyes. She always felt awkward, not knowing what to say. Sril had a wide grin on his feline face and suddenly grabbed her in a bear hug.

"OK," gasped Tyran, "seems you know a few Earth customs too well." She caught her breath as he released her. "What if he comes back? The Collector, I mean," Uttering a gruff chortle, Sril shook his head.

"You'll see when the ship takes off. I left a present on board for Varran. It's an upgrade system for your Dagger shuttles' engines. You'll travel further and faster. I think you're going to need it." Tyran frowned, studying his face for a clue as to what that meant. He just gave her a wink. "Goodbye Tyran. Keep well."

"You too," she smiled, giving him a kiss and a hug. With a final wave she stepped into the ship.

Moments later, she was above Ether, sitting in a chair that had seemed to grow from the floor. It allowed her to sink back into it reminding her of her favourite sofa back home, a terracotta one her mother had bought from Leckey's Sofa World. The air in front of her shivered and she could see the planet below.

It was beautiful, shaped with strange land masses and cotton like clouds. As she watched she saw a faint shimmer spark at the most northern point of the planet. It expanded and rolled across the surface, encapsulating everything. Ether became a mass of colour. In seconds it was gone, the stars bleeding through where it had stood moments ago.

Of course, she breathed, they couldn't have always been here if they had existed for eternity. The planet must shift position regularly to avoid detection. But then, how did the Collector know where and when to strike? Lying back in the chair, which molded to her shape, she glanced at the white knobbed box over to her left. What did Sril mean? They were going to need his present? Although the temperature was lovely, she wrinkled at a shiver down her back. She recalled what the Collector had whispered to her.

"I know where Earth is."

EXPERIMENT FOUR PART 1

It was high summer in the middle of July and the night had fallen like a blanket on the island of Farron.

It was an idyllic picture.

The rough cliffs searing upwards like ancient kings as the docile sea lapped at their feet tossing white crests like jester hats. The air was warm as the island sweltered beneath a heat wave, islanders sleeping with their windows open and even a few camped out beneath the stars.

The black sky made the stars sparkle with the fierce white of precious diamonds crowned by a half moon so clear you could see the features on the surface.

Perhaps on nights like this when people looked up at the sky and saw the moon; it gave rise to the old man in the moon stories.

A solitary jumbo jet flew overhead en route to Florida with eager holidaymakers excited at going to Disneyland and the few passengers that looked out the cabin windows saw chains of golden lights that looked like giant necklaces.

Some wondered what the people below were doing and how they lived on an island. What sort of life did they lead? Most people that lived in the country or the cities and towns that cluttered the mainland could not comprehend the appeal of living here away from civilisation.

They imagined little background stories for those who lived there and what their lives were like. It passed the time if you didn't like the latest movie played in flight or had grown bored with your book.

It was that or go to sleep. Silently the plane left the island behind and as the distance grew, the stories left them. But none could dream up Ernie Reavey's story.

The sound of laughter and music filtered over the night air, flowing from the golden spill of the pub's white wood panelled windows which cast shadows over the gravelled ground.

The stench of beer carried through the night breeze as someone played a fiddle rendition of an Irish jig.

Shadows jerked like struggling puppets as some customers danced bringing screams of laughter.

The thatched roof and white painted walls gave it a picture postcard quality, the owners having kept most of the original structure. The squeak of rusty hinges brought attention to a sign above the door.

It was an old style painting of a boat in which sat a man in a navy pullover and black cap smoking a pipe with two grey dolphins swimming at his bow. Above it was painted the words Sailors' Keep. But they were few and far between these days.

Farron had been a major fishing power some years back but new ideas from university graduates spoke of economic restructuring and relocation. Costs and figures had lessened Farron's importance.

While it still had a fair amount of trading with the mainland companies, most of its attraction was tourist based. With its historical ruins and myriad of sea bird wildlife that roosted in the giant cliff faces, the island had a regular influx of people that toured and rested.

Some of the passengers aboard the jet may have wondered why people lived here but the tourists knew after a stay. It was tranquil where the pace of life was so laid back no one seemed miserable.

When the sun beamed down from the clear blue skies, igniting the water with a serene quality, you could walk the litter free sandy beaches without falling over crowds or sit on the cliff tops gazing out over the vista of perfect sea and enchanting sky.

You forgot there was a world out there where people lived in fear on overcrowded estates and cities. Where pensioners froze to death because their pension wasn't big enough or slept on cardboard streets, a shaking hand extended for small change.

Of course, in the winter, life could be harsh but the population of over a thousand always looked out for each other no matter what. It was a sight to behold when the sea raged and slammed against the cliffs in bellows of white, causing even the birds to huddle as thunder growled cruelly and sharp white flames of lightning slashed the sky.

But it was the stuff documentary makers lived for and to behold such a sight truly left one breathless with fearful awe.

But tonight was different. It was calm with the slightest of warm breezes dancing across the island. The part moon bathed the island in a soft hazy glow.

No clouds, no storms on the horizon, just nature slumbering peacefully in quiet contentment. A coffin of light broke the partial darkness as the Sailors' Keep's door opened and a dark figure stumbled outside.

Tugging his flat tweed cap down over his head, Ernie pulled the lapel of his worn beige overcoat tighter round his neck as he steadied himself. He waved in answer to the cries of goodnight from inside the pub.

The door swung shut, leaving him in darkness once again. His eyes adjusted to the dark and he saw the welcoming light of his cottage. It wasn't far, only a few hundred metres and he always kept a light burning in the window.

He looked forward to getting into his bed, the central heating having been on since he left for a pint four hours ago. At his age it was always cold even in this heatwave.

He caught the smell of Guinness and brandy shots on his breath as he set off down the gravel path, the crunch under his worn booted feet sounding sharply in the night air.

Flowering bushes rustled lazily as he headed in the direction of the footpath that took him to the cliffs. Today was a special day for Ernie. It was July 21st, his wedding anniversary.

He had worked on the fishing boats for years and had met Lily on one of his trips to Farron in 1951.

His first memory of her was on the jetty, walking with some friends, the sea breeze making her curly black hair shimmer. Her brown eyes locked on his as he climbed the steps to get a better look at her while pretending to work with a crab keel. Ernie slipped and fell on the watery steps and Lily had rushed over to help him.

Gasping in pain, he had gratefully accepted a lift to the local doctors. He was told he had broken his arm. Having had it set, Lily had taken him to her parents' cottage to rest and had a cup of tea.

He recalled her slender fingers round the brown mug as she handed it to him, the slight brush of her skin against his and was inwardly relieved not to see a ring.

Unable to work, he and Lily spent the next six weeks inseparable and shared their first kiss on Shannon's Point, a local spot frequented by blossoming couples. Most liked it for the abundance of bushes which afforded them privacy. Ernie could not believe how much Lily had captured his heart and he was totally entranced by her.

She was his world.

Her infectious giggle, the way she flicked her hair away from her forehead, the gentle touch of her fingers as she constantly smoothed Ernie's unkempt blond hair.

Sometimes he saw her watching him when she thought he wasn't looking. The look on her face gave him butterflies. It was a look of absolute love and warmth. And he wasn't going to let it go.

On September 10th, he had taken her to the Golden Mile, a stretch of beach that sat adjacent to the sea like a tiara. It was dotted by green spiky bushes and shells, the sweet smell of brine travelling on the breeze as gulls cried excitedly overhead.

He laid out the tartan blanket and spread their picnic of tea in a flask and cucumber and tomato sandwiches and homemade sponge cake between them. They had eaten in silence, giving each other the occasional gentle look.

Ernie took his shirt off and Lily pulled her skirt to just below the top of her legs. They lay under the lazy sun tanning nicely.

Gingerly, Ernie slipped his hand in hers and intertwined their fingers. He looked sideways at her. Her eyes were closed but a slight smile lit her face.

"Lily O'Reilly. Would you marry me?" Her eyes snapped open and she stared at him, shielding her startled gaze from the sun. She took one look at his screwed up face, squinting in the sun and smiled.

"Yes," she said simply as if it were the most natural thing in the world. "Pass me a slice of sponge cake."

Ernie brought his other hand over and opened it. They sat up as Lily put her hands to her face, stifling a grin. It wasn't sponge cake he held out to her but a simple brass band.

It wasn't encrusted with diamonds or pearls nor was it fancy; it was plain and simple, just like Ernie. But it was hers. He slipped it on her finger and they kissed.

They had been married eight months later, a simple ceremony but one infused with love and hope for the future.

They decided to stay on the island, they liked life here, it was uncomplicated and the party had been attended by most of the islanders. They rented Mister Shane's old cottage and set up home.

Within the year, Lily was pregnant but unfortunately, the birth was difficult and that day in July, Ernie lost his beloved Lily and infant son. They were buried in the local graveyard and Ernie fell apart.

He had stayed on Farron and still lived in the cottage. He had never remarried, not even dated. The pain was too much living without Lily and his child and he couldn't face it again with someone else. He had often thought of taking his own life but he just couldn't.

God no longer existed for him, for no god of love could be so cruel as to take all Ernie loved and leave him alone. He continued to work on the boats and lived a meagre life style but had been left a substantial amount from his parent's estate.

As long as he had money for a pint he was alright.

He shuffled along the gritty path, his circulation not what it once was, and in the gloom he saw a battered wooden bench with metal arm rests. It was just on the verge rusting, with the grass growing up round it. Sitting himself down, he took off his cap and held it in his lap.

Staring up at the curtain of crystal stars that sparkled like tear drops from heaven, he smiled.

"Well, Lily. It would have been 48 years today. Had a few brandies for you, hope you don't mind."

He sat in silence for a while, letting warm memories wash over of him of their scant years together .He often talked to Lily. He firmly believed she was still with him and had raised their boy in a better place.

He recalled the baby's eyes, brown like his mother and how he had held his stillborn son at the bedside of his deceased mother and soaked in every detail about him before the doctors took them away.

He called his son, James and he was the spit of his mother, same features, and same soft hair. If someone had looked in, they would have thought it was a father cradling his son while the mother got some sleep.

"How's James? Playing you up I suppose. He probably has your spirit. I miss you Lily. Even after all these years, I still love you."

His eyes welled sadly and he broke down as he stared at the sky. If the stars could be so bright, surely it could only be a gateway to heaven. He imagined Lily and James smiling down on him, patiently waiting for the day they would be a family again.

And sitting on this cliff top watching the starry sky glimmer on the slate like sea, Ernie truly felt he was close to his family.

He imagined that if he just reached up, they would take his hand and tell him how much they loved him and he would hear James' stories of all the wonderful things he and his mother had seen in the next life and how much they had longed for Ernie to be with them to share it.

He sobbed lightly, rocking slightly; failing to see the dark shape that slithered up the cliff path behind him.

It saw him in a red hue, alive with colour and energy. It gurgled softly as it seethed forward. Ernie wiped his eyes as the stars seemed to glow with such brilliance he thought the pearly gates themselves were opening. Beyond would be Lily and James, smiling and loving.

He felt a flood of the deepest peace he had ever known and in a second Ernie fell into the open arms of his wife and son.

Rosie McMahon stood side by side with her husband, Joe.

She was a large chested woman with a round cheery face, inset by deep green eyes and a wave of rough black hair that sat rigid on her head.

Middle aged and slightly overweight, she was taller than her rotund husband by six inches but as she always said, it didn't matter when you're lying down.

Sliding her arm round Joe's, she stared at her sniffling spouse. She noticed his hair was thinning in a pope cap and his chestnut brown curls were fading to slivers of iron grey. He was short but compact and Rosie always felt warmth when he stripped his shirt off. He was sagging with age and gravity but still a fine figure of a man who spoke his love for her with a simple smile.

They had been together for thirty years and still Rosie fancied the pants off him and told everybody so, much to Joe's embarrassment. Being the landlords of the Sailor's Keep, they were the centre of everybody's lives and knew more about certain things than respective partners did.

Rosie and Joe were integral to life on the island and there was very little they didn't know. That's why they liked it so much;

the intimacy and general feeling of family and now three days ago, one of their family had died.

Joe and Ernie had been drinking partners since they took over the pub so Rosie was well aware of his history.

She invited the old man over for Christmas every year along with a few others and the craic was always great as Ernie told stories of his days on the boats and some of the characters and situations he'd encountered over the years.

But Rosie always saw that glint of sadness in Ernie's face as his mind anchored him to his beloved Lily. Often she had hugged him for no reason, the smell of stale beer and cigarette smoke caked to his clothes but she didn't care.

It would keep him alive in her memory and a picture of Ernie, Lily and James fleeted through her thoughts.

But she didn't shed any tears despite the hollowness in her chest. She could only hold her husband as the cheap mahogany coffin with false brass handles was lowered respectfully into the ground by the pall bearers.

It seemed the whole island had turned out, even Colin McPeake, a sheep farmer Rosie disliked intensely ever since she'd witnessed him beating a Labrador with a blackthorn walking stick. She hated cruelty to animals.

Father Collins's sermon droned in her brain, the words failing to register, despite the lovely heartfelt service.

Her thoughts flowed like white water as all the rumours splayed about her mind. She looked across and saw Inspector Gough head of the local Garda, standing solemnly in full uniform, hands folded across his groin.

It was a beautiful day and a soft warm breeze whispered dutifully in remembrance. Numbly tossing a yellow rose down into the grave, Rosie and Joe stepped back into the crowd to allow others to follow suit as the milling crowd slowly dissolved.

They would head to the pub for a pint the first of which was free and they would toast Ernie's memory. Rosie had already got a photo enlarged to 10 x 8 and framed to put behind the bar.

Her eyes never left the Garda as McPeake wandered over to him and had a heated discussion before Gough waved him away with an assurance he was working on it.

Gently nudging Joe, Rosie made in Gough's direction without making it obvious she was doing so.

Gough never noticed them until they were at his shoulder. Giving him a small smile, Rosie nodded at him in greeting.

"Alright, Arthur," she said quietly. "How's it going?" The Garda shook his head mournfully, his face etched with fatigue.

"Had better days," he replied in a thick Dublin accent, his gaze wandering towards the open grave. He barely registered the carpet of flowers and wreaths, each with a handwritten note. The colours shone in the sun, the outpouring of grief obvious.

"Did you see the body?" asked Rosie bluntly, ignoring Gough's startled expression. He had experienced Rosie's fierceness many times and he stared at her.

"Rosie!" he answered softly but sharply. "This is hardly the time or place." Rosie stood resolute, Joe's teary glare joining hers.

"I think this is exactly the time and place. Need I remind you who's in that grave and the times he helped you over the years, Arthur?" she pointed sternly, watching his brow crease.

How could I forget? he thought wryly.

"I can't discuss it Rosie, I'm sorry." His tone was firm, his tired expression suddenly hardening. The landlady stiffened at his refusal and tightened her grip round her husband's arm. She breathed heavily through her nose as she gave him a savage look.

"Do you know Arthur that I haven't cried yet? I want to, it's sitting there behind my eyes ready to come out but it can't. There's a rumour that Ernie was in a bad way when he was found and he never had an open coffin. Now unless eight pints and two whiskeys can cause a man to die so badly, he can't be displayed for his last goodbyes, then something else happened and I want to know what! It's Ernie we're talking about Arthur, not some lost soul washed up on the beach."

Gough cleared his throat and avoided their gaze for a second.

"It was a massive heart attack according to the coroner." His voice gave Rosie little reassurance.

"Bull."

Joe had spoken and with that one word let Arthur know what he thought. That's my man, thought Rosie proudly. He doesn't say much but when he did, it counted.

"And the rumours about the state he was in: are just that are they? Or do you know something else? Please Arthur." Her features softened and for a second Arthur thought she was going to cry.

"I can't discuss it. Sorry." His tone was resolute. Rosie's lips pursed angrily. There were too many strange things happening in the last few weeks just to leave it at a red tape brick wall.

"Fine but your mother would beat ten bells out of you if she could see you now. She knew what family meant. By the Duke himself, I wish I had a wooden spoon!"

Arthur rolled his eyes nonchalantly. Rosie poked a finger in his face. "And if you roll those sexy brown eyes at me again, you can get your pint from the mainland!" she hissed.

Tugging the tensed up Joe, she stormed off, throwing Arthur a hateful stare in her wake. They reached their black Ford Focus at the top of the path and got in. Rosie stared at the lines of head stones, grinding her teeth as she thought. Joe lit a cigarette and took a deep draw as he watched Arthur's blue and white police car move off.

"If he's not going to do something, I am!" she growled determinedly. "Joe, give us your phone."

With a shimmer of blue light, four figures solidified beneath the shadow of the Sailor's Keep.

Dusk was falling and the sky was a gorgeous spray of orange and pink with strings of white cloud adorning the endless breath of the blue sea. Gulls were but small dark silhouettes gliding in the evening wind that was gradually cooling the island.

"I love the teleport!" declared Michael as he hoisted his navy sports bag over his shoulder, his face almost alive with delight. Tyran patted his slight paunch.

"That's why that happens," she said. He fired a sarcastic look as Varran looked about him.

Dressed in a checked shirt and plain black trousers with matching boots, he nodded satisfied as he examined his hand unit before pocketing it.

"This is the place," he said as he surveyed the landscape, "looks normal enough."

Jacke pulled a doubtful face. "I've learned by now nothing is normal when we're involved." She fumbled with her carry all. "I can't believe someone literally phoned you to come here."

Smiling, Varran looked at her, his sapphire eyes glittering in the dusk.

"That's the advantage of a network. Everyone knows how to reach me if they ask the right people. How do you think I was able to get help with the repairs when the Numaran attacked? It's no big deal; in fact it's rather nice to know that I'm not alone and haven't been forgotten."

Michael shook his head wryly.

"Ok Bette Davis, are we going in or not?" he nodded toward the mahogany door with its wrought iron latches.

The murmur of a crowd filtered through the double glazed windows, the light throwing a cross shadow over the new arrivals.

"I've never been to an Irish pub," revealed Michael, looking at Jacke. "Is Guinness nice?" Smiling to herself, Jacke cocked her head at him.

"It's an acquired taste," she said teasingly. "Which reminds me, don't get drunk."

He gave her an incredulous glare. She knew he thought himself infallible but she also knew she could drink him under the table any night. Pushing politely past her, Jacke heard him mutter "we'll see."

The smell of beer and smoke hit them as soon as they opened the door. Michael entered first, holding the door open for the others. The murmur died as they received a number of cautious scowls. The air was sullen, muted by recent events; fear a silent companion to them all.

"This isn't going to be An American Werewolf thing is it?" griped Tyran as the door clicked behind them. Defensively, she held the customers' looks.

It was brightly lit, the walls a deep cream with pictures and portraits scattered randomly around the bar walls, some colour, some black and white of various folks past and present.

There were photos of cowboys and fishing boats and a large painting dominated the wall directly across from the bar.

Looking about, Tyran wondered why old pubs seemed to have brass work stood like sentries on a gnarled black wood shelf that ran the length of the pitted wall above the bar and optics run wherever you went.

They were interspersed with dried flower arrangements and odd little knick knacks but what caught their attention and really made an impact was a huge anchor that was embedded into the bar itself.

It gleamed from what was obviously a recent shine up and it looked as if the bar had grown around it.

"Hell of a job that," muttered Michael admiringly as Tyran shifted her carry all onto the ground, rubbing her palm where it had dug into her.

Michael smiled broadly as Varran crossed boldly to the dark stained bar, nodding to people as he went.

Joe smiled at him and shouted for Rosie. She emerged from the back like a flustered typhoon, scraping her hair back as she looked to see what her husband had called her for.

Immediately, she beamed, almost too enthusiastically, thought Michael at seeing her guests. Bustling Joe out of the way, she came round the bar and smothered Varran in a bear hug. His face pressed into her chest and he turned bright red as she whispered her thanks to him.

THE TIME WARRIORS – FIRST FOOTSTEPS

Putting her arm round his shoulder, she announced to the bar that the four new arrivals were her cousin and his children.

"So make them feel welcome!" she threatened.

Immediately the atmosphere changed and there were shouts of greeting and calls for drink. Embarrassed by the welcome, the Warriors shuffled uncomfortably as they gave tiny waves of acknowledgement.

"Makes a change from the usual welcome," chuckled Tyran, feeling a bit overwhelmed. Jacke clapped her on the shoulder.

"That's the Irish for you!" she laughed. "Rosie, can we leave our bags upstairs?"

Immediately, Rosie flew into her organisational mode, super flustered.

"Joe! Bags!" she barked. She clipped a young man at the bar. "You too Jim Welsh, give a hand or everybody will die of thirst. Chop, chop!" With a less than enthusiastic manner, Joe and Jim scooped up the four bags and lumbered round the bar and up the back stairs to the guest rooms. Rosie clapped her hands in front of her, her white blouse tightening as she did so. Varran looked away graciously, his face a picture of locked happiness.

"Are you hungry? Can I get you something?" she asked, eyes widening. "Of course you do, come on through to the back." She led the way behind the bar past the rows of bottles and optics. "Davey Sloan! If you're going to be sick, do it outside so the dogs can clean it up!"

Tyran saw a thin wiry man jump as if his mother had caught him with his hand in the biscuit tin. He nearly slid off his stool but composed himself and hung his head guiltily. This is going to be fun, Tyran thought amusedly.

The kitchen was dominated by a huge black range stove which Rosie had spent the last thirty minutes playing like a pianist.

It was a big old fashioned country kitchen and Michael could only stare round him amazed at the space and how much was crammed into it. The floor was dark stone tiles and the walls an off white green. Dark wood shelves lined the wall above the range where rows of spices and sauces stood like soldiers on parade clinking as Rosie whipped various ones down without even looking and replaced them the same way.

On a hefty looking dresser made of oak were framed photos and ornaments along with opened mail stacked along one end. An array of faces and places smiled out at the warriors as the wide oak table filled with plates of crusty bread, wheaten, sauces, salt, pepper and vinegar.

The biggest larder they'd ever seen stood on the other side of the white panelled door that led out to a back hall containing the fridge freezer, a chest freezer, washing machine and tumble dryer.

Who do they feed? wondered Michael, his jaw virtually hanging open. He took a drink from the frosted tumbler as he watched Rosie ply their plates with lasagne, salad and chips.

They whizzed like bullets onto the wicker placemats as Rosie wiped the work tops before plonking herself down. Michael expected her to be out of breath, her face beetroot but no. She must have been doing this for years.

"My nan's living room and hall would fit in here," he told her as he buttered a slice of wheaten. Giving him a sympathetic look, she urged them to tuck in. Varran smiled at her as he looked at his plate.

"This really is too much, Rosie," he chided, patting her hand lightly. She dismissed his humility with a screwed up face and wave of her chubby hands.

"You've come a long way, literally, to help us. Least I could do." Tyran was staring as she chewed. Concerned, Rosie leaned closer asking if she was alright. Nodding, Tyran swallowed.

"I've never had wheaten bread before. It's gorgeous," she said as if she'd tasted the elixir of life. "You never told me about this," she directed at Jacke who shrugged. She glanced at the round false marble clock on the wall with its Roman numerals before returning her attention to the chattering Rosie.

"I don't know if it's anything really bad but I just can't get any answers from the Garda," she was telling Varran.

He was nodding politely, savouring his food as he listened to her. As they ate, Joe joined them, having left Suzie and Ryan in charge of the bar. He filled a green flowered patterned plate with soda and cheese before taking his place at the top of the table.

He ate slowly as he perched like a watchful owl listening intently.

Rosie told them of Ernie's death and how the coffin had been closed.

By tradition, a corpse was laid out for their final respects in the best suit and waked for two nights before the funeral. Ernie had been held in the coroner's parlour until his funeral and no one saw his body.

Emma O'Reilly who worked as a receptionist for the undertaker, who happened to be her father, said she had never seen anything like it.

Her father had been summoned and given the measurements for the coffin and despite his perfectionist demur, was refused access to Ernie. The Garda, namely Arthur Gough, had dressed the body and sorted the coffin. Rosie and Joe had gone to the parlour to pay their respects to their old customer.

Not happy with what they saw, Joe had tried to open the lid but it was firmly and most definitely shut.

There was talk that the body had been mutilated and was beyond recognition but the official report was a massive heart attack. Tears welled in her eyes but she blinked them back.

When she found the truth then she would grieve.

Varran listened, ignoring the puzzled looks from the others. A closed coffin was hardly enough to summon them here, thought Michael. As if he had read his mind, Varran took Rosie's hand.

"Rosie, I saw our world die and vowed that it would never happen again. And sometimes a dying world is more than a rock circling a sun. I understand loss better than you could imagine."

"But what if I'm over reacting?" she fretted. "Maybe the stories are just that –stories."

"What do you mean?" asked Tyran. "What stories?"

Rosie slapped the table cursing her own stupidity. "Joe! Laptop please lover!" Joe ambled out with the computer and plugged it into a socket by the work top before running the lead across the floor and onto the table, laying it gently before his wife, earning him a see you later in the bedroom look. Jacke tried not to smile.

It was wonderful to see older people in love but Rosie's way of putting things made her laugh. She thought of her mother and wondered what she was doing right now, a tinge of regret that she didn't ring home often enough but then again things had been a roller coaster recently.

Tapping the keyboard, the land lady brought up her document files and opened them.

"Sorry, I was so flustered, I forgot to tell you." Settling down again, she composed her thoughts as she picked at the serving plate of chips.

"At the funeral, I saw Colin McPeake; he's a local farmer, awful man, talking to Gough. Now over the last few weeks, some of his sheep have been found dead, totally healthy animals that just drop dead overnight. Barney Tilly, the vet, says all the animals were drained of something in their bodies." She paused, brow crinkling as she tried to remember the technical name but failed. "Some fluid, or something, I'm not sure but there is no reason for it."

"Vampire?" chimed Michael. For a second, Varran thought he was joking but he wasn't.

"Vampires don't exist," he said calmly, his eyes warning Michael to pipe down. Rosie looked at Michael face on and said quite seriously.

"Banshees do though." Exchanging a smirk, the Warriors looked at each other, remembering the first time they'd met.

"Too right," muttered Tyran.

"Do you think something killed the sheep and Ernie?" Jacke asked earnestly. Rosie's face hardened as she carried on her story.

"To anyone else, it would seem crazy but some of the people here have said they've seen strange lights around the island and frightening sounds echoing in the night. Gabriel Fisher, who actually is a fisherman, said he saw a large shape in the ocean which nearly hit his boat and he has no idea what it was. I've downloaded and stored all the stories for you to read." Her face was mournful and a little scared, not something usually associated with Rosie. "If you could just look into it, maybe it's nothing but I don't want anyone else to die, not like that."

Helpless to the feeling welling up inside her, Jacke got up and put her arms round Rosie, lightly kissing her on the head.

"There's no alien invasion this week, so of course we'll help."

Gratefully Rosie patted the coloured girl's hands.

Exchanging a look with Varran, Jacke saw him smile proudly at her before swivelling the computer round to study. She checked the time.

"Listen, the dinner was lovely but I have to make a phone call," she announced.

Rosie rose to clear the table but Michael and Tyran moved to do it under a hint ridden glance from Varran. He gently sat Rosie down who told Jacke to use the phone in the hall.

Jacke pulled out her slim line silver mobile.

"It's ok," she said, sliding it open. "I'll have a shower and meet you in the bar."

Varran nodded and sat thoughtfully as he absorbed the stories on the laptop. Something was going on, he mused before being distracted by a tap from Rosie. She leaned close to him, her eyes wide with anticipation.

"Is there really an alien invasion every week?"

Time seemed to have very little meaning to Farron, Jacke decided. They had been here only for a short time and yet it seemed like they'd always been there.

She was sitting in the bar watching the others. Eric Pearce had brought out his guitar and was playing in concert with the barman Ryan who was furiously working the fiddle.

The air was alive with whoops and cheers as Michael spun round arm in arm with Suzie.

Joe was watching from the bar, an almost indiscernible jig in his stance. Varran was sitting with a group of older men, spinning tales about his travels over the world and Tyran was chatting with a group of younger men in the far corner, trying to ignore Michael's sudden passion for the Riverdance.

The only river he'll see is the one he pukes up, Jacke thought to herself as she took a sip from her pint glass.

She wasn't a big drinker, she hated the hangovers after a bad experience with a session of black Russians a couple of years back. Her knee was jerking subconsciously in time with the music and her head bobbing.

As she surveyed the crowd, she realised how far they had come in only a few months. Varran would never have embraced company as he did now and Michael had really come out of his shell and was opening up more. Tyran was Tyran and no one would ever change that. Jacke was the big sister and even she felt more at peace with the life they now lead.

Aliens, space ships and time travel were common place for some races and it surprised her how comfortable she had become with it.

Only a short time ago, her closest encounter had been watching a movie. It was probably her alien genetics but it felt normal to her. She thought of her family back home in Belfast, wondering what they were doing and if they missed her as much as she missed them.

When Varran had offered her the chance to work with him, she jumped at the chance but it was becoming more difficult to juggle her studies with whatever the universe threw at them.

She knew Varran didn't expect her to give everything up and she had made a point of not thinking of the quarters on the Juggernaught her permanent home.

Going home to continue her studies kept her grounded; it was important to her to finish them, another hurdle she had to overcome.

If, when, she did it, it would give her the opportunity to help change people's lives, on a more personal level than she was now with every fight they won. This life gave her the chance to help keep people safe and allow children to grow up without knowing that monsters were out there. It was her job to stop them.

A shape sidled over to her and slipped into the adjacent seat. Rosie was smiling at her.

"Hate to see anyone sitting alone in a bar!" she beamed. "Did you make your phone call alright?" Jacke nodded.

"Yeah, just ringing home to check everyone's ok and let mum know I haven't been eaten by a squid monster," she said. "Mum's a worrier."

"Mothers worry til the day they die." Her voice grew wistful. "My daughter's at university in Cork and I make sure we talk every day."

"That's nice." Rosie pulled a face.

"Nice nothing. It's to stop her getting pregnant and a motherly talk every night does no harm. She needs an education first."

Laughing, Jacke glanced over to see a tipsy Michael downing more Guinness.

"By the duke, girl, smile!" prompted Rosie, slapping her arm.

"I'm fine," Jacke assured her. "I just get homesick sometimes."

"Then get home to see your folks when you're done here. Life's too short," declared Rosie with an insistent nod of her head. "You're very lucky you know."

Jacke raised her eyebrows. She hadn't expected that.

"You live a life I can only dream of. Oh, I know it's scary sometimes and dangerous always but the very fact you have it, it's wonderful."

"I know what you mean but it's strange. We're not human but I think of myself as such. At least I thought I was, up until the racial memory thing when I was 18. Yet I live as a human does and obey the laws and pay taxes. Sometimes it's a little difficult to get my head round it."

Rosie shook her head and put on her motherly advice face that many a customer had benefited from.

"It's very simple." She gestured towards Varran whose face was getting redder from whiskey. "There sits a man who saw his world die and hasn't aged a day since. And I do mean a man. There is no difference between human and Xereban D.N.A...I mean look at you. You're black and Irish and alien, it's a wonder your head doesn't explode!" Her face grew sincere as she leaned closer. "You cross so many prejudices and what would you say you are?"

Thinking for a moment, Jacke could only think of one answer.

"I'm me."

"Exactly!" boomed Rosie and for a second Jacke thought she was going to applaud. "Think of my pub as the world; humans and Xerebans all in one place, talking and drinking, forming bonds all the time. And does it matter who came from where?" She fixed Jacke with a smile. "We bleed, we fart, we piss and we get grouchy, we fight, we love."

Jacke nodded in realisation looking round the pub. "We're all in it together."

Rosie pointed at her. "Right!"

Turning round on her chair, Rosie pointed to a 12 x 10 framed picture hanging behind the bar. It was a black and white photo with writing on it of a man in a tweed cloth cap. "See that? That is the greatest man that ever lived, outside of Joe of course. John Wayne, the Duke." Her voice dropped to reverence as she stared at him for a few moments. "And do I care where he was born? Had a ladies name before he changed it to John, you know."

"John Wayne," caught Jacke as she noticed the western memorabilia. She saw movie posters, all John Wayne films scattered about the walls, lovingly framed.

Tyran had thought they were paintings earlier on, Varran would be annoyed she hadn't been vigilant.

"I'm only catching that now. That signature must be worth money."

"I paid 320 euros on Ebay for that signature. God, he was gorgeous. He never actually said; get off your horse and drink your milk but I would anytime." She lowered her voice conspiratorially. "Between you and me, I get Joe to dress in a cowboy hat and gun belt to spice things up." Jacke's face dropped as Rosie burst into guffaws of laughter.

"He's better than the pony express!"

Clapping her hands over her ears, Jacke giggled. It was too much information for her as an image of Joe naked with his beer belly and belt haunted her, his Stetson and colt 45 at the ready.

In that second, Michael toppled over and fell trying to copy Suzie's Irish dance moves. Rosie and Jacke buckled with laughter.

Jacke was brushing her teeth a couple of hours later when someone knocked her door softly.

She opened it to see Varran standing there, his eyes slightly fuzzy.

"Just checking you're alright and to let you know I've scanned the island for temporal anomalies but it's clean. So get some sleep and I'll see you in the morning." The sound of retching interrupted them. "See Michael didn't listen as usual," he grinned. "Sleep well," he waved a little unsteadily as he headed to his room.

"You too," replied Jacke easing the door shut.

It had a creak that Joe had given up long ago trying to fix. She finished rinsing her mouth out and wiped it before putting her gold necklace and rings on the pine bedside table.

Pulling back the lilac quilt, she snuggled into the soft double bed, the pillows cold against her cheek. It was almost two thirty in the morning and she soon slipped into sleep, her thoughts on her family.

It shifted across the rocky ground quickly and determinedly, the thirst burning its being as surely as if it were on fire. Skittering silently over the edge of a hillock, it paused, its senses probing the chilling breeze, filling itself with every scent, every sound as it trembled beneath the moon, its bright grey white surface blaring down accusingly.

A bleat made it freeze, poised to run or strike, such hunger, such need. The shuffle of hoofed feet on grass boomed like thunder in its mind though it made no difference to the night air.

Moving like a cobra, it sniffed the air and targeted the noise.

With a startled cry, the sheep fell beneath its attacker's bulk as quivering tendrils pierced its flesh, drawing blood from the almost surgical incision. The sheep convulsed with a plaintive whimper as it succumbed to a blissful blackness, oblivious to the quelled sucking as the creature feasted.

With a start, Colin McPeake leapt to his feet as he heard the fearful cries of his flock. He leapt out of the worn pine rocking chair, snatching his rifle as he moved. He was fully clothed, green body warmer buttoned up and cap pulled tight to his black haired scalp.

Sickened by the lack of action on the Garda's behalf, he had stood guard over his flock, catnapping and taking a few hours of sleep during the day. His wife lay soundly upstairs in their deep divan bed as he slipped the latch on the door behind him and hurried into the night towards the terrified flock.

Beneath the moon and shivering stars, he could just about see the dim run of frightened animals.

Raising his rifle, McPeake flicked the torch on that he had taped to the end of his weapon. A baleful beam of yellow light cut the darkness, sheep's eyes reflecting the sudden beam. Scared by this new arrival, they scattered bleating as they went, leaving the farmer to focus the torch on the shape on the ground.

Fear gripped him, as his scalp crawled with a chill as he heard something suckling. His eyes widened as his aim wavered. Whatever he'd been expecting, it wasn't this, nothing could have prepared him for what lay before him.

With a defiant yell, he fired!

With a start, Jacke sat upright in the bed, the quilt cracking with the sudden movement.

She froze, listening intently.

What was that?

There it was again, a gunshot, distant but carried on the night air.

Leaping to the window, she peered out onto the moonlight landscape but the encroaching darkness was too deep to reveal anything.

Firing off her pyjamas, she quickly pulled on jeans and a black jumper and red padded jacket. She patted her jacket to make sure she had her hand unit.

Her window opened onto a yard filled with empty kegs, pallets and Joe's silver jeep.

Dismissing the idea of waking the others, Michael especially would be no help; she opened the window and jumped out, her boots making a soft scuff on the paving stones.

Running to the end of the gable wall, she paused listening for another shot. It never came. Maybe it was nothing, probably hunters or poachers. Damn, she cursed.

She was almost about to go back when a gurgled scream sliced the air.

It was hard to tell how far away, sound travelled far in the still summer night and it was hard to judge.

Jacke nervously weighed her options and realised there was something else, the dull reverberation of an engine. Glancing upwards, she could just about make out a dark shape thread the starry sky, barely making a noise.

What the hell was happening out there? She stumbled against something and instinctively reached out and grabbed it, smiling as she felt handlebars beneath her grip.

Swinging her leg over, she kicked off, her hand unit steadily following the engine wake of the mysterious craft. Jacke paused, flicking on the front light and wedging the hand unit in the wicker basket attached to the front.

It was only when the darkness got thicker; she realized she may have made a mistake.

Crouching in the thick hedge, Jacke peered at the small screen. The engine wake had ended in this area somewhere.

Pushing the bike tighter into the hedge, she kept still, her ears straining for any sound.

Only the creeping hiss of the sea and bland sheep bleats broke the air. She wasn't even sure if the gunshots had come from here. Berating her stupidity, she walked along the edge of the road; the bicycle torch gripped tightly in her left hand but switched off.

Her eyes flickered to the hand unit as it scanned the surrounding area for anything anomalous. The tarmac gave way to grass and sand as she made out the glassy black shield of the ocean.

There was nothing in the sky bar a commercial plane flying across the horizon, its navigational lights blinking rhythmically.

Knowing she was getting nowhere, Jacke turned to leave when the flicker of a light down on the beach caught her eye. Checking her scanner, she saw it was picking up a group of people and a craft of some kind but there was nothing like it in the database. Aliens, she thought.

A dread made her stomach knot but she crouched down, getting as much as she could. The towering cliffs and hills were too steeped in darkness for her to see anything but the scanner was picking them up.

Never the fool, she decided to go back and tell Varran.

She never saw the black shape that swooped up behind her.

Her startled scream was stifled by a rough calloused hand, cold and sweaty. A stale breathed voice hissed in her ear to not cry out.

Calming herself, Jacke slowly nodded, her heart racing, her body tense. Her self-defence classes swirled in her mind as she readied to cripple her assailant but the moment she felt the long hard shape of a rifle lightly touch her leg, she changed her mind.

Pulling her lower to the shrub filled ground, Jacke wiped her mouth as the hand pulled away slowly, as if the very motion would alert something nearby.

With a frown, she turned to look at the dark heavy coated shape beside her and surprise caught her face. She didn't recognise the man with his sweaty lined face but she recognised fear when she saw it.

Eyeing the rifle, she composed herself and fixed him with a defiant stare.

"Do you usually creep around in the dark with a rifle?" she snapped, with more confidence than she felt. His eyes never met hers as he scanned the darkness, his frame poised for action.

"I don't know you," he said, his voice low and gravely, his breathing shallow.

"That's ok, I don't know you either. Jacke's the name and you are?" The man stared at her as if seeing her for the first time, his pale green eyes looking at her from a shadowed mask.

"Colin McPeake, I live here." He answered curtly. His features were distorted in the torchlight.

"I take it you're not out rabbit hunting at this time of night," prompted Jacke, "it was you I heard shooting." He fixed her with that distrusting look, his grip on the rifle tightening. He didn't answer and Jacke sighed ruefully. "I'm a friend of Rosie."

Instead of relaxing him, Rosie's name seemed to tense him up even more.

"Her," he gritted, instantly betraying his ill feeling toward the land lady and making Jacke dislike him.

To hell with this, thought Jacke as she manoeuvred around to face him. "What were you shooting at? Is it anything to do with whoever is on the beach?" she demanded, keeping her voice low but her tone stern. McPeake's face fluttered slightly as if remembering a nightmare, his head lowering as the memory flashed before him.

"I found what was killing my sheep and by Jesus, girl, it wasn't anything I'd seen before." His face broke into sheer horror. "It wasn't human and the way it just sucked the life out of that poor animal, Satan himself would be hard pressed to think of such a thing."

For a moment, Jacke realised how calmly she took this news.

When had she become accustomed to monsters as everyday occurrences? She smiled to herself before realising the only thing between her and whatever it was, was a pedal bike and a freaked out sheep farmer with a nasty looking rifle he was not afraid to use.

Her smile faded quickly as she took his arm.

"We need to get back to the pub and tell my friend. He'll know what to do."

McPeake didn't respond. Instead he stared at her as if she weren't real.

"It looked at me," he rasped, his voice awash with nerves. "I shot it and it just looked at me. But it had no eyes and it was looking right at me!" His face scrunched as he saw it in his mind's eye, cold, malevolent and utterly devoid of emotion.

"It was an alien!" he hissed, his eyes wide, his face pleading for someone to say he wasn't mad. Despite herself, Jacke felt sorry for him and lightly touched his arm, the padded material smooth beneath her touch.

"Let's go!" she urged, forcing him to his feet and moving him back down the road. "Whatever's down on the beach can wait," she decided, "just move!"

Stumbling over his own boots, McPeake allowed this girl to propel him forward.

Behemoth blackness shrouded the beach below them but Jacke didn't care. She was suddenly too afraid to care. All she could think about was not ending up like Ernie or the sheep and how stupid she now felt.

Suddenly, the hedgerow before them erupted with a gurgled snarl as a massive shape reared up in front of them.

It stood over seven feet tall, its quivering bulk alive with hunger as it swayed like a cobra, a low rattling hiss accompanying its movements. In the moonlight, Jacke could make out a body covered with thousands of tendrils amid a jelly of silver and crimson.

She could see the powerful muscles rippling below the surface as it seemed to sniff the air, seeking a scent. She could see no face, no features to speak of as the creature slithered across the black tarmac cutting off their escape.

McPeake yelled in terror as he raised his rifle and fired, the shot sparking the night like a mini nova. The bullets hit the creature's underbelly, making it screech. The sound was like glass shattering, making Jacke's scalp crawl. Her heart raced as McPeake let off another volley which only seemed to anger the monster.

Its tendrils seemed to shake like raging fists as Jacke felt the air slice as it lashed out, the tendril striking the road with a sharp slimy crack. She hadn't even seen it coming.

"Run!" she yelled, pulling the farmer with her toward the hilly path that led to the blackened beach.

There was something else down there but she and McPeake could do no more than run blindly for their lives.

With a primeval snarl, the creature surged after them. Realizing she had dropped the torch when the creature appeared, Jacke leaped off the edge of the road onto the rocky path, worn by decades of people travelling to the beach for fun. McPeake was right behind her, his breathing laboured and fearful.

With a cry, she fell over a rock and tumbled helplessly down the slope, her hands cut by sharp rocks as she went. A sharp blow to her thigh made her cry out in pain. She could hear the creature reacting to her voice and it charged like a train as it churned the ground to find her. McPeake called for her but she couldn't tell where he was in the dark.

Scrambling to her feet, she kept heading downward, tripping and stumbling desperately trying to stay ahead of the monster.

The fear in McPeake's eyes was enough to convince her to keep running but her leg ached and she felt blood stick to her clothes. She cursed as she remembered the hand unit.

Slapping her pockets as she fled, a knot gripped her stomach as she realised she couldn't find it. Please don't let me have dropped it when I fell, she pleaded to the heavens. Her cold fingers felt the slim rectangle shape in her inside left pocket and she gratefully whipped it out, flipping it open.

"COM mode!" she shouted. "Colin, follow my voice, keep heading down!" Her only answer was the guttural snarl of the creature as it caught her scent and headed towards her.

Shit! she thought. " Computer, lock on and beam me and closest human up now!" she yelled, the roar growing closer, the air alive with the putrid smell of the thing as it bore down on the helpless girl.

"Computer, teleport now!"

She saw the dark bulk shred the hill as it thundered toward her. Her body ached from the fall, her face torn by terror and within seconds the creature was rearing over her.

She could see the tendrils squirming like suckling pigs. She froze as the creature hissed triumphantly, its bulk blotting out the weeping stars above.

It reared upwards into a kill position, almost dragging out its prey's final moments sadistically. Jacke lay helpless as it lunged at her.

Suddenly, the air around was filled with a swarm of high powered darts that smacked into the creature's body like hail stones.

With a squeal, the creature lurched to the left in agony, losing its grip and tumbling down the slope with a high pitched shriek like a thousand terrified piglets. Jack watched it as it fell before finding its grip again and whipping itself back into a defensive stance.

A group of black clad figures rushed past Jacke and took up formation to unleash a second volley which the creature, despite its bulk avoided as gracefully as a ballet dancer before vanishing into the dark with a roar. Too stunned to move, Jacke heard one of the figures shout orders. Military, she noted before she realised her body was enveloped in a blue swirl of light and the night disappeared.

Deftly, she kissed the floor panel of the teleport chamber as its light faded and she rematerialized on board the Juggernaught.

"You left that a bit late!" she shouted at the air, giving the computers a reproachful glare.

Sitting upright, she jumped at McPeake's breathless awe.

"Sweet Jesus," he breathed almost reverently. "Where are we?"

Grinning, Jacke allowed herself to relax; delighted the farmer had been swept away with her. In a second, the hexagonal chamber flared back to life with a soft purr of power as the blue rain of double helix light permeated both of them and the familiar spread of Rosie's bar sprang into existence around them.

Jacke smiled widely as Varran's reproachful stare. He held his hand unit in front of his face, waving it at her.

"Just as well I had this linked into yours just in case any of you tried something silly like, oh, I don't know, running off into the night after strange ships, alone, unarmed, defenceless." His stern tone made it clear he wasn't happy with her.

Despite herself, Jacke blushed like a scolded child. McPeake jumped to his feet, brandishing his shot gun menacingly at the Xereban scientist.

"Knock the attitude on the head, mate. If it wasn't for your daughter, I would be dead right now." Almost dismissively, Varran gave him a withering look.

"Actually, Mister Whoever you are, I saved both of you and just in the nick of time it seems," he trailed off, seeing Jacke's torn bloodied jeans. She dismissed it but Varran insisted on tending to it. She pulled a face as he muttered something about infections and sly flesh eating germs.

"Put that down right now, Colin McPeake!"

Rosie's growl made them jump and despite holding her hateful stare, McPeake did as he was told.

Dressed in a light blue frilled house coat and hair standing on end, Rosie looked more scary than usual. She was glaring at the sheep farmer defiantly, willing him to fight back but he nodded at Varran and Jacke and made to leave.

"You can't go out there!" protested Jacke, turning her head to look at Rosie whose angry countenance hadn't faded at all. "Rosie, There's something out there and I think it killed Ernie."

"And my sheep," gritted McPeake, sliding onto a pine chair and rubbing his dirty face wearily.

Varran listened intently as a bleary Tyran wandered in, having been awakened by the sound of their voices. Her face lit up, alarmed at the sight of an injured Jacke.

"Bloody hell, what happened to you?"

With a wry grin, the Irish girl shrugged at her.

"The usual; monsters and men in black with big rifles."

"Same old then," came the reply as Tyran sat next to McPeake, looking him up and down with a hello.

Rosie hadn't moved.

"Won't your wife be missing you?" she shot pointedly at her old enemy.

McPeake returned her glare with a sly smirk. "Worried about me, are ya?"

"Hardly," she sliced back, her voice dripping with distaste as if she had just swallowed a pint of lemon.

Varran stood up. "If you two are quite finished, I believe we have a problem." He looked down at Jacke. "Tell me," he said tenderly, relief flickering across his face.

Rosie looked guiltily for a second and moved to put the kettle on as Jacke composed herself.

"It was Colin here that saw it first," she said, nodding at McPeake to continue.

Rosie looked about to say something but kept her silence under Varran's gaze.

Shifting uncomfortably, as if unaccustomed to public speaking, McPeake's eyes glazed as he remembered the thing feeding on his sheep and the baleful, malevolent stare it gave him.

"Two rounds I put into it and it still came," he mused before realizing he was talking to himself.

Mumbling an apology, he cleared his throat and told them how he had stayed up to protect his flock and catch whoever was killing them. There was big money in sheep and he couldn't afford to lose any of them especially as the Garda were doing nothing to help.

But he hadn't been prepared for what he had found.

"It looks like a giant jellyfish," added Jacke, "covered in tentacles and suckers. If it hadn't been for the soldiers in black, we were finished."

Her voice trailed off as she realised what she had said and how close she really had come to dying.

"Could it be an alien?" asked Tyran, yawning and rubbing her cheek. Looking undecided, Varran shook his head.

"Maybe but I don't think so, not with soldiers involved."

"How do we know they're soldiers?" Rosie put in as she poured tea into five mugs with purple flower patterns. McPeake looked at her.

"Because they were all in black, shouting orders and had very powerful automatic weapons. Not to mention the big black helicopter. I'd say some sort of special ops sent specifically to find this thing."

Unimpressed with his sarcastic tone, Rosie held herself back from throwing his tea over him. Instead, she breathed through her nose and turned to Varran handing him his tea.

"Six sugars?" he asked hopefully.

"The only way," she answered. McPeake watched them and it suddenly occurred to him that Rosie was almost in awe of this strange man with the white hair. He had an air about him, something he couldn't put his finger on but he definitely held court in Rosie's eyes. She always was a shallow cow, he thought bitterly.

Varran sipped his tea, considering what had been said, a swirl of possibilities in his head.

"Government experiment maybe," suggested Tyran.

"Something escaped, you mean," breathed Rosie.

Jacke shook her head uncertainly, "It could be a sea monster, something never seen before or a mutation."

"The pollutant level in certain parts of the world could certainly justify that theory but we need to find out. Tyran go upstairs and get dressed. Jacke, are you ok to go back?" She nodded, giving a prompting nod in McPeake's direction. Varran caught on. "Mister McPeake, are you up for it?"

Noticing, Rosie's disapproving stare, Colin took a chance to goad her and agreed to come.

Besides, he had a family to protect.

"Before anyone else dies," he said grimly.

EXPERIMENT FOUR PART 2

"What about Michael?" Jacke asked, thinking they could use all the help they could get right now.

"He's drunk," Varran replied with a rueful tone.

"That's alright then," came a bright determined voice. Rosie stood tall, her ample chest puffed out. "There's room for me."

Varran made to protest but she shushed him with a single word, warning finger in the air.

"Ernie."

Ten minutes later, they gathered back in the kitchen. Standing in a semi-circle as per Varran's instructions, they stood like sentries about to face the rampaging enemy.

"Colin, I don't believe in titles so I'm going to call you by your first name," Varran told the farmer who acknowledged with a small bow of the head.

He held his shotgun tight to his body, poised to fight. His thoughts were of his wife and sons and prayed they were alright. He had few friends and little respect but by God, he was going to help kill that creature with a bunch of strangers and loud mouth Rosie.

No matter what anyone thought, he was going to protect the island and everyone on it.

At 42 years of age, he was feeling the decades creep into his bones day by day but a fire enveloped him, a rush of youthful determination, he had not felt in many a day.

And somehow he trusted the man with the white hair and youthful face. He inspired something in him and he was willing and ready to stand with them to the last.

Varran smiled as if he could read McPeake's thoughts and glanced at Rosie in her knitted green jumper, jeans and black puffer jacket which had clearly seen better days.

Her eyes shone with excitement and she squeezed Jacke's hand joyfully.

"I've never teleported before," she breathed in short gasps. Jacke thought she was going to jump up and down with glee.

Leaning closer to whisper, the coloured girl hissed teasingly, "I thought Joe teleported you all the time." Rosie seemed taken aback but her face melted at some memory that flashed before her.

"No love, Joe's warp speed. The Duke himself has nothing on my Joe's engine!" Closing her eyes regretfully, Jacke threw the image out of her head.

"Be quiet and do exactly as you're told," warned Varran as he set the teleport for Jacke's last location. "Let's go."

Blackness melted under the vivid blue swirl of the teleport as the five figures solidified from thin air.

In a second, it was gone and darkness swamped around them.

"Down!" hissed Varran, making them crouch down, the wiry brush of shrubs scratching Tyran's face.

Opening his hand unit, Varran fiddled and worked with it as the others watched, breaths collectively held for fear of alerting someone or something.

"This isn't where we saw it," Jacke whispered in his ear, her breath hot on his skin. He didn't acknowledge it as his eyes followed whatever was on the tiny screen.

"Is that a mobile?" wondered Rosie, craning to get a better look as his fingers danced deftly across the small keys, the white tinged light carving a rectangular shape in the shadow of his face.

"Better than that," said Tyran, her darting around the darkness, alert for the slightest movement. Her heart pounded in a mixture of fear and excitement; giant jellyfish monsters and secret death squads, by God, this life never failed to surprise and frighten her.

"Anything?" whispered Jacke. Varran said nothing as he studied the readings.

"Varran," prompted the large landlady, "the lady asked you a question and you're being rude." The hint in her voice was enough to snap him out of it. He stared at her for a second then at Jacke.

With a smile, he lightly squeezed her hand in apology.

"I put us down on the beach where it's nice and dark," he beamed as if it was supposed to reassure everybody, totally ignoring their blank stares. "If the creature and the soldiers are still here, we have the advantage; they'll be looking in the wrong place and you did say the soldiers must have landed on the beach."

"Do you think they are some sort of covert op?" asked McPeake softly, his grip still tight on his weapon.

Varran considered, his head tilting to one side thoughtfully. "I don't know but we have one thing in common," he said voice trailing off.

"The alien!" said Rosie with more enthusiasm than she meant, earning her a grab to her arm to keep it down. The Xereban looked at her curiously, his face alive with revelation.

"It's not alien. Whatever that creature is, it originated here on Earth."

"I saw it," breathed McPeake fiercely, "that thing was alien." He shuddered, the image of his sheep being bled dry while alive flashing before him. Varran shook his head.

"I scanned Jacke's clothes as she had the closest contact with it."

"Too close," pointed Jacke.

"But close enough. Ever watch CSI, Mr McPeake? What you don't see often contains the key to separating fact from fiction. The cells that fell from this creature when it was hovering over Jacke, and I'm very glad it only hovered by the way, are from the jellyfish DNA range and that only originates here on Earth." Varran was rattling along like a train. "However, there's something different about them. Someone's been tampering and mixing."

"Genetic experiment, you mean?" realised Tyran. "Is that possible?" Jacke shrugged.

"Why not? Dolly the sheep may have the first step of something bigger which they couldn't go public with, discounting the rumours of successful human cloning previous to that."

Rosie let out a shocked breath, her cheeks red. "They tried to make a sponge cake and found dynamite," she reasoned, her mind racing.

Was Joe ok? Was this what killed Ernie? Sucked dry was how McPeake described his sheep. Was that why the coffin was closed?

A saddened rage welled up in her. "We have to kill it before anyone else dies!" she said determinedly and looked at McPeake, "human or livestock." McPeake held her stare in the gloom and nodded in agreement.

"Can you find it with that mobile thing?" he gestured towards the glowing device in Varran's hand.

"I'd prefer it not to die without getting the full story first, Mr McPeake," Varran said steely.

"Tell that to Ernie," Rosie glared at him. He held her gaze. He gave Jacke and Tyran two sleek silver weapons with black curved handles and a tapered snout. Three black buttons ran along the finger line.

"They're set to stun. Follow me and stay quiet!" The threat in his voice was like a slap in the face to Rosie and McPeake.

The farmer watched this stranger and wondered exactly who they were? He had been beamed up like something from Star Trek and been attacked by a monster and it didn't faze these people and now with a mobile they were going monster hunting.

McPeake shook his head. It didn't really matter; he trusted these people and knew they had the same objective as him. Wherever the man with the white hair led, he would follow.

Keeping close to the cliff face with its spread of over hangs and recesses, the five made their way slowly up the beach, Varran holding his hand unit before him like a talisman, his expression betraying no feeling.

The moon gave little light here and the shadows coiled like sleeping dragons, the soft lick of the ocean on the mottled sand the only song in the night concerto.

With a quick rise of his hand, Varran signalled them to stop.

He looked upward, hearing the sound of boots on rock. The others heard it too, the girls gripping their weapons tightly as McPeake raised his rifle in readiness.

After a couple of minutes, Varran gestured them forward.

They had only taken a few relaxed steps when a dark shape fell from above them to land with a squelch before them.

Varran paled as he saw the twisted cadaver, its flesh scrunched like a prune, the expression of horror still evident. It smelt of dead fish, its black uniform hanging grotesquely on its frame.

The sound they had heard had been the poor soldier kicking uselessly as the thing had fed on him. There was the crash of shouts from above and the smack of high compression rifles in the night air. Rosie gripped Jacke's arm terrified as another two shapes fell before them.

A weapon smashed to the ground along with the convulsing soldier, his strangled gurgles being smothered by the bulky creature that was sucking greedily off his body.

Rosie screamed as Tyran recoiled.

McPeake let off two rounds as Varran shouted for him to stop. With a gut wrenching snarl, the jellyfish thing rounded, squealing as the bullet impacted on its flesh.

Jacke and Tyran fell to their knees and aimed their weapons, the night flaring as twin red beams lashed across the beach and hit it square on.

It writhed, screeching as it flung the crippled soldier at them, its bulk twisting in an impossible way as it recoiled like a leech underwater. Varran stared almost awestruck as it righted itself and reared up, its underside exposed with its hundreds of tendrils, each shaking angrily and hungry for revenge.

"Fire again!" screamed Rosie, her hands to her face, helpless to move. McPeake fired again as Jacke and Tyran followed up with another double shot of laser.

The creature's flesh smoked and buckled where the beams hit but it was like a bee sting to it. It flopped forward and began to sift over the sand towards them.

Desperately, Rosie looked about her but there was nowhere to go. The monster hissed, knowing they were trapped and almost savouring every last second.

Its flesh rippled, powerful muscles gaining ground as it shrugged off every bullet and laser beam.

"Beam us out!" yelled Jacke, as Varran shook the hand unit in frustration.

"I can't! Something is blocking me!" Jacke looked at him, drawing Rosie and McPeake back.

"That's impossible," she said, her eyes wide with fear as the creature slithered closer.

"Tell me about it," he hissed back.

Something cut the moon out as the darkness became even more foreboding.

An almost inaudible pump of engines whipped the air and a swarm of bullets sliced the salt air viciously and all in the creature's direction.

With an angry screech, it veered away from its prey and vanished into the comforting haven of thick shadow along the cliffs.

"Run!" ordered McPeake and they ran along the cliff base.

The craft hung for a second, then swooped lower, powerful search beams slicing through the dark and catching the five racing figures in its bloom.

"Thank Big John himself!" shouted Rosie, pointing to a shadowed shape close by. It was a jeep or truck, they weren't sure but it was their only hope.

The craft bore down on them, its beams blinding.

Any second now, it would unleash its weapons and they would die here now alone. Rosie thought of Joe asleep, snoring, not ever realising what had happened to her; McPeake thought of his wife and how he had snapped at her today over something stupid, bitterly regretting it now. All Varran could think about was how his hand unit had been blocked, it wasn't possible.

"We won't make it!" cried Tyran as the black shape bore down from the sky.

Without a sound, another shape launched itself from the cliff above and swooped through the air before smashing into the craft.

With a shudder, the ship dropped out of the air like a brick and crashed onto the beach along the shoreline, the water crashing up in a white plume. The creature screeched infuriated as it tore at the craft, great sheets of ripped metal flying into the air, terrified screams echoing in the chaos.

It had smashed through the exterior and reached inside, its tendrils forcing into the space and tearing into the occupants bodies. Jacke closed her eyes, realising how close she had come to ending up like that.

McPeake reached the truck and ripped open the driver's door. He jumped into the cab along with Varran while Jacke and Tyran helped Rosie clamber into the back forcing back a heavy canvass.

They jumped as they were met by a frightened face, huddled in the corner, dressed in black. It was ginger haired man of about thirty and he was terrified.

"Please, it killed them all," he whimpered pathetically. The girls felt no sympathy and Rosie grabbed him by the scruff of the neck.

"You can join them," she growled venomously. Leaping forward, Jacke grabbed her, restraining her gently.

"We need him," she said softly. "He may know what's going on." Rosie glared at her, her lined face puffed angrily before nodding and releasing him.

"You better do," she told him coldly, "or I'll show you how good I am with a rolling pin, son."

McPeake turned the key in the ignition and glanced at Varran who was sitting transfixed, staring out the passenger side window.

Following his gaze, McPeake saw the creature silhouetted against the night sky, rearing triumphantly into the air, splitting the quiet with its unearthly screech atop the shattered hulk of the helicopter which lay like a dead gazelle.

Then it did something totally unexpected.

It began pulling the crew's bodies out one at a time and tossing them onto the wet sand.

"What's it doing?" muttered Varran, his hand unit pointed at it, scanning for every second he could.

"They're not dead," realised McPeake as his eyes adjusted to the dark. He could see the fallen soldiers struggling to escape by crawling away but barely able to move.

"It broke their legs, crippled them," Varran watched with a mixture of revulsion and fascination. "Why?"

"Hurry up!" shouted Tyran from the back. "We have another passenger."

"In a second," retorted Varran gruffly. He winced as the creature gave a high pitched shriek but this one different in tone to the others.

It reminded Varran of a whale song, morose and mournful which hung in the night like a death shroud. Jacke and Tyran peeked from the tarpaulin as the sound filtered across the beach.

They saw the crippled soldiers and helicopter wreck. They heard the plaintive cries of the people for God and family.

And they watched in horror as from the cliff base they had ran along, emerged more of the jellyfish creatures, each slurping and screeching hungrily as they homed in on its mother's call and the meal that squirmed helplessly.

They had never noticed the cave in the dark, had not known how close they had been to the nest.

Over a dozen creatures, smaller than the mother, rippled forward and snatched the soldiers up like dolls, feeding on them ravenously.

McPeake put his boot down and the truck thundered off in a spray of sand. Pale, Varran sat unable to speak.

"I think the shit just hit the fan," muttered McPeake.

The farmer vehemently insisted on going to pick up his wife and children, as much as Varran was disagreed, he was helpless to stop him.

The dishevelled woman clambered into the truck with the others in the back along with two little boys, each the spit of their father.

They were dressed in pyjamas and wrapped in blankets. Rosie cuddled the youngest while Mrs McPeake clutched the other.

The two women exchanged brief but civil glances.

"Don't worry, Sheila, Everything will be fine," soothed Rosie. "Are you warm enough, sweetie?" she soothed the little black haired boy, his face a mask of bewilderment. He nodded and she held him tighter.

Jacke smiled. Rosie was a woman of powerful convictions and yet her protectiveness of the children belayed her good nature.

Twenty minutes later they reached the pub.

McPeake and Varran helped the others out, all the while checking the creatures hadn't followed.

Bustling everyone inside, Rosie locked and bolted the door, shouting for Joe. Tyran forced the shaking soldier into the back scullery while McPeake gave his wife and kids a reassuring hug before following Tyran. Joe appeared in stripy pyjama bottoms, his hair sticking up, his face bleary. His bare chest was covered in white black hair and his beer belly drooped over his waist.

Michael emerged, woken by the shouting, clad only in his black boxers.

"Michael, women present, cover up and wake up!" blared Jacke, locking the windows shutters. "Hurry!"

Suddenly sober, he bolted as Joe began putting heavy tables against the door without knowing why. If his Rosie said do it, she had a good reason.

"Is that everything locked?" bellowed Varran. Rosie nodded. "Everybody into the back!"

Jacke took him to one side.

"That thing took down a helicopter. I don't think tables against a door will stop it." He smiled reassuringly and for a moment she was convinced he knew exactly what to do and everything was going to be alright.

His young old face framed in the shining white hair held a calm she didn't feel. He winked and led her by the hand after the others.

Out in the warm night air, seared only by a light salty ocean breeze, she watched her youngsters gorge themselves on the twitching bodies of the animals from the metal box.

The waves seemed to shush the slurping and squelching as mother sighed with a pride born of her children's independence.

Soon, the bodies had stopped whimpering and flinching, and the sound of her mewling children filled the air. It was a whale song as heard out of the water and a plaintive cry echoed all over the animal kingdom as the young's insatiable appetites never seemed to waver.

The mother shifted her bulk, spraying sand as she did so and with a calming shriek, led them up the cliff face.

The sight of McPeake pointing his rifle in the captured soldier's face disturbed Varran as he sat down at the oak kitchen table.

He had never agreed with the heavy handed methods of the military on Xereba but had learned over the years that those kinds of methods were a sad universal constant.

However, he had also found himself desensitising to certain things over the years and right now, they needed information. A gnawing feeling in his stomach told him time was short. He gave his hand unit a quick study and gave a frustrated grunt.

Jacke was by him in a second. Her eyes were filled with concern and he did his best not to seem too worried.

"Something is blocking me. I can't access the Juggernaught's systems," he said so as not to alarm the others.

"But there's no technology on Earth capable of bypassing yours," she answered.

"I know." Varran's tone left the implication unspoken between them but she caught the heaviness in those two words.

She glanced round. Michael had joined them, looking worst for wear, while Rosie had secured Mrs McPeake and the two boys in the upstairs spare room, the boys' fears squashed by cola and crisps. McPeake had reassured his wife before joining Varran and the others downstairs.

Right now, McPeake and Joe hovered over the black clad soldier who was tied to a wicker seated oak chair, his eyes wide with fear as the barrel of the rifle held steady in his face.

"We need answers sir," Varran said directly to the soldier, his youthful face damp with sweat, his ginger fringe caked to his forehead.

The terrified young man stared at the man looming over him, taking in the swept back white hair and piercingly determined sapphire eyes. He had never seen eyes quite like them before.

Standing tall over him, Varran fixed him with his hardest stare. Tyran was watching the windows and the glare unnerved even her.

"As you saw from your comrades unfortunate demise on the beach, we don't have a lot of time here, so I would kindly ask you answer my questions as quickly and as fully as you can, otherwise my friend with the rifle here will do anything to protect his children in the next room. We only met tonight so he has no allegiance to me. I can't control him. Now, what are those creatures?"

The soldier breathed heavily through his nose, his eyes locked on Varran's but he said nothing.

Sighing, Varran bowed his head slightly and glanced at the others.

"Look, sir, I don't care who you are; I don't want your name or where you come from. I don't care if you are part of a shadow squad or a full blown celebrity. All I care about is stopping those creatures and I need your help to do it. There are over a thousand people on this island, most asleep in their beds, hapless victims if those things out there decide to do a supermarket sweep. And I can't believe you'd let whole families be murdered in their beds, children who can't defend themselves. Please sir, help me understand this, I can stop them."

"You can't." The soldier had a gravely element to his voice, whether from fear or exhaustion, Varran couldn't tell. "You saw what it did to us, what can you possibly do?"

"More then you know, mister!" snapped Rosie, handing out tea, her face tired and anxious. "And just so you know, I'll buck this teapot over you if you don't talk."

The soldier knew she wasn't messing about. Her face had glazed into a determined scowl, one he'd seen many times, and still haunted his thoughts on a lonely night.

"What the hell? Those things come here and I'm tied to a chair, I don't think anybody's going to stop and untie me."

"Probably," Varran said softly, his calm tone thick with quiet intent. The soldier bit his lower lip, a bead of sweat tracking his left cheek. His years of training yelled at him to keep his guard but no amount of training had prepared him for giant jellyfish monsters.

No matter what else he knew, everyone in this room were as helpless as him, the consequences could wait until later.

"I'm part of a vanguard, the name of which I'm not prepared to disclose," he began. Varran's head snapped up.

"I don't care. Tell me about the creature."

Noting the steely fire in this stranger's eyes, the soldier frowned slightly before continuing.

"We were sent to retrieve the creature. Easy mission, so we thought. It was part of an experiment, I don't know exactly what and somehow, it escaped. We traced it here and have been searching the island for a few days now."

"That explains the U.F.O. sightings," McPeake glared. "It isn't military issue, is it?" The question was more accusation than query but the soldier just gave him a thick stare.

"As I said," he hissed, "I can't disclose it."

"Continue!" bit Rosie sharply, her hands wringing nervously. Tyran gave her a reassuring smile before returning to her vigil. It didn't help.

"I don't know how but it got out. It was supposed to attack livestock to evaluate its ability as a biological weapon. Bullets can't stop it and it is fast for its size but we never realised it had bred, we never knew."

"Spontaneous pregnancy occurs in nature all the time, it's nothing new," Michael added, his pallor still pasty, "But surely whoever created it gave it a built in weakness, some sort of Achilles Heel."

"It was programmed with basic animal instincts but you saw it. It knew how to fell the copter and break the others' legs so its young could just feed."

Varran stood up and immediately began working on his hand unit, producing a tiny blue pouch with mini tools from his jacket pocket.

"It's worse than that. Every person on this island is lying asleep in their beds, blissfully unaware of what's coming and helpless before it. Farron has just become their larder."

He said no more and worked furiously at dismantling the little machine. Clicking his fingers he motioned for Michael to hand his over and took it apart too.

"Do we know how many of those things there is?" asked Michael.

Jacke gave him a look and he knew right away she had been face to face with one of the creatures. "One was bad enough," she said quietly.

"Mister Soldier, will you help us?" Varran asked pointedly without looking at him. His brow was furrowed as he reworked the little machines on the table before him, his fingers moving with chaotic certainty. "There's no strings, no conditions. You can disappear wherever you came from when it's over and we won't stop you. If anything, it's important you survive to tell your commanding officers exactly what happened here. Agreed?"

"Agreed," he answered, grateful for the choice. Varran nodded consentfully.

"Mr McPeake, would you kindly untie our new friend?"

Hesitantly, Colin did as he was bid and the soldier stood up wearily, rubbing his wrists. Rosie gave him a stern look, indicating the boiling pot of tea on the stove.

With a wry smile, he pulled out a revolver hidden down the back of his combat jacket and checked it was loaded.

"Is alien D.N.A. part of the creature?" wondered Rosie. "There's nothing like it on Earth, and to cut you off, there has to be alien technology somewhere. How did you get here?" she asked the soldier.

"Submarine," realised Joe. "Don't you remember Darren telling us how the fishing fleet said they saw a sea monster off the island? It passed right under the boats causing a massive wake; nearly capsized them."

Varran nodded thoughtfully. He knew no experienced seaman would mistake an ordinary submarine for an animal, not even a whale.

Whatever type of sub it was, he bet it was bigger than and as classified as the copter they saw crash to the beach.

And to mutate any animal's biology to such an extreme was beyond lawful means.

He had heard about secret human cloning and rumours that the chupacabra of Mexico was in fact an escaped genetic experiment utilising alien cells but proof was as fleeting as snow on a summer's day.

If he had learned anything about the human race over the last 100 years, it was that they were a constant source of surprise, creatures of deep ambition that strove against all odds to realise even the sickest dream.

But something niggled at the back of his mind, something else he couldn't picture.

Something had blocked his technology, whether by accident or purposely, he wasn't sure but a dark agency capable of doing all this was a frightening prospect and he had seen enough of that whilst working for the government on Xereba.

With a cry of delight he fused the two hand units together with a wide smile. His yell made the others jump and he was suddenly aware every pair of eyes was fixed on him, demanding silent explanation.

"Why the glum faces?" he grinned, "we have our first weapon!" He shook the little sliver mobile like object excitedly. It didn't elate them as he thought it would.

"Rosie, keep the tea coming!" he ordered and glanced at the kitchen clock. Four eighteen. Time really does fly, he thought. It was only a couple of hours until dawn.

They slewed across the grass like huge watery snakes, their senses scraping the summer air for the scent. The mother growled at its babies to stop their mewling. They would have food soon, the mammals on the beach having failed to quell their thirst.

Through hawthorn hedges they slithered, clutching every scent like a drop of gold.

She paused, sniffing the air and realising a large rectangular shape loomed before them, nestled in the darkness. It could hear the woolly animals bleating and the barks of distant dogs as the noise echoed in its senses like a dinner gong.

But it screened them out and caught the other scent, the one given off by the two legged creatures that had tried to hurt it on the beach.

It was faint but tangible. They were still, it knew, because the scent rose when they moved about, heightened by their adrenalin and emotions.

When they were like that, the two legged animals were like ripe fruit, teetering on an abyss of succulence and decay.

The mother knew the two legs were resting inside their stone buildings. With a low hiss, mother led her children towards the building.

Feed here, it told them and we move to the next nest and the next and the next.

Paradise.

Suddenly, she froze, her senses turning back towards the ocean, all black and wrinkled under the moon light.

They were out there, she knew, coming for her and her children and she would never allow that. They were free and they would never be caged again.

Determinedly, she turned back to the structure and it was gone.

Confused, she swayed uncertainly, her senses screeching as it tried to find the elusive scent again, the mewling of its young becoming annoying as nothing came to her. Where had the nest gone? Had these two legs the same abilities as her tormentors?

Quivering desperately, she caught a faint scent, like a whisper dying on the wind. Squealing to her children, she ploughed onwards determined not to lose it again.

McPeake had stood for a few brief moments watching his boys sleep, their mother's arm curved protectively around them. His heart swelled lovingly as a dark fear gripped his heart. He would not let those creatures take his family.

Rosie stood regarding him in the dim hallway and catching his expression, felt her bitterness dilute slightly.

Whatever disdain she had for him, she realised in that moment he was a father with feelings and loved his family deeply.

And she knew anyone worth their salt would always put their family first and do whatever it took to protect them and keep them safe. She tapped him lightly on the arm and gestured for them to return downstairs. She pulled the oak door over quietly and clicked it shut.

Colin let out a weary sigh as his expression softened.

"Sam, the youngest, is a fire cracker, so independent and headstrong," he said in a low voice.

"Just like you then," Rosie answered with a hint of sympathy in her tone.

McPeake nodded with a wry smile. "He thinks he's indestructible, typical boy. He'll leave one day to see the world and I don't think he'll come back. At his age nothing's impossible and everything is his for the taking." He paused at the bottom of the stairs, looking at Rosie directly. "I'd do anything for my boys, keep them safe and help them make the impossible a reality. But Sam was attacked by one of my sheep dogs, a golden Labrador. It bit him badly because he tried to ride it like a horse and it was a crotchety old bastard. That was the dog you saw me beat and you've hated me ever since."

"I didn't know," Rosie stammered, her cheeks blushing, barely able to return his look.

"You never bothered to find out, you just assumed." McPeake's words were neither severe nor angry and that made Rosie even more uncomfortable. "I just thought you should know in case… well, just in case." He padded off down the hall leaving Rosie feeling like he'd punched her in the gut.

Tyran and the soldier were still holding their positions by the window when they reached the kitchen. The others were staring at Varran's device which he had attached to the main phone connection.

Varran's face was a picture of delight like a pupil whose project had just won the science fair. He had offered no explanation for what it was, keeping a smug silence.

"Guesses, anyone?" he challenged.

"Nice to see you are not worried about monsters crashing in here any second," griped Michael sarcastically. Jacke eyed him and the device.

"Every home on Farron has a telephone line which also means most of them have home computers, internet etc," she reasoned. "Would that be a fair assessment, Rosie?"

For a moment, Jacke thought the jovial landlady seemed a bit red in the face, her eyes slightly teary. Composing herself, Rosie nodded.

"It's the 21st century, my dear. God, the nights I've spent on John Wayne's websites. Did you ever see that programme where they went looking for his ghost? You're so lucky, Varran. You can go back and walk his life a million times over, see what history has missed."

Tyran caught Jacke's train of thought and sidled over to get a good look at the device.

"You must have got something on the beach and you're sending some sort of signal to every home on the island, something connected to the creatures."

Pride swelled up within Varran as he watched his friends work things out for themselves instead of him leading them by the hand.

His smile grew wider as the two girls' deductions blossomed into perfect logic.

Squatting down on her hunkers, Tyran watched as data scrolled along one of the small screens. She raised her eyebrows, looking suitably impressed.

"You're sending a bioelectric field to every house via the phone lines, very clever." Varran nodded gracefully, arms folded across his chest. Realising what her friend meant, Jacke glanced at the others who stood bemused, their blank expressions saying it all.

"It's okay. The creatures can't attack anybody because they can't sense them. This is generating a blanket if you will, keeping humans off the creatures radar. You got that from when they killed the soldiers didn't you?"

"The creature uses a bioelectric field to hunt. When it brought the helicopter down, the field was huge, nearly blew my unit off the scale. The signal I'm generating disrupts their field, rendering humans invisible to them. Now all I have to do is work out how to bypass the signal that's blocking us from the Juggernaught."

An audible relief shimmered round the room as they realised their neighbours would be fine. Losing Ernie was more than enough for them to stomach. Rosie sidled over to Varran as he began fiddling with Jacke's hand unit and gently leaned close to his ear.

For a second, the scent of his cologne grabbed her.

"Just one thing, does your magic blanket cover Xerebans too?" Like he'd been hit by a hammer, Varran's smile crumbled.

With a screech like a thousand banshees, the mother smashed through the makeshift barrier across the window, showering them with vicious shards of wood and glass.

Its thick bulk weaved through the gap and tendrils lunged round the soldier's head and yanked him back outside.

He never had time to scream as a horde of suckling squeals ripped the air and the children heaved through the window.

Joe and McPeake fired almost simultaneously as one of the babies scattered them like bowling pins and reared towards a screaming Rosie. She whirled round and in one fell movement grabbed the tea pot and hurled it at the creature.

It screamed as the boiling liquid burned its flesh and it fell back.

She grabbed Joe and pushed him toward the stairs. McPeake scrambled to his feet and let off another round before bolting towards the stairs.

Part of the wall exploded and collapsed as the mother slammed into it like a freight train, plaster and brick cascading like a storm into the room. Their hungry screeches tore at the air.

Jacke, Michael and Tyran stood side by side and fired their pistols, red beams lancing across the dusty air and striking the jelly like bodies.

It had little effect, merely making the creatures hesitate and recoil for a moment but it was enough to allow Varran to push them towards the stairs, his hand unit gripped in his left hand.

Racing up the stairs, Michael grabbed a fire extinguisher attached to the landing wall. Unclipping it he crouched at the top of the stairs and let fly, the white foam uselessly washing off the lead creature's bulk as it heaved itself up the stairs.

The girls flanked him and fired another barrage of laser fire which lasted longer and seemed to burn brighter than the last just from sheer determination.

With a disheartening snap like bones, the banisters collapsed as the creatures all tried to get up the stairs at the same time which only caused them to jam themselves against the wall and begin fighting among each other to get to their prey.

"Come on!" yelled Varran, his fingers flying across the hand unit, his face twisted in desperation almost as if heard the last seconds of life clicking down.

They tore down the corridor as the air filled with the nail on a blackboard screeching of the creatures. Jacke's scalp crawled at the sound as she reached Rosie and the others.

"Rosie and Joe, you're with us!" barked Varran. "Mister McPeake, stay here with your family, lock the door and keep quiet!"

Jacke saw the terrified children, woken by the noise, and immediately had an image of them trapped by the advancing creatures.

A whole family wiped out. She grabbed Varran's arm and whirled him angrily round.

"We can't leave them!" she blasted furiously. Varran gripped her by both arms and fixed her with a stern glare.

"Trust me." She hesitated, looking at the family.

"I do but it took the soldier."

"I know," came the grim reply. "Colin, lock the door."

With a fearful look, McPeake nodded trembling. He looked briefly at Rosie and Joe.

"Good luck." He slammed the door as the noise of the creatures grew louder as they reached the top of the stairs.

"This way!" cried Rosie, grabbing Joe's hand like grim death. She ran to the window at the end of the corridor and pushed it. It didn't move.

"I told you to oil this thing!" she snapped at her husband. He moved her aside and shoved it. Its white painted hinges heaved outwards. About two feet below was a sloping roof.

"Fire escape," she explained as Joe jumped out first, then reached back to help his wife through.

"Go next," Michael told Tyran. She saw the shadows fill the corridor and she jumped into Joe's strong hairy arms. Jacke followed.

"Michael, go!" Varran shouted firing down the corridor as the creatures filled it like one giant gelatinous shape.

"No, you're the best chance to stop them!" Michael answered pushing him toward the window roughly. "Hurry up!"

Varran hurled himself out, missing his footing and falling backwards onto the gravel. Head beams blinded him as Joe started up his jeep.

Michael landed with a grunt beside him. "I'm definitely never drinking Guinness again," he muttered as Varran grabbed him by the jacket.

"It's an acquired taste," said Varran shoving them both towards the jeep and clambering into the back with the girls.

It was a tight squeeze but the upper part of the wall shattered, spraying the ground with rubble and a thick cloud of dust which fell like dead snow in the head beams.

The creatures squirmed through the hole and flumped to the ground, twisting and turning to find their prey. As if realising what was about to happen, they filled the road, blocking the jeep's path.

"Put your boot down!" screamed Rosie. Michael and Tyran leaned out opposite windows and fired at the ground, shards of burning gravel spraying up and forcing the nearest creatures to retreat with high pitched screeches.

His sweating face like stone, Joe revved and shot the jeep forward, the jerk smacking Michael against the frame of the window and cutting the small of his back.

He fell back into the jeep, grimacing painfully. Gravel spewed as the tyres spun but the mother twisted at the last minute and smashed her bulk into the vehicle and flipping it from the back end.

With a sickening crash the jeep tumbled over, slamming into the gravel, glass flying everywhere.

In seconds the creatures swarmed over the wrecked vehicle with delighted squeals as their prey cried out in terror.

One by one they were dragged out of the wreckage like dolls and hurled to the ground.

Helpless, Jacke managed to look at Michael, his face full of regret and fear yet she found comfort from his wink. Varran had lost the hand unit and Rosie was trying to control her sobbing as she reached to grab Joe's hand one last time.

I love you Mum, Jacke grimaced as a tendril leeched round her neck. Varran stared helplessly, his mind racing for that last desperate chance as the world filled with the creature's quivering bodies and hungry shrieks. Tyran shut her eyes as she felt the tendrils creep over her body, relishing every scent, every drop of sweat as the creatures closed in, ready to suck the life right out of them.

Two things happened at once.

The haunting tones of a horror movie theme cut the air and a flare of heat struck them as a ball of fire showered the creatures' bodies.

With a chorus of squeals, they scattered in all directions as another fireball exploded above them, lighting up the night air like the dawn.

The roar of the creatures was deafening as they reared into haven darkness in a flurry of heaving bodies.

Varran was on his feet in a second, scooping up his hand unit in his trembling, sweaty hand. With the other, he grabbed Tyran and bundled her back towards the pub.

Joe had Rosie, her face twisted in terror, perspiration streaking her dirty face. As Jacke pulled Michael to his feet, he winced in pain, limping where one of the creatures had nearly crushed his leg as it pinned him down.

Not looking back, they saw McPeake and his wife in the ruined doorway of the pub, their expressions grimly determined. The sheep farmer had his rifle tight to his shoulder, his eyes glowing hatefully as his wife tossed an aerosol can high over their heads.

McPeake trained his rifle like an extension of himself. The bullet sparked as it fired, followed by a dull pumph as another fireball lit the area like hellfire itself.

"Sheila was captain of her camogie team!" beamed McPeake. "She has a great right hand."

"Here they come again!" yelled Michael as a low determined gurgling hissed out of the darkness as shadow peeled back to reveal the mother cautiously checking for her victims, the excitedly squeals of her babies coming from somewhere behind her, eager for the kill but wary of the fire.

Jacke realised it was her mobile ringing. She held her mobile disbelievingly, staring at it. She had always hated that ring tone but had never gotten round to changing it. Pressing the yes button, she put it to her ear with a wide smile.

"Mum, you will never know how good it is to hear your voice!" she smiled. "Why are you calling at this time of the morning? It's freaky." She listened to her mother as Varran dashed to the table, dismantling the hand unit at record speed, while the others began moving furniture into the gaping wall but they knew it wasn't enough.

"Varran, any joy with breaking the signal yet?" Tyran yelled desperately. Her question was answered with a solemn nod and a blank expression. Fine, she thought, keep fighting. She turned to see a quivering Rosie clutching Joe's hand and kissing it.

Tyran heard her tell him she loved him and always had. Don't give up, Rosie, she thought, her stomach churning fearfully, not yet; it's not over yet.

More harshly than she intended, Tyran shouted, "Rosie! Gather up all the aerosol cans in the pub!" she ordered, her petite frame shaking despite her bravado. "Michael, have you still got your gun?" He nodded, wiping his dirty hands on his jeans; he looked terrible. "Jacke, have you?"

To her amazement, her friend was talking on the mobile, her body slightly turned away from the main group. The clatter of aerosols thrown on the table made her put one hand over her free ear as she strained to hear whoever she was talking to.

Varran was still amid the clatter, his fingers straining to keep from shaking as the tiny pieces of machinery were taken apart and reshaped. He asked a single question.

"Rosie, I take it the pub is insured?" She nodded, exchanging a quizzical look with her husband.

"They're coming closer!" cried Sheila, backing away from the barricaded gap. Like a storm, Varran shot up and began barking orders.

"McPeake, take your wife and children and go home." They floundered and his face hardened. "Move! Rosie, Joe, go with them! The field is still generating, so you will be alright. After tonight these things will be dead."

McPeake took his wife by the arm and herded her toward the doorway, shouting for the kids to come down. Rosie stopped and gave him a peck on the cheek, her face speaking volumes.

"Out through the bar!" she said, " and grab the Duke's autograph on the way out Joe or no more pony express for you." Her husband's dismayed look said it all.

Pausing to watch them go, Varran whirled round to Michael, pointing to the large black range. "Loosen the pipes then take the girls out of here." The gurgling was growing louder and his face ghosted with a hint of panic. He looked round to see finish her call. She had a stunned look on her face. He was facing her in a second, the whiff of gas building up all around them. Jacke stared at him bemused.

"That was my mum. She had a dream we were being attacked by monsters."

"As much as I would love to debate physic powers, this isn't the right time, you all have to go!" he said breathlessly but Jacke fixed him with a steely look.

"She saw us burn to death." Allowing himself a wry smile, Varran felt an inner calm swell within him.

"At least I know I'm on the right track. Give your mother a kiss for me when you see her." She gripped his arm tightly, holding him back with a force that made him wince with pain.

"Have you got a death wish? First the Numarans and now this; we need you." The gas was more powerful now and the creatures could clearly be heard shifting the rubble outside the gap.

"No you don't. You have come so far, all of you, and I couldn't have wished to have met better people. Whatever happens, I know you are more than capable of dealing with it." He pressed the reconfigured hand unit into her pocket. "This will give you access to everything on the Juggernaught. Use it wisely." His expression hardened. "Michael, get them out of here."

Michael stood where he was, Tyran moving to stand with him, their faces determined. To make her point, Tyran folded her arms and stood tall.

The piled furniture fell as the mother lunged through the gap, her tendrils waving through the air, scenting her prey and gurgling greedily.

"They all have to be in," breathed Varran softly, backing away with the others.

Stealthily, hunger drove all the creatures forward, the mother keeping the children in check as she warily watched the figures, waiting for another burst of flame and her children had been hurt enough.

They piled in squealing as no fire came and the prey stood like the fragile white animals in the fields.

The mother paused, memories of running through a field with another shooting through her mind.

She remembered a tender touch, a touch that she had for her children and the faces, faces that brought her pain and anguish and changed her, made her what she was now, the hunger screaming in her as she screamed and the love for her children forcing her forward towards the prey.

The building had fallen easily as one these prey would now do.

She stopped as she saw one of the prey raise its arm and point a pointy object, not at them but the wall behind them; another sound, a high pitched bleep that made the prey jump.

"The signal has stopped! I can reach the Juggernaught!" cried Tyran. With a delighted cry, Varran snatched the hand unit out of her hand and activated the link.

With a screech that ripped the air apart, the mother reared up, tendrils writhing angrily.

Like a light from heaven, the room blazed in a double helix dazzling light that solidified like sapphire ice around the jelly like creatures, piercing every fibre of their bodies and freezing them where they stood, the mother locked in an attack stance, her ferocity as solid as the light.

"Michael, cut off the gas supply!" shouted Varran as the girls opened whatever windows that were left. Jacke looked at Tyran and burst out laughing. Tyran couldn't help but give in to giggling.

"What?" she asked, eyeing the frozen monsters only inches away.

"We're opening windows," she pointed to the ruined wall, the warm night air wafting through it like a grateful angel.

They held each other, as much in relief as humour at being in one piece. With a renewed sense of childish curiosity, Varran walked round the creatures locked in the teleport beam, the sparkling helix light making their translucent bodies dance with spiralling blue energy. It was as if they had been carved from the power of the universe itself and even in this state, imbued nobility born from the most primal essence of nature. Michael watched silently, mesmerised by the size of the creature, his mind racing with questions.

"What are we going to do with them?" Varran stopped, his face running with blue, making his white hair shimmer, shadowing his wide eyes.

He sighed staring at the mother and her brood respectfully. They were beautiful but knew nothing else but to survive.

"They're as much victims as poor Ernie and those sheep. Someone did this to them, someone with the ability to cut us off."

"Well, there have been rumours of secret experiments going on for years, most of which the authorities don't even know about," said Michael. He grimaced wryly, smiling to himself. "Still, they're the best hangover cure I ever had."

"We can't release them. They'll just keep on killing." Jacke's voice was flat, the implication unsaid but caught by the others.

"What about relocating them to another planet, an uninhabited one," suggested Tyran, moving closer.

With a sad glance, Varran shook his head. He had sworn to do good; protect the less fortunate wherever he could and he had drawn these three youngsters into it with him.

These creatures were victims as he had said, but their blood lust to turn them into weapons was too strong, too fierce. Even those that had created them had lost control.

If he closed his eyes, he could almost hear nature itself quiver fearfully.

A dull ache grew in his chest as he knew there was only one thing he could do. He raised the hand unit and gently pressed a button.

With a high pitched buzz, the blue lights swirled and spat as it became a cyclone, its wraith edges collapsing and compressing and as they watched the creatures began to dissolve and collapse as the beam tore them apart and spread their molecules across the ether.

It was silent. It was painless. It was the only option.

It didn't stop a single tear roll down Varran's weary face.

The glacial ocean whipped froth and foam as a new dawn greeted the day with a pink and orange sky tipped with white.

It was going to be a hot day, a day filled with hope and an embrace of the joy of just being alive. As the world rose slowly from its slumber, the lapping sea watched as a great shape slipped silently beneath the chopping waves away from Farron.

Within seconds it was gone, lost to the ancient depths that harboured its secrets well, its purpose defeated and still unknown to the world.

But for a moment something glinted in the sun, an emblem; it was a wolf's head howling at the moon surrounded by a gold circle.

Renovations had begun on the pub the next day and as usual Rosie and Joe stood proud as the islanders gathered to help.

None would know what had happened or of the four strangers that had saved their lives as they slept soundly in bed.

It had been a gas explosion that had damaged the pub, so they believed but they would have it repaired in no time. McPeake and Sheila had arrived to help also and he and Rosie exchanged a knowing look, a look of a new found respect.

Jacke had helped with painting the new look kitchen and she had phoned her mother to tell her the whole story.

Of course, she had moaned about Jacke going off on her own and putting herself in danger but Jacke could hear the unspoken pride in her voice. Keep dreaming, mum, she thought. She thought Rosie had looked tired.

If it hadn't been for her asking them here, everyone on Farron might have died and no one would have been aware of it, for a while at least. Varran had been the best site manager in the world and hadn't lifted as much as a brush, although he had used some of his technology to speed the repairs up. After all, there were tourists due to arrive tomorrow. Jacke looked at Rosie and Joe.

They seemed tired and had almost sacrificed everything to save them all. Varran could do something for them, something special, Jacke smiled to herself as she realised he could give Rosie and Joe a thank you no one else could.

The sun blazed down from the crystal blue cloudless sky as the horse pounded over the desert, sand beating the air beneath powerful hooves. The heavy set rider hunched over his steed as he suddenly railed him back and in one swoop, leaped from its back and fired his Colt 45.

A rough unshaven man fell back clutching his chest in a death throe, landing heavily on his back as blood stained his shirt.

"And cut!" The man with the megaphone got off his canvas chair his face beaming with excitement. He pushed his hat back from his forehead, black hair stuck with sweat. "Great job everyone!"

A number of crew bustled about amid the movie cameras, lights and whinnying horses. Two buzzed about the tall man as he dusted himself down and the dead man got to his feet, swiping at flies.

The director walked across to the big man and slapped him on the back gleefully.

"Great job, my friend," he said in a thick American accent that indicated he was from New York. "Could you do me a favour? There's someone I'd like you to meet."

Rosie stood in her best frock, sun hat covering her face from the sun. She was clutching a large straw weaved bag like her life depended on it.

Joe stood slightly behind her as the two figures approached.

The sun was in her eyes but her view was filled by the big man, his broad shoulders belaying a powerful build and he walked with a swagger which radiated a gentle strength. His neck scarf fluttered in the breeze as he took his broad Stetson from his head.

His smile was like a thousand suns and his blue eyes sparkled with a deep love for life and respect for those around him.

The director caught Varran's grin and nodded. It was good to see a fellow Xereban creating a movie millions would see and remember forever. Xereba had nothing like that in all its history.

"John, I'd like you to meet Rosie and her husband Joe. They're your number one fans." John Wayne nodded and shook Joe's hand and took Rosie's and kissed it lightly. Rosie blushed and put her hand to her chest giggling.

"It's an honour to meet you Mister Wayne. I've seen all your movies and my pub is dedicated to you," Rosie blurted. John gave her a curious look.

"You're Irish, aren't you? I had a swell time in Ireland filming the Quiet Man," he said. "You've come a long way." Rosie returned his deep smile.

"Oh, further than you think, sir. May I have a photo?" she asked blushing with delight.

Watching Rosie made the last few days almost worthwhile, thought Varran as he watched Jacke, Michael and Tyran gather round Rosie's idol, getting autographs and having photos taken.

Varran couldn't shake the feeling that gnawed at the back of his thoughts about the creatures. He had been responsible for killing an entire species; genocide.

No matter how he justified it, he knew in his heart of hearts he was totally justified but it still disturbed him.

Why were they created and by whom? Why had the signal broken at that moment? It felt controlled somehow, regulated.

In the last few days, he had studied the readings he had taken and had discovered some disturbing coincidences.

The jelly creatures indeed had alien D.N.A. crossed with two other genetic genomes, one of which had human traces.

He had revealed as much to the others but had held back something that unnerved him greatly.

The creatures had come after them; they had recognised Xereban biology and hunted them. And the soldier they had captured should have alerted Varran straight away something else was amiss. He had scanned him when captured for hidden devices but found none. He should have been looking for something else.

And in the confusion, something happened he hadn't even noticed and only realised afterwards.

When the monsters attacked, the biocloak was still active, making every human invisible to the creatures. When it took the soldier, the selection had been deliberate, it could see him. And that could only mean one thing.

A chill gripped Varran's spine.

The soldier from the black ops was a Xereban.

THE INFINITY WEB PART 1

Orange skies darkened by thick stone clouds and heavy black smoke held parliament over the shattered landscape. Massive craters were everywhere and the dank rocky ground was littered with the bodies of the dead.

War had dragged its relentless claws across Europe, turning quaint villages and towns into battles for survival where the biggest battle for people was what they were going to put on the dinner table that evening and keeping their families free from the fallout of war.

One dark day, grey uniformed storm troopers and tanks rumbled into their lives and brought everything crashing down.

Families were shattered as the bombs fell and bullets ricocheted. Blood flowed in the streets as skies blackened. Women fell weeping to their knees cradling loved ones fading corpses.

The Nazis had changed the world and plunged it into hell on Earth. They had thundered across country after country, destroying life after life, plundering resource after resource and sucking all it wanted into the Nazi legacy.

The giants had been toppled leaving the smaller countries helpless.

But even in an earthquake, the smallest of flowers can survive. And the storm was met head on by good souls that dared to stand up and say, "Enough!" And the battle was on, determined troops clashing.

Young men, far from home and feeling small and afraid, died in fields that reminded them of home whether it were the dales of Yorkshire, the heather plains of Scotland or the quilt spreads of the Irish countryside.

Countless battles, trenches filled with the brave and too many lying dead, good enough to fight for their country but not good enough to go home, would never be buried in the steadfast soil of their birthplaces.

It wasn't deliberate, just unfortunate.

Millions died and this was just one of those battles. The ground had been ripped apart by salvo after salvo of bombs and bullets.

Murky clouds of mustard gas crept along the air, seeking the last of the living. Mighty trees, centuries old, lay black and withered over trenches lined with broken barbed wire and brown uniformed cadavers bloodied and burned.

Body parts lay strewn over the area and the sad pelting rain formed puddles of red in a feeble attempt to wash away the carnage. The opposing sides had clashed here and in the end, what was left of each battalion had scattered back to their safe houses reporting a great battle where they had severely depleted the other side's numbers.

Nature wept floods of tears as it gazed upon what was left of a once glorious meadow where families had picnicked on sunny days.

Parts of the sky glowed red with distant fires as battle raged on but this was its wake.

Such was the rain; you could no longer make out which side was which. The air was mucky with death as a harsh wind drove the rain even harder. The bodies were everywhere, enemies lying rotting amid enemies, heads open, faces gone and limbs blasted off.

The silence was so profound it was as if Mother Nature had curled up in a ball and refused to admit how quickly her beautiful creations had been raped by man's evil.

Against the red and grey skies, black shapes flew closer to the scene, the scent of death carrying on the wind like an open invitation.

Cawing, they swooped onto the fallen branches, the rain making them blink as yellow eyes scanned the carnage for danger.

But the beasts weren't moving.

They cawed excitedly, bringing others to them. They descended like angels of death, the rain dripping off their large black feathered wings.

Hooked ridged talons flexed as they hopped heavily across the muddy ground, heads tilting curiously as to why the men didn't move.

The crows were used to the bang of rifles from irritated farmers or the gaunt skeletal figure of the scarecrows but here, there was nothing like that.

They could hear the distant rumbles of battle miles away but they knew they were safe here. It was nature's first stage of reclaiming the land as the scavengers ate the flesh of the dead.

One pecked at a soldier's bloody hand and jumped back ready to take flight. There was no reaction so it pecked again, tearing a morsel from the body. The sharp black beak swallowed down the meat, traces of blood staining its beak. Others flapped down to join it, the rain melting off them.

Soon a raucous feeding frenzy had begun, their delighted squawks breaking the silence. The hard metal things gave no sustenance but they didn't care as the bodies were pecked greedily.

Something changed.

The carrions froze, sensing a sudden vibration in the air. It was not natural and their bodies stiffened. Some flapped their wings apprehensively as a vast shadow fell over them in a haze of red light.

A high pitched throb culled the air as the crows realised the rain had stopped. Their heads flicked upwards. Their eyes filled with fear and with panicked screeches launched upward, wings pounding the air frantically.

A rat, its fur streaked with blood and bits of brain, poked its head out from a soldier's broken skull. It squeaked fearfully, its meal forgotten as it scurried for its life back across the terrain, running over other fleeing rodents to escape.

The dark shape circled slowly over the battlefield, carefully and deliberately. It crackled with energy as the rain lashed against it. A low powered hum rippled the air as something began to build.

Bright yellow beams of light shot over the ground, sweeping and searching. Green sparks scarred the air as the beams trailed purposefully and silently.

In seconds, they were gone, the darkness rushing back in.

As silently as it had come, the shape vanished and the rain pelted down again. Silence carved the site again as the crows watched from their drenched perches.

After a few minutes, they bravely swooped back down to continue their feast. They hopped about, heads cocked quizzically, blinking rain from their eyes. There was nothing left. All the bodies had gone.

Varran was trying desperately to avoid Tyran's interrogation.

She had seen some of the archive material of Xereba and had, despite her racial memory, been bombarding him with a stream of questions about life on the planet.

He'd been happy at first to talk to her but that had been four hours ago and now he felt like he had been the subject of one of Solos' interrogation sessions. He knew youth and curiosity went hand in hand but was there no end to Tyran's questions? How could one so young talk do much?

At this point they had discussed the final day on Xereba and how the survivors had survived when journeying through space before finding Earth.

"So," continued Tyran without pausing for breath, "since everyone but you assimilated into Earth society and lived by their customs..." She checked herself. "I'm spending too much time with you."

"You are, definitely," agreed the weary scientist. But she ignored him.

"I keep calling them humans but I feel as human as the next man." She and Varran stared at each other. "Of course, I'm not a man and you're not human, neither am I but that's beside the point." Her eyes widened as a thought struck her. "Of course, that opens up a whole new question as to exactly what makes a human, human. Technically, I'm not human but I am in a way. Does biology dictate what it means to be human or is it a state of mind?"

She was stopped as Varran suddenly stumbled, holding his head, gasping in pain. She leapt up and reached for him and he leaned gratefully against her.

God, I've made his brain explode, she panicked. He straightened and fell back against the nearest console.

Blinking several times, he watched the command centre grow fuzzy and indistinct. Tyran's anxious questions faded as suddenly the room was filled with personnel, all rigged out in full Xereban military gear; men and women attending their stations.

He watched as a tall black haired man stood centre of the room, irradiating strength and authority. He was dressed in red leather body armour with gold trimming, his black cloak over one shoulder and trailing to the back of his knees. The left side of his chest bore the insignia of the Xereban militia, a sun with a dagger through it.

Varran gasped as he recognised the man.

It was General Solos.

It wasn't possible. He had died with millions of others over a century ago. How could he be here, now?

The holoscreen before him was active and showed the image of a small red planet.

Solos barked an order and a huge fountain of energy streaked through space to the planet surface.

In seconds, the planet exploded in a hail of fire.

"Weapon test successful, General. The Juggernaught is fully operational." Staring at the lieutenant giving the report, Varran recognised him as Terrol, one of the soldiers on duty aboard the Juggernaught the day Xereba had exploded.

He had saved many lives with his quick thinking, setting the teleport to scoop as many people aboard as possible within such a short time. Varran would have died that day had it not been for him.

Solos was as sleeked looking as Varran remembered and the smug power mad smile on his face stirred old hatred in the scientist.

A sharp pain shot through his head again and the room went misty again. The personnel vanished and everything was as it had been.

Shaken, Varran turned to look at Tyran but found himself facing an old woman, cursing him for destroying her life.

"You should have left me alone, let me live a normal life instead of wasting my life fighting your damned phantom vision. You were wrong damn it and you dragged me down with you." Varran recoiled as she raised a knife above her head. He saw the light glint off it before it plunged toward him.

Screaming he fell to the floor, arms raised to save himself.

"I swear to god, I won't ask you another question!" declared Tyran, standing over him, hands open innocently.

He blinked disbelievingly, his breathing quickening, his mind racing.

"Get the others," he croaked before collapsing.

"My first aid course didn't really cover this," cracked Jacke as she examined the slender ice blue console before her.

A tired looking Varran lay prone on top of it, his dark ringed eyes staring upward, glistening with moisture.

Two small round circles were attached to his temples, registering his brain activity, as a holographic representation of his body and its innards rotated above him. Tiny green dots flashed at various points showing his major organs. An agitated Tyran looked on, arms nervously folded across her chest, as if hugging herself.

Her frown betrayed her concern. Now and again she would tug nervously at the sleeve of her green striped top, almost dancing from foot to foot.

"Would you stop fidgeting? It's hard enough to figure this out without you doing the Riverdance," Jacke snapped at her.

Rubbing her hands on her denim jeans, the young girl muttered an apology. Letting out a short sigh, Jacke looked at her side on, her dark almond eyes rueful. She had forgotten the girl before her was exactly that, a young girl.

With her short cropped blond hair and light blue eyes she looked younger than she was and Jacke realised she probably hadn't had to deal with sudden illness before and had grown close to Varran over the last few months.

She knew Tyran battered him with constant questions and had seen him control his patience at times but when someone you like suddenly collapses in front of you, it can be a traumatic event.

Having known it herself only too well with the death of her grandfather, Jacke felt a pang of regret, the painful memory flashing in her mind suddenly. Tyran looked every bit the little girl lost. She smiled reassuringly.

"Sorry for snapping. I'm just not sure what's wrong." Almost like a lamb, Tyran looked at her from under her eyes.

"Is he dying?" Glancing back at the medical readings, Jacke drew in a slow breath.

"Well, he told us he hadn't aged a day since his accident when his time experiment went belly up," she said thoughtfully, "but whether he can die or not is....I don't know." Tyran edged closer, peeking over Jacke's shoulder at Varran.

"Maybe we should call a doctor and beam him up," she suggested.

Like a corpse in a horror film, Varran shot upright with a loud gasp. Screaming the girls jumped back and grabbed each other.

"I think I wet myself," bleated Tyran as she giggled nervously, her stare fixed on Varran.

"Mop mine up first," shot Jacke, letting her go.

Varran's head was in the hologram of his body and he looked at them from his ribcage, the red and green lights playing over his pale features.

"You have no idea how gross that is," chided Jacke, pushing down the sleeves of her red jumper.

A puzzled look crossed Varran's face before he cottoned on to what she meant. He told the computer to stop the medical scan before pulling the sensors on his temples off.

He swung his legs off the table and jumped to the white mottled floor as if he had never looked at death's door mere moments ago.

"You two look like you've seen a ghost!" he said.

"We thought we were about to," pointed out Jacke. "Are you alright?" Frowning, Varran recalled the things he'd seen. He looked at Tyran.

"You're a tetchy old thing," he said, smiling at her bewildered look. "No. You're partly right Jacke. Ever since I was caught in the temporal explosion, I haven't aged but it did something else. Maybe it was the tachyon levels but I'm sensitive to ripples in time."

Tyran looked perplexed. "Prefer Maltesers myself. What do you mean?" Leaning on the lip of the medical scanner, Varran composed himself, letting the images wash over him.

"It's like a sixth sense. I know when something is wrong with the flow of time, when someone interferes with it. This," he gestured round, "is our present but I saw the Juggernaught with a full military compliment with my old friend," this word was dripping with sarcasm, "General Solos in command."

"Maybe it was a hallucination," offered Jacke, her Irish accent almost soothing to Varran's senses.

"No, for a second history had changed, then it was Tyran as an old woman." Tyran's eyebrows shot up.

"Bet you I'm gorgeous." The look on Varran's face said otherwise. "Don't want to know," she said quickly.

"What makes that happen?" asked Jacke curiously. "We didn't notice a thing."

"You wouldn't. Life carried on as normal for you because that would have been your life if you'd never have come here. So, for you nothing changed. Something is causing ripples in time rather than actually ripping holes in it."

The intercom gave a high pitched whine. Michael's voice filtered through.

"You'd better come up to the command centre," he said, a slight urgency in his voice. "There's something you should see."

"Nessie alive and well! Tourists claim to have filmed the legendary Loch Ness monster while on a boat trip this afternoon."

The newsreader with her feathered brown locks gave way to a jumpy video camera in which a large creature with a long neck and humped body was seen rising from the water, letting out a roar from its jaded teeth filled mouth before crashing back under the murky surface.

"My god, they got him at last," breathed Michael incredulously as he sank back into the padded black leather seat, his eyes locked on the monitor. Varran stroked his chin thoughtfully, his expression neutral.

"Maybe, what else is there?"

"Computer, cross reference unusual phenomenon with today's news reports globally and play." Michael leaned back in his chair, winking at Tyran. Whatever he'd seen had clearly excited him.

A Japanese newsreader appeared next, the computer automatically translating his words.

"Witnesses claim the UFO hovered over Tokyo for several minutes before vanishing to the north." The report was accompanied by a picture perfect shot of a large rectangular craft passing over the city. The screen changed.

"Manchester was brought to a standstill by reports of a large dinosaur in the city centre while in the United States, the town of Birmingham claim they were invaded by a Sioux war party on horseback. Spokesmen for the reservation totally deny all knowledge."

"A naval frigate came to the aid of a passenger liner which was under attack by a pirate galleon. The liner took damage from cannon balls but there were no casualties. The said ship has yet to be identified."

"A newsagent was attacked today by a Roman centurion. CCTV footage shows the man did not speak English and threatened the owner with a sword. He then ran out of the shop before vanishing. Police are appealing for information while experts examine the footage."

"Computer pause," Michael said. He swung round to the others.

"There's a tulip farm in Amsterdam that claims its tulips became giant Venus fly traps and ate the owner's dogs and in Australia people claim a volcano erupted then disappeared. There are also reports of islands appearing and disappearing, strange lights in the sky and caveman in Dublin."

"No change there then," muttered Jacke, remembering an encounter with a salesman called Phil. Varran crossed swiftly to the central command table.

"Computer, begin temporal scans of Earth. Relay image with localised weaknesses and cross reference with reported events in the last 24 hours!" Within seconds a rotating image of the Earth appeared with a yellow wire frame surrounding it.

At several locations red dots pulsated slowly with more appearing in seconds.

"Those red dots correspond with the strange reports," explained Varran, pointing them out.

"What does it mean?" asked Tyran, seating herself at the table.

"Think of time like a web stretched tight like cling film and those dots show where time has weak spots, where its fabric, if you will, is weakest. Sometimes, it's weak enough to allow the past or the future to just touch the present and let two time zones meet."

Michael scratched the back of his neck slowly, the collar of his blue denim shirt irritating the skin. "You mean the people on the boat were actually seeing a dinosaur and not Nessie. That for a moment was a window to the past," he reasoned. Varran nodded.

Michael cursed. "Thanks for blowing that dream," he muttered. "I always believed in Nessie!"

Throwing the briefest of sympathetic glances, Varran continued, "Time was weak enough for them to watch a dinosaur swimming in the water but only for a moment. Events like this are rare and seem isolated, just odd stories to fill the news but it's not. What I saw and what all those people saw is someone interfering with the fabric of the time/space itself."

Jacke caught the gravity in his voice. It made her feel uneasy.

"Deliberately?" she asked. He looked at her, his brow concerned.

"If it is, the walls of reality will collapse and you really will have hordes of dinosaurs roaming the streets or worse. The future will move into the present. Reality will be wiped out in a massive temporal implosion. Everything will cease to exist."

They watched through the specially tinted cockpit window at the swirling maelstrom that swarmed all around them. Primeval colours exploded across their hull in silent crescendo as their eyes scanned the area.

"So this the space time continuum," whispered Tyran, sinking back into her black padded seat nervously as solid boulders of red skimmed the Transport Dagger's surface.

They were only optical illusions caused by the power of the forces that surrounded them but seemed real enough. She fully expected one to smash through the cockpit at any second.

Michael gazed awestruck at the panorama outside.

He had hardly spoken since Jacke had guided the ship into the vortex, though vortex didn't really do this place justice.

It reminded him of paintings of Dante's Inferno with its fiery reds and yellows. It spread before them in chaotic symmetry like a collusion of suns exploding, never ending in a kaleidoscope of impossible brilliance.

The dark armadillo shape of the Dagger hung motionless; almost huddled in the storms like a rabbit in a hurricane.

It seemed in constant danger of being swept away in a tsunami of time but stayed where Varran had sent them. He had probed the vortex, the ability somehow linked with his accident and its consequences; he had told them and found something was punching across the threads of the continuum, reckless and uncaring.

He had described it like a child stomping across an ant hill gaze fixed on some distance goal. The child was doing one of two things, he was either deliberately destroying the hill and the ants or he was unaware of the damage he was doing; either way someone had to stop him.

The warriors sat like officers in a submarine during silent running, the computer scanning the vista for anything unusual. Of course, how anyone could make sense of the exterior forces was beyond Michael.

"Just think. You can go anywhere, anytime in all that. It's a doorway to creation itself." Jacke looked at him, her legs curled up under her in the front seat. She swivelled round and smiled at his wonder struck face.

"Where would you go?" The question took him by surprise and he looked at her, mouth partly open, "If you had only one chance."

Lifting his head in thought, Michael grinned as his furrowed brow unfurled.

"Dinosaurs. I'd go back to see what killed them." His face ghosted as he pictured it, his grin widening as the possibility became almost tangible.

Scratching the side of her ebony face, Jacke glanced at Tyran unable to resist.

"I always fancied the exploding spaceship theory. The meteor one's too boring," she teased, catching his widened eyes.

"A spaceship exploded?" he gasped incredulously. "When?" Stifling a grin, Tyran watched Jacke reel him in. The Irish girl's face was as impassive like the best poker players.

"It's in the Juggernaught database. Varran took a trip back and saw it for himself," she spoofed. "Anti-matter vessel ripped open on impact, very messy, he said."

"Really?" Michael gawped childlike.

"When we're finished here, why don't you ask Varran to send us back and see for ourselves," she suggested, her face a mask of honesty and helpfulness.

"Bloody right!" he declared resolutely, "should have thought of that myself ages ago."

Leaning forward, Tyran peered at the readouts on the half-moon controls in front of Jacke.

"Speaking of explosions, are those shields still working?"

In a second, Jacke's hands flicked over the console, her head nodding reassuringly. Tyran watched her long chestnut hair flick across her shoulder as she turned and briefly thought of growing hers. Hers hadn't been that length since she was ten. Short hair was easy to manage but sometimes she wondered. Maybe it would make her seem less of a tomboy.

"That's not all!" Jacke said urgently as a red light flashed on the upper right console and a shrill alarm sounded.

She spun round calling for the computer to isolate and identify the source of the alarm. An image the size of a football shimmered into being above an indent in the middle of the controls.

Amidst the temporal storm fronts a shape had materialised and was drifting silently in the violent flows. They all leaned forward for a better look as the image was enlarged, projected onto the cockpit window.

It breathed fear.

Its enormous iron grey bulk was enhanced with layer upon layer of armoured plating from which bristled fierce looking weapons. The blazing colours flickered off them almost charging them with an air of viciousness.

It almost challenged them to show themselves. Along the sectioned circular hull was a row of ten metallic arms that looked like cargo containers.

A few blinking navigational lights gave it any colour as it slid silently across the relentless flames of the continuum. The trio held their collective breaths as it hung malevolently like a demon in heaven.

Veracious green sparks the size of planets curved about it as it seemed to come to a halt.

Having spent a lot of time teaching herself how Xereban technology worked, Jacke was able to make an initial assessment.

"According to these readings, it has some sort of time engine but it's as if it's not attached properly. It's giving off massive displacement waves," she said, leaning closer to the console to make sure she was getting it right. Michael reached across her and tipped an indent on the console with his finger.

"Varran, computer's tied into the Juggernaught's systems," he said, cocking his head slightly. "Are you getting this?"

"Very clearly," sounded the Xereban scientist's voice across the communication system. He paused as he studied the images. "I don't recognise it."

Jacke glanced out the window. "I think it's the source of the damage. The power readings seem erratic to say the least," she offered. It was obvious from Varran's tone that he was impressed with her reasoning.

"That's exactly right. I suppose the closest analogy is driving a car through a shop window," he explained. Tyran mouthed teacher's pet at Jacke who stuck her tongue out at her. "Every time they jump through time they shatter it," Michael thought out loud, pointing in mid-air, "which is why people are seeing Romans and Nessie."

"What do we do?" asked Tyran, a hint of concern in her voice. Jacke noticed she was wringing her hands. Giving her a reassuring smile, she promised they wouldn't beam over – yet.

"Definitely doesn't look friendly," remarked Michael. "I think we need more information before we make any decisions."

From the com system, Varran told them to stay put. "I'm bringing the Juggernaught to meet you. Maybe we can reason with them."

"You hope," muttered Tyran, hugging herself. She still had nightmares about the Numaran ship and what they did to her. She had no desire to repeat that experience.

Without warning, the ship curved across a plane of energy and swooped directly for the Dagger.

From its back, a volley of laser missiles flared and shot towards the little ship. Moving quickly, Jacke kicked the Dagger's engines into life and the ship darted forward, leaning into a downward curve.

The missiles exploded harmlessly but seemed confused by the continuum's energy flows.

Like a shark, the alien ship surged forward, releasing another array of missiles.

Ducking and weaving, the Dagger screeched with the strain to the engines as it bucked the time storms and returned fire. Her shots bounced off harmlessly as the ship filled the window with its bulk.

Michael glimpsed darkened windows of various shapes but little else as Jacke weaved them across the bough, evading the nests of weapons.

"Varran!" yelled Tyran, clutching her seat harness. "Get your arse here now!" She grimaced as the Dagger made a stomach churning spin. "This is the worst rollercoaster I've ever been on!" she gritted.

"Hold on!" shouted Jacke as she steered the transport towards a crackling spiral of cloud that choked with glacial plumes of blue flame. If she got cover it might give Varran the time he needed to get here.

"It doesn't look safe!" Michael cried as they shot closer to the billowing cloud.

"No option," Jacke snapped back angrily as the Dagger shuddered under a sudden barrage of fire.

The shields faltered and as if smelling blood, the alien ship stepped up its attack. The cloud's power crashed about them thunderously, striking both hulls.

Like a cliff diver, the Juggernaught slid angrily into the continuum, barely pausing before sweeping toward the battle.

"I hate bullies," muttered Varran as he urged the station forward, all too aware the Dagger was buckling under the alien assault.

Like an eagle targeting a mole, the Juggernaught dived, its weapon ports opening up.

"Computer, target Dagger and occupants and beam directly here."

A trail of sparks on the holoscreen made his head snap up. In horror he watched as the Dagger trailed the cloud's edge and lit up. The alien ship's lasers were relentless.

With a final shudder, the Dagger exploded in a ball of fire, the fallout spreading through the cloud, drawing its inherent energies like a magnet and engulfing the alien ship. Varran froze as new fire burned in the continuum and both ships shattered in a nova of blue flame.

"Computer! Teleport!" yelled Varran, the colour draining from his lean face.

Silence.

He glanced at the teleport pad desperately, his ice blue eyes wide with fear and pleading hope. The computer answered; its tones flat and uninvolved.

"Teleport unsuccessful; there is nothing to lock onto."

With a start, Jacke bolted upright, her heart pounding, her breathing shallow. What happened? she thought.

She could feel the hot sun on her face and a warm breeze flitting all around her. There was soil beneath her fingers and vegetation that made her flattened palms itch.

Her expression grew more concerned as she glanced around. Getting to her feet, she called for Michael and Tyran but no reply came. It was then she realised the ground was covered in tiny metallic fragments, wraith wisps of smoke curling skywards.

She was surrounded by giant trees as far as the eye could see. Strange coloured shrubs grew amid them like trolls emerging from a forest. The leaves were shiny and green, almost oily and they shivered in the breeze as if whispering to each other about the strange arrival.

A savage sun burned in an orange sky with clouds that hung skeletally under its intense rays.

Jacke followed the terrain with her eyes as she saw a spread of jaundice coloured plants with large orb like spores run up the floor of the valley towards a network of caves in the mountain side.

Jagged ancient mountains crowned the skyline, their imposing forms staggered by eons of erosion, some with snow tips, others, naked rock that threatened to gut the sky.

A mist crept down through the tree tops like a myriad of giant anaconda, bringing with it a stale scent like burned wood.

Even the coppery tinged grass seemed rough and uninviting with its sharp tips. Thick leathery vines ran up the trees as if to suffocate them. Wide veined leaves trapped the sunlight that fell through like frozen golden rain and hung rigid in the ghostly breeze.

She staggered as she rose unsteadily to her feet, her throat raw, and her joints aching. The debris was scattered everywhere and a slap of nausea made her knees buckle slightly. It was all that was left of the Dagger and the sudden realisation made her heart race with fear.

It was obvious they had crashed, so where were the others?

She'd seen footage of plane crashes and the horrible yellow sheeted coloured bodies. No, she thought, put that out of your mind now, she chided herself.

Putting her head in her hands, Jacke breathed deeply.

She moved deeper into the shivering foliage, careful where she tread, fearful the next step would reveal dead flesh beneath her foot. The long thin fronds of palm like plants curved upwards in a coral arch, obscuring her view.

Jacke pressed forward and froze.

She saw a sneaker sticking out from beneath a ledge of moss.

It was blackened and twisted at an awkward angle. Jacke knew who it was before she shoved the net like foliage out of the way, her stomach churning. Tyran's blank eyes stared up at her from a burnt face, her blond hair blackened and scorched, her right eyelid torn away and teeth broken like glass.

Jacke screamed and fell to her side, immediately trying to make Tyran comfortable, gently cleaning her face, hopelessly unaware how futile it was, stroking her hair before gently cradling her and rocking slowly back and forth, weeping like a baby.

Jacke wasn't sure what hurt more, the fact Tyran had died so young or how torn up she seemed, her beautiful face like a burnt saucepan.

Deftly laying her down, Jacke knelt by her, wiping the hot salty tears from her face as she looked around.

"MICHAEL!" she screamed.

She stumbled around the area, dead to the scratches on her arms and face. And there he was. If she hadn't have known better, she would have sworn Michael was sleeping.

He lay on his back, clothes ripped and scorched, his skin virtually untouched, save for the deep head wound, steeped in congealed blood. Jacke screamed and screamed before vomiting her guts up.

She had no idea how much time had passed, she didn't care.

Her body trembled with slight sobs as she sat cross legged beside the mound of earth. She had used a piece of wreckage, the only decent sized scrap there was to scrape a hole deep enough to lay both the bodies inside and heave the dirt back over them.

There was nothing to use as a head stone or grave marker, no single item left from the crash. The force of the impact had virtually vaporised everything inside the Dagger.

Jacke was shaking despite the sweltering heat, her thoughts with her friends and how those faceless aliens had wiped out people she held dear in a second, without cause or reason; and now she was alone, all alone with no hope, no chance of communicating with Varran.

She would never see home again, never watch Corrie nor sit in a Moviehouse cinema eating a giant bucket of popcorn. And what of her mother and father, would they look to the stars and wonder where she was or stand by an empty grave? She sat in the widening shadows and wept.

Not knowing when night would fall, Jacke had made for the caves high above her.

The terrain was hard going, the plants catching her boots as if to drag her back down the hill. She had fallen countless times, her legs and hands covered in scratches but she pressed on.

With a startled cry, she pitched forward into an orb plant, its sphere of spores bursting into the air with an audible sigh. They stung her eyes and stuck to her clothes.

Soaked with sweat, Jacke pulled her dirty red jumper off and sat in a white sweat stained muscle vest catching her breath.

Pulling her hair back she fastened it with a scrunchie and wiped her face. Squinting up at the cracked sky, she realised night was a bit away yet but how long she wasn't sure. Halfway up the mountainside she could see the caves above her.

Not that far, she thought as she swept her gaze over the valley below her. It was a beautiful sight, full of colours and weird shapes from the flora but it seemed thick and oppressive to her, as if the trees were huddled together plotting dark plans.

It struck her there were no animals to be seen. Surely birds of some sort would be nesting in the plentiful canopy, soaring the burning sky in a defiant screech to the world. But there was nothing, not even insects.

If this was another planet, Jacke could be the only life form here and that scared her.

The solitude didn't scare her, it was the fact she had no idea where or when she was.

Maybe a passing exploration ship would scan the planet and find her; at least then she would have an idea where she was and maybe contact the others. Sadly, she recalled how Michael had described the continuum as a stepping stone to countless times and places. If somehow the alien ship's attack had sent her somewhere over the rainbow, there may be no chance.

She stiffened as she realised something. If Jacke had been thrown here, then so could the aliens. The possibility spurred her on and she resumed her climb up the mountainside, its crags and out crops staring down mockingly at her.

Over an hour later, Jacke grunted as she hauled herself over the edge of a crag overgrown with a purple weed.

The biting rock scraped her elbows, drawing blood as she rolled over onto her back with a heavy breath.

Lying still for a few minutes to catch her breath, she turned her head to see the gloomy entrance to a cave, warped, yellow vines hanging over the entrance, shivering slightly in the breeze. It wasn't until she sat up and looked over the edge, that she realised how far she had climbed and how steep it seemed.

Drenched in sweat, she brushed herself down and got her bearings.

The harsh rays drummed upon her as the Irish girl trudged across the grassy ground to investigate the entrance.

It reminded her of the shape of a lopsided man and she immediately recalled her father's friend, Charlie who seemed to spend most of his adult life in that shape three times a week.

He was a fat, red faced man, his blood pressure obviously too high, who made Jacke and her two sisters laugh a lot with his funny faces and tall stories. She liked him a lot especially when he slipped them a handful of coins or sweets which Jacke's mother lightly scolded him for.

With eight kids of his own, Jacke wondered now where he had gotten the money to drink so much. But that was life, she mused, you always managed somehow.

The black and grey rock was pitted with a myriad of tiny holes which pressed into her palm as she leaned on them to peer into the darkness. She dug into her combat trouser pocket a she remembered something and smiled as her fingers closed around a familiar object.

She was not a smoker but always carried a disposable lighter around with her ever since the electricity had gone out at home one night and her mum hadn't any matches to light the candles.

Jacke had huddled on the sofa for over three hours with her sisters and parents that night, her mother's bosom her comfort zone as dad told them stories about growing up in London and their slightly eccentric grandparents.

He recalled how he had met their mother working in a bar in Wembley.

She had come over from Belfast for work. He insisted it was love at first sight, for him anyway, and wooed her for weeks until she agreed to a date. Having got married, they had moved back to Belfast to be near her family and to raise theirs.

His stories had made Jacke feel safe, but she always kept a lighter with her, just in case the lights went out again.

A musty aroma wafted from the bowels of the cave not unlike damp carpet but Jacke didn't care. It was shelter and no sign of animals. The sky had buckled to a deep pall which probably meant night here.

Her attention was caught by a sound. She tensed, head darting round. There it was again. Creeping as softly as she could, she followed the rock around a corner and let out a sigh she hadn't realised she was holding.

It was a stream, the clear water tickling down the mountain side into a pool that had formed in the rocks, before carrying on its journey down into the valley.

Jacke knew there had to be a river down there somewhere but the foliage was too thick to see it.

Squinting upwards, the rock reared above her like a bird puffing its chest out in a throng of dangerous looking boulders and rocks. She didn't fancy going up any further so decided this would do for the moment.

The pool was about four feet deep and stringed with dozens of green lichen around its edge. But on the surface were large spongy leaves like water lilies that bobbed the slight currents lazily.

Squatting down, Jacke reached across the edge and realised she stank of sweat. Her hands and knees were scratched and sore and she filthy.

With a quick glance to the darkening sky, she stripped off and dived into the water. It was surprisingly warm and she washed herself as best she could. Not being a shy girl, Jacke couldn't have cared less who saw her now.

The water invigorated her as she ducked below the surface and was able to break the root off one of the leaves. The bottom of the pool felt like sand and she heaved the leave onto the dry ground.

Managing to break off another two, she lay back letting the water wash over her. Not wanting to waste any more time, she climbed out and began dragging the leaves back towards the cave.

It didn't take long to dry in the humidity, so quickly dressing, she foraged for any scraps of wood she could find lying around.

Even up here, the trees grew; their perches on the edge of the plateau making them seem like great animals overlooking their realm.

Using the heel of her boot, Jacke managed to crack off sheets of bark. They felt thick and solid, not like bark on Earth. A lot of the thinner branches she was able to break off by grabbing the end and using her weight until it cracked and peeled off.

Piling some inside the cave, she made a bundle, surrounded by a circle of rocks and with a bit of effort, managed to light them. Throwing any leaves or twigs she could find helped the flames build and as the orange sky finally paled into a blue black, Jacke stared into the flames, the giant lily leaves wrapped round her.

They acted like a quilt and as exhaustion ebbed over her, she lay on a leaf she spread out flat to act as a mattress. The soft sponge shaped to her head as her eyes seized closed, thoughts of her family dancing in her mind.

She awoke confused as you do when your dreams become a turbulent tornado and leave you with the certainty you dreamt but couldn't remember about what. Her eyes fell on the smouldering ashes of the fire as she remembered what had happened.

Pulling the leaf tighter round her comfortingly, she closed her eyes wondering what to do next.

"You never were a morning person!" Jacke let out a slight scream as she shot upright and scrambled back away from the voice.

She grabbed a fist sized rock and held it threateningly. In the cave mouth, silhouetted by the creeping orange red dawn, sat a figure.

It was about four feet high, dressed in a white short sleeved top with a frill of pink lace round the neck the straps of a pair of dungarees over the shoulders. One blond pigtail in a pink ribbon trailed across the front while the other hung down the back out of sight.

Pale blue eyes were fixed on her in the half shadow matching a set of smiling white teeth bar the front one which was missing. A little girl, dainty hands crossed behind her back stood smiling a perfect Shirley Temple smile.

"What's up? You think you'd seen a ghost?" she said sweetly.

Jacke stared incredulously. "Lizzy?"

Jacke could only gape at the small figure silhouetted in the breaking orange dawn, the bleeding sun giving her blond hair a halo effect almost like an angel. Her innocent features were shadowed but the eyes shone with a self-satisfied fire.

Lowering the rock, Jacke got to her feet and stared at Lizzy who smiled back at her as if nothing was unusual.

"Either I'm going nuts after less than a day or something in the air is affecting my mind," Jacke reasoned aloud, her thoughts a rush of jumbled events. "Or there could have been something in those spores from the plants I fell into." Coming from an age where science fiction was abundant in movies and television, Jacke had watched that much of it, she could comfortably relate those stories to the new life she was leading. Uhura in the classic Star Trek reruns and movies was a personal favourite. Jacke loved her grace and beauty though Michael liked her short skirt and red knickers better.

Typical bloke, she thought.

"Maybe alien spores are affecting your mind and making you see things," offered Lizzy, poking the ground with her white shoes. She tutted as it left a mark and she rubbed furiously at it with her small fingers. Her head lifted cockily as she watched Jacke's dilemma. "Or maybe you're somewhere over the rainbow but without the whole dog and ruby slippers thing." A ghost of a smile lit Jacke's ebony face.

"That's Dad's favourite movie," she recalled, memories of Christmas at home playing before her eyes. "He got us hooked and we watched it for months on end until the video snapped. I always thought the machine ate it deliberately because it was the only thing we played." Putting her hands on her face, she snapped herself back to reality. "What am I doing telling you this?" she chided, "You're not even real."

A hurt expression dulled Lizzy's face and she pouted.

"I was real enough to you for a long time. You brought me to your life when you needed me, so what's the difference now?" Fixing her with a disparaging look, Jacke almost growled.

"You were my imaginary friend, Lizzy. Everybody has one," she pointed out.

"So?"

"So? I was a child and made you up. You didn't scuff your shoe and wipe it off and I can't believe it now. You're not real."

A half smile carved the little girl's face as she listened lazily.

"So you find out you're descended from the survivors of a doomed alien race, you travel in time and meet all sorts of aliens," she listed, counting off her fingers. "You used to watch that sort of stuff on telly and now it's real. Yet," she purred dramatically, "you have a cheek to dismiss me as an illusion because you're trapped alone here at Jurassic park!" She paused, "without the dinosaurs or Jeff Goldblum that is."

Closing her eyes, Jacke refused to believe and knew that when she opened her eyes, Lizzy would be gone.

"Still here!" the girl beamed sunnily.

Sighing, Jacke approached her and gingerly poked her shoulder. Lizzy protested, prodding Jacke back who winced in pain.

"You can't be real," she murmured. Increasingly frustrated, the little blond girl scowled.

"Listen up. I have never left your mind. I've always lived there. Jacke, you made me up during your dark time as a conduit for you. You told me things no one knew and we played and went on adventures and we were happy. Nothing could come to our world. So why is it so hard to believe that you wouldn't call on me now, even subconsciously?" She frowned as she looked at Jacke's softening face.

Gently, she took her hand and gazed as only a little girl could. Her expression was open and honest, her eyes like a fawn's. "I don't know why I can touch you or feel the warmth of your hands either. All I know is I'm here and somehow I'm real. So thank you very much for stranding me as well. I was quite happy in there," she said, indicating Jacke's head. "I had plenty of company and could go anywhere. Did you know the older you get the wilder your imagination gets?" Lizzy gave Jacke a disapproving mock scowl. "Especially your memory of Peter O'Neill…"

"Don't even go there!" snapped the black girl quickly. "Some things are best left to the imagination." Grinning naughtily, Lizzy chuckled.

"If you say so," she said to herself.

Jacke couldn't help but stare at Lizzy. Shocked as she was, she found herself actually glad to see her imaginary friend.

At least she had someone to talk to now. Tom Hanks only had a basketball so at least she wasn't that far gone.

She realised Lizzy was right and she had always told the truth. She had no idea where she was or how the trip in the continuum had affected her.

With all those turbulent time waves and vortices, reality itself could be rewritten and she had indeed ended up somewhere over the rainbow where dreams did come true, even the dark ones.

Over the last few months she had discovered the universe was rife with creatures, so was this really so unbelievable?

"We have to find food," she decided. "Any ideas?" she asked raising her eyebrows quizzically. Lizzy threw her a pitiful glance.

"I'm sorry," she bleated innocently. "Did we forget I just got here?" Jacke found herself smiling in spite of herself. "Besides," Lizzy trawled on, looking around at the expanse of foliage. "It looks like vegetarianism is going to be our new life style."

Her wit and language made Jacke shake her head amusedly.

"You never talked like that before." Giving Jacke that sunny smile, Lizzy chortled.

"Told you, I never left your mind. I quite like 21st century culture; the language is so vibrant. Pity we didn't know Tyran when we were young, she's so …fiery." Mention of her friend stopped Jacke in her tracks as a sadness and fear rumbled in her stomach. She realised she would never see Tyran or the others again. And it scared her.

The gentle touch of a hand jerked her back to the present as Lizzy lovingly wrapped her hand in Jacke's and smiled encouragingly up at her. Jacke tightened her grip knowingly.

Looking out at the valley below, she nodded to herself.

"Let's go."

The darkening sky burned like an inferno, its lurid orange and pink colours melting beneath the silent wakening of night.

A few nervous stars peeked from cauldron clouds as the seething breeze sighed through the colossus trees of yellow and green like a lover's breath.

Jacke closed her eyes as the breeze wafted across her face like an angel's wings enfolding her in soft, warm tranquillity.

Her mind drifted to home and of family holidays to Portstewart and her Dad marching them all along the Giant's Causeway in the middle of a summer heatwave. Summers as a child seemed to last forever and every day was sunny.

She remembered standing atop the hexagonal giant stones and looking out to the horizon, the red sky melting into the lapping sea.

Her Dad told her the wind was Mother Nature breathing a sigh of relief for another glorious day. He was always telling porkies like that; babies under gooseberry bushes, storks delivering babies and the like.

The best was Christmas Eve when they were driving back from midnight mass along the mountain back roads leading into the city.

As they came over the winding hedgerow flanked roads, the television mast that stood invisible in the star spangled night atop the mountains was seen only by a solitary red light.

She was wedged between the two front seats as her brothers jostled for her space, desperate to be home and leave Santa out milk and cookies.

The irritable jittering was silenced by her Dad who indicated the red glow that seemed to hang in the sky and told them it was Rudolph's nose, guiding Santa to their house.

The awed silence was deafening as the kids gazed in wonder looking for the tell-tale sled with its flying reindeer.

For an instant, Jacke swore she saw it but the others started yelling at their Dad to drive faster or they'd miss Santa. The race was on. Her mother had stifled a chuckle as she reinforced her husband's story with a stern warning that all good children should be in bed and asleep within the hour.

"They were good times weren't they?" Jacke snapped out of her musings at Lizzy's dulcet tones. Her eyes jerked open to see the little girl staring at her, her face painted in a soft smile that conveyed an inner contentment.

For a fleeting second, Jacke thought the little girl had read her mind.

"I did," Lizzy confirmed, wrapping her arms round her legs and hugging them to her like a safety blanket. Her head tilted thoughtfully. "Well, not read your mind exactly, more I can feel the images and the emotions attached. Such joy and familial strength, oh you are so lucky. Of course, you probably didn't realise it was bittersweet for me." Her blue eyes fixed on Jacke sadly. "That was the last time you needed me."

Swallowing, Jacke felt those memories become caustic as she recalled the years previous.

"It wasn't like that and if you really were in my head, you'd know." A wry smile broke her features deftly as she felt a rush of contentment. "The nightmare was over."

Shifting uneasily, Lizzy gave her an accusing stare which Jacke failed to notice.

The shadows cast by the tall flora sidled over the little girl's face, flaking her features gloomily, making her expression hard to read.

"Amazing; you still believed in Santa Claus."

Defensively, Jacke glared harshly at her. This time, she hugged her legs to her protectively. Her brow furrowed, hiding her eyes in darkness. Her shoulders slumped almost indiscernibly as her face became haunted.

"That's because I knew there was a bogeyman."

The earth exploded around Tyran's fleeing frame as she was showered with earth and debris.

The compressed boom slammed her ears as she stumbled as a mortar detonated mere feet from her, knocking her hard to the cloddy ground, smashing the wind from her.

She lay there stunned as another whistle sliced the air and the ground disintegrated in a ball of hissing flame. She felt the heat drag over her and it pushed her on. She had no idea where she was going or who was firing these mortars.

The air was rank with dirt and thick clogging smoke that seemed to lurch after her, striking her lungs like a match on sandpaper and making her choke with the acrid fumes.

What had seemed to be an idyllic countryside panorama had rapidly descended into a war zone and she was in its epicentre.

She had woken on her back over a cluster of boulders, the heavy sun gazing raggedly down on her tanning face.

She could see a flock of some flying creatures far in the distance but no other animals in the spread of patchwork fields and pastures with its concentric swirls of what looked like willow trees that splattered the area. Huge formations of boulders and rocks scaled the air and she recalled a game her mother played with her where she had to find the shapes in the rocks; the crouching giant and the kneeling elephant were her favourites.

Of course, thousands of kids did the same thing with clouds but the rock game was better; only Tyran and her mother knew about it and it was their special thing, the one thing where nothing came between her mother and her.

Now, those rocks were being blasted into the sky by the cascading fuselage of fire.

She fell over the root of an upturned tree and slammed her elbow off a jagged rock that slashed through her jacket and drew blood. She bit back tears as she forged on and tensed as another teasing whistle crept somewhere behind her. The ground fell away into a steep slope of granite and quartz rocks that spread like shark's teeth, awaiting her uncertain footing to give way and plunge Tyran onto its vicious edges, ready to slice her to the bone.

Unable to stop her momentum, she desperately struggled to keep her balance as the shingle crumbled beneath her boots and slowly tipped her over the edge into mid-air.

Suddenly a dark shape swooped out of nowhere, blotting out the flames.

With a last gasp of surprise, Tyran toppled over the edge. She looked astonished as she fell backwards, shutting her eyes as she waited for the impact that would kill her.

Something lashed round her, rough strands digging into her exposed skin as it tightened around her swiftly. She was jerked upward as the shape veered upward and outward across the diamond like rocks that glistened angrily at being deprived of their prey.

Black slabs of smoke careered through the air behind her as Tyran closed her fingers around the net that held her and held on for grim death.

She could barely make out the ground below her as her eyes stung and watered from the rushing air as she was dragged helplessly beneath the craft above her. It was like water skiing but much less enjoyable.

She swore they passed over a large lake shaped like a sausage but time was lost as she concentrated on holding on, the harsh knotted rope cutting into her face and hands and burning like acid.

She heard the deep wheeze of engines as the craft slowed, firing its thrusters and she began to sway downwards.

God, now I know how Nemo felt, she thought ruefully as a vast plain of mountainside slipped into view, its surface dotted by large red and green shrubs that quivered in the biting wake of the craft's roaring descent as it skimmed the ground then curved upwards towards an overhang laced with a thick curtain of ropey roots saturated in a mould like growth that wove an intricate web of camouflage that parted as the craft flew straight through it.

A hologram realised Tyran, her tears clearing. Very clever, she admitted to herself, hoping the owners were as friendly as they were smart.

They were in a cavern of sorts, hewn out of the luminescent green rock.

With a drop more gentle that she hoped, Tyran fell to the ground and immediately fought to untangle herself.

The net came away easily and she stood as the craft came to rest with a sigh, its landing thrusters whipping up a swirl of dust.

Looking about, Tyran saw the cavern roof swell above her, stalagmites hanging like cloisters amid a brush of purple and grey lichens. The walls were rough and she saw circular metallic devices embedded on other side of the walls, a dull red glow pulsing serenely within them.

The craft looked like an ovoid hovercraft, black in colour with heavy armourments mounted on either side of its pointed shark head front.

Narrow darkened cockpit windows curved like sly accusing eyes and the hull was pitted and scarred with weapons fire. Whoever this was, they were no strangers to battle.

Had she been thrown into someone's war?

She tensed, knowing there was nowhere to run and besides, they had just saved her life for reasons best known to themselves so maybe they could help her find a way home. A bulky knotted hatch hissed as it heaved open on the side of the ship like a pensioner rising from a chair.

Peering closely, Tyran could see dull shapes moving in the gloomy hatchway almost hesitantly.

"Move forward!" boomed a voice, rife with menace.

Hesitantly, she took tentative steps closer to the ship until she was at the foot of the ribbed extended gangplank.

A humanoid shape hovered just out of the light. It made a noise, almost like stifled laughter.

"Typical. You'll be late for your own funeral!" teased a man's voice.

She recognised it but couldn't quite place it. It was slightly hoarse but familiar. The figure came into the light, his broad frame clad in black trousers and jacket and light tan round neck top.

His face sported a nautical beard and his brown hair was matted and more greasy than normal. Her face fell as he ran down the ramp and grabbed her in a big hug, laughing heartily.

"Should have known you'd turn up eventually," he said, voice thick with emotion, "god, I've missed you!" He stood back, holding her at arm's length, staring at her, scrutinising every inch just to make sure she was real and not an illusion.

His face was locked into a wide smile and he looked as if he were about to cry.

Tyran stared in disbelief, her face falling as if slapped by a fish. He was older by about ten years but she knew that smile, that twinkle in his eyes that let her know a verbal spar was coming. Her hanging jaw managed to click back to life.

"Michael!" she breathed in disbelief. "I hate the beard!"

Tyran hadn't realised how hungry she was and was now scoffing a nutty bread and ham sandwich along with water in a blue plastic handled mug.

Michael sat watching her, his face alive with delight at seeing his old friend. He had led them along a network of tunnels laced with the same luminescent plants that lined the cavern.

The ground was covered in shale and the confined space made their footsteps seem louder than they were.

Electrical cables bolted at intervals along the passages were hooked to a series of wired black cased lanterns that gave out a pale yellow light.

Three other people had joined them from the hovercraft.

Jentos was a squat bald man in his late forties. His face was heavy set with pale grey eyes and a heavily furrowed brow and he gave Tyran the impression of a man who had seen great tragedy and was tired of fighting.

Sela was in her twenties with long blond hair and piercing almond green eyes and her whole frame seemed constantly ready to leap to combat and she looked Tyran up and down. I'm ready for you bitch, thought Tyran, straightening her dusty jacket.

She had slipped her arm round Michael's waist suggestively and his comfortable reaction made Tyran uneasy which surprised her.

Ruba was an overweight woman in her thirties with short bobbed black hair and podgy chapped lips.

She nodded at Tyran nervously as she gripped a canvas shoulder bag. The metallic clunk gave it away; the bag was filled with weapons and maybe tinned food. They had walked in silence along the tunnels meeting a few scruffy looking people along the way, each with an air of fatigue.

They had entered a chamber furnished with simple plastic chairs and a table. It was lit from an overhead naked lamp, the sort that was used, Tyran knew, by miners. The ground was smoother here as if overlain by some sort of plastic sheeting.

A computer something similar to a laptop sat on a chunky wall unit while three monitors attached to the wall showed various locations and people at work.

Some were working on electrics, others engineering consoles and a large object that looked like a laser cannon from Star Wars. Michael had crossed to a hatch in the wall and spoke into it and in a small shower of golden light, the sandwich and water had materialised.

"Handy," quipped Tyran as Michael motioned for her to sit at the table and tuck in. Ruba and Jentos had disappeared somewhere, giving cursory acknowledgements to Michael.

He's different, realised Tyran as she watched Michael dealing with various people who showed him reports of something and talked about Calderian movements. He seemed much more confident and they regarded him with an air of respect.

Whatever had happened, it had seemed to do a world of wonder for her friend. He had definitely become bulkier and his face betrayed a world of experience that she couldn't even guess at.

And, she noticed, he was watching her like a child with a new pet and from Sela's catty glances, not a welcome one.

"Girlfriend?" she asked, nodding at the blond.

With a grin, Michael fixed her with a teasing stare.

"Jealous?"

"Please! You'd never keep up," she retorted with a grin. He folded his arms in a mock scold.

"I seem to remember the answer was not if I was a bike," he smiled, catching her suppressed grin. "Bit obvious to see if you can catch me out," he added disapprovingly. She gave him a mock look of innocence. "You're not sure if it's me. Here I am ten years older and may I add, better looking, and you don't know how because to you, we were together only a short time ago."

"When did you become all F.B.I. profiler?" she teased, a slight tremor in her voice betraying her fears.

Sighing, Michael sat back in his chair and regarded her with mournful eyes, an expression that spoke volumes.

"You have no idea of what has happened in the last ten years, Tyran. I've done things I never thought I was capable of and carved a life as best I could."

Tyran glanced about. "Seems to me you've done alright. People here see you as a leader; pity about the accommodation though. What happened to us in the vortex? Why was I being bombed and how did you know where to find me?"

"Now I know how Varran felt the day of the accident," grimaced Michael, rolling his eyes. Sela slinked over to his side like a cat and ran her hand across Michael's shoulders, giving Tyran a superior glance.

"I'll leave you two alone," she purred. "Don't do anything I wouldn't do." With that she took his chin in her slender hand and kissed him full on before pulling away and swishing out of the room.

"There's probably nothing she hasn't done," bitched Tyran. She pointed a finger at Michael as he made to defend her. "And don't you start; she gave me the attitude, right?"

Holding his hands up in surrender, Michael leaned forward and sat with his hands clasped in front of him. He took a deep breath as Tyran listened intently.

His eyes seemed to cloud as his thoughts moved across the years and to different times when life was simpler.

With a slight jerk of his head, he gazed at her and she saw the old Michael, unsure and lost. Then it was gone.

"The last thing I remember was a firestorm when the alien ship attacked us. I thought we were dead. I felt the Dagger split open and being pulled apart from the inside. The next thing I knew, I woke up here."

He continued in a low voice as if this was only meant for his and Tyran's ears. He had found the Dagger intact not far from where he had woken but of Jacke and Tyran there had been no sign.

He had tried to contact the Juggernaught but hadn't been able to reach Varran.

The engines still worked and he had flown to find someone that could possibly help. He had been attacked by a squad of Calderian fighters but they had been no match for the Dagger's systems and sheer manoeuvrability.

Escaping, he had fallen in with these people and discovered a world crippled by tyranny.

The Calderian Supremacy had beaten the people down with crippling taxes and laws, stripping people of their very dignity and will to live. This society was basically a giant slave market where citizens toiled in mines and poverty to keep the Supremacy in a life of luxury.

It had gone on for so long that the ordinary person knew no different and the majority accepted this as the norm.

Being wary, Michael hadn't blindly accepted the story and had gone to find out for himself.

It was when he saw one of the Royal Guards coldly murder a little girl who had asked for water did he decide to turn things around.

Utilising the Dagger's technology, he had joined the rebels and began to attack strategic targets and disrupt the cosy lives of the elite.

But the Supremacy's hold had grown deep over the years and Michael had come to realise it wasn't like the movies where the evil empire gets overthrown in an hour and a half.

Retribution was swift and brutal and an entire team had been publicly skinned to quell any more rebellious thoughts.

However, the rebel forces had grown and they had survived, operating from this base using the Juggernaught's shielding technology, scavenged from the Dagger.

In ten years, Michael had found himself a symbol for hope and if it took centuries to fell the Supremacy, then the rebels would be prepared to do exactly that.

There had never been any word from the Juggernaught or the girls so Michael had forged a new life, falling in love with Sela and always planning the next attack.

Plants were destroyed and slowly the Supremacy was being destabilised. But he had always held out hope that Varran, Jacke and Tyran would swoop in and help him rescue this world.

So he set up a detector system keyed specifically to their life signs so that no matter where they appeared, he would know.

"That's how I knew where you were," he said. "I assume the time vortex dumped you here ten years in the future. Do you know what happened to Jacke?"

Tyran shook her head wearily. "I can't believe Varran has never come to get you." Michael made a face.

"Tyran, in ten years I still don't know how to work out their calendar. We could be thousands of years in the future or the past. All I could do was fight to live and I was damned if I was going to be a slave to an alien race. I'd rather be Spartacus than Braveheart." Tyran stared at him with a wry grin.

"They both died." He bit his lip thoughtfully.

"Yes, but the principle's the same." A great bellow of laughter erupted out of Tyran as she collapsed in hysterics across the table. Michael couldn't help but join her. He grabbed her hands and held them tightly, his eyes watering. She looked gratefully at him.

"I am so happy to see you," he said, tears welling.

"Don't start wailing, Braveheart," she encouraged, returning his grip. His hands felt rough but comfortably real.

His face screwed up as a sudden thought struck him.

"Do you know what I miss?" he said.

"Condoms?" she sparked, thinking of Sela's smug grin.

"Jam doughnuts. You can't imagine how often I have thought about the moment when you bite in and the sugar clings to your mouth and the jam bursts out and falls down your chin."

"You always had the eating habits of a cow choking on grass," chided Tyran. "Michael, tell me this. Why didn't you ever just fly into space and pick a direction? Surely the Dagger's database could have picked the most probable star constellation and guided you home." It seemed so logical yet it amazed her he hadn't even tried it.

Her eyes narrowed as his face crumpled slightly as if despair had crushed his soul.

He looked up at a clock on the wall with fourteen numbers in a circle rather than twelve, two hands at different positions.

He patted her hand lightly and got to his feet, the chair making a flat scraping sound on the floor. He took her by the hand and led her out of the room.

From the shadows, Sela watched them leave, her face a masque of fury.

Michael walked in silence, his sweaty hands keeping a firm grip on Tyran's. At one point he stopped and tutted as she saw a wall light had gone out. He muttered that he would have to get someone to fix it and continued on.

They came to a nexus of passages and he guided her upwards to a set of carved stone steps that spiralled up the wall like a great snake.

It levelled off to a flat landing of sorts and Michael finally let go of her hand to push open a rusting grey metal hatch that creaked as it was pushed open. They climbed the small ladder.

The rush of fresh air hit them as Tyran saw they were on top of the plateau, the landscape stretching far below them for miles in a swath of linen clouds. It was dark, night had obviously fallen. The petit blond looked at her friend confused.

"What are we doing here? What's this?" He stared ahead, not looking at her. His voice was low, laden with regret.

"I'm giving you your answer Tyran." He reached down and picked up a torch that spewed a yawning jaundice glow over them. Tyran stepped forward, scanning the darkness but not seeing anything.

"Calder is a planetoid, small, dying in its own decay. Calder translates as Tomb. Look up." Tyran did and saw a sky blacker than hell's abyss itself; a black so solid that she felt as if she could reach up and touch it. Michael was a

disembodied voice in the dark. His face was cloaked in shadow, his eyes pin pricks in a veil.

"That's why I didn't leave. I couldn't, neither can you. There are no stars. There's nowhere to go."

THE INFINITY WEB PART 2

Sweat soaked Jacke's face as she pushed aside a concave red leaf, one of a sheaf that hung from a gnarly tree.

The sky had been awash with pink and white as the new dawn broke.

Jacke had fallen asleep just inside the cave entrance with a quilt sized lily leaf that blanketed her in a cosy motherly heat that brought sleep quickly.

She had smelt almonds when she woke, the scent given off as the leaf dried out. Best thing next to pot pourri, she decided as she stretched awake, looking round for Lizzy.

She saw the little girl's snoozing form nestled amid the great leaves.

Quietly, Jacke had sat up and watched her sleeping; Lizzy's face angelic in the breaking dawn.

A warm fuzzy feeling embraced the dark skinned young woman as she was glad to have company even it was her imaginary friend. Bizarre was almost a way of life for her now but even she had limits.

Jacke wasn't someone who craved the company of others but she welcomed it whenever possible.

She'd had several boyfriends, none of which were lasting but she wanted children one day and she sometimes wondered if there was something she was sub consciously doing to sabotage all her relationships as a result of the past. Of course, since there was a good chance she was going to spend the rest of her life here alone, there seemed to be little chance of happy ever after.

"You couldn't have got stranded on a paradise world or one where a car or space ship was just lying about," complained Lizzy as she threw the intrusive foliage a hateful glare as it slapped her in the face once again.

She was smaller than Jacke and found the terrain harder going.

"I don't remember you being such a moan," teased Jacke, holding the foliage back for her to pass through. "You used to be so resilient, so happy."

Lizzy stopped dead and put her hands on her hips, directing her glare to her tall friend.

"I didn't have to tramp round alien worlds looking for nuts and berries just to stay alive so you have someone to talk to," she growled.

Jacke sat on a green mossy boulder and pulled her shirt off and wiped herself down.

"Lizzy, the whole point of an imaginary friend is you can conjure them up any time you want; death isn't really a big option for you." She tapped the side of her temple. "You'll just go back in here." Lizzy folded her arms crossly.

"Whatever," she mouthed. Jacke burst out laughing and fell into an uncontrollable fit.

Turning on her heel, Lizzy found herself face to face with a large shrub riddled with fist sized nectarine like fruits.

"Finally," she muttered, cupping her top into a basket and scooping them into the make shift carrier. "Any chance?" she fired at her shaking friend. Jacke wiped her eyes, wondering why she found that so funny. Stress, probably. She helped Lizzy, using her shirt as a holder.

She squinted up at the burning sky with its crown of mountains and sighed. The green covered hill seemed a lifetime climb with this heavy heat; she would definitely be having a swim when they went back.

They picked together in silence until Lizzy broke the quiet.

"Remember when you said the nightmare was over that Christmas," ventured Lizzy. Jacke slowed slightly, wondering what was coming. She hummed in response. "Was it? Really over, I mean."

"I said so didn't I?" replied Jacke a bit more sharply than she meant to.

"Okay," Lizzy rolled the words slowly off her tongue. She was going somewhere with this, realised Jacke. "It's just, something like that, it can't ever be forgotten. You think you have, think it's just a passing memory like a train disappearing into the sunset but it doesn't do that. They sink into your sub conscience and fester like a tumour that never goes away. I've seen them Jacke and I know you're lying when you say life was back to normal from that Christmas on."

Angrily, Jacke turned on her and pointed a finger into her face.

"You never forget but you go on. No one could ever go through that and live a normal life again but I did. I went on and finished school and got the qualifications I needed to do the psychology degree. I vowed never to let what happened to me happen to anyone else." She pushed into Lizzy's face. "I was so lucky. I could have gone under, many do but I didn't. My family were my life line and a few months ago I was given the most amazing chance to make the world safer and do the right thing."

Lizzy looked at her impassively. "Then why are you pointing a finger in my face? Aren't you doing exactly what you swore to stop?"

Jacke froze, her eyes falling to her half fisted hand and accusing trembling finger.

She slowly straightened up and let her hand fall to her side. Her face was a confusion of emotion as Lizzy's words struck a chord. Why had she reacted like that? She looked at the little girl.

"I'm sorry," she said flatly, her cheeks burning.

"Okay," accepted Lizzy gracefully, "only asking."

Tyran sat silently staring into space in the recreation room.

Her mind was awash with disbelief. Bad enough to wake up with bombs going off but to be told there was no way out; that this place was a ship in a bottle and she and Michael were doomed to sail on it until they died was too much to take.

A shadow fell over her, startling her. A hand placed a mug of tea in front of her; at least it looked like tea, its slight steam wisping gently from the mug. Tyran masked her surprise as Sela slipped into the seat next to her, her face carved with a smile that failed to warm Tyran's heart.

"I thought you might need this," she purred, the words syrupy with an undercurrent of malice. "Michael has a flare for the dramatic," she continued, "in every department," she added wryly.

Fixing her with a pitying look, Tyran took a sip of the tea. It tasted sweet but seemed to be the first real thing since she got here.

"Sela, Michael isn't my type and quite frankly, the fact you see me as a threat has made my day. You don't know me from Adam and if you want to drop your knickers to stay in with him, go right ahead. I'm sure he's not the first and won't be the last. Where I come from we have a label for girls like you and it involves pricks and a dart board."

With a flash of anger in her narrowing eyes, Sela leaned forward in her chair and came right into Tyran's face. Her breath smells of fish, Tyran thought cuttingly.

"You don't know Michael. He's not the same man you knew. Ten years have passed since you last saw him and a lot has happened. I may share his bed but I love him. He has given my people so much hope and kept us alive all this time and I believe he will lead us to a better life and overthrow this regime that makes us live like rats."

"You're the best dressed rat I've ever seen," countered Tyran steely. A smirk cut the other woman's face as her eyes flickered up and down Tyran.

"I have never met a man like him. Let me tell you how we met. I was gang raped by one of the Supremacy's squads; they see my people as something they can use and abuse at their pleasure." Her face crumpled as the unpleasant memories stung her heart and Tyran saw the pain flicker across her green eyes clouding them. "Michael stepped in and killed them where they stood." She noticed Tyran's shocked expression. "Not the story you were expecting?"

The blond girl shook her head.

"No, not the Michael I knew but then he was always a man of principles. I know what you mean when you say you had never met anyone like him. He," she paused trying to think of the right words, "was unlike any fella I'd ever met." Her expression softened. "Sorry about the dart board thing, better you forget it."

"He is not the man you knew, Tyran, so be prepared," warned Sela, pushing her blond hair back across her head.

Tyran stared at her cooling tea, pursing her lips thoughtfully. An awkward silence hung between them.

"Sooo," Tyran said slowly, lifting her eyes to meet Sela's. "Is he really that good in bed?"

Michael glanced up from his bed as Sela slinked in. The room was big enough for a double bed and a gun grey metal cabinet with two pitted doors bolted against the left hand wall which acted as a wardrobe.

Inset above the bed was a small light which cast a pale light that streaked shadow across the room.

Setting aside the plastic blue sheet onto the granite stone floor, he watched his partner peel her red jumpsuit off and drop it casually before slipping into bed beside him, nestling against Michael's naked body. He stroked her hair as she sighed.

"Ok?" he asked softly. Sela nodded, his chest hair rubbing against her cheek. She sat up and looked at him.

"I can understand why you like her." He smiled wryly as he kissed her.

"She is one of a kind," he murmured as he stroked her body, nuzzling her neck. Sela drew him closer, tingling beneath the trace of his lips.

Roughly, she grabbed the back of his head and stared Michael in the face, moving on top of him.

"Have you told her yet?" she hissed. He shook his head, his brown eyes focused on her. She felt his longing and pressed herself tighter against him, urging him on.

"She won't object. I know how she thinks." He kissed her hard before rolling Sela onto her back, and pressed hard against her. "Not jealous are we?"

Sela's eyes hardened, digging her fingers into his back, and smiled.

In the next room, Tyran lay fully clothed on the bunk she'd been given. She closed her eyes as she tried to ignore the noise from Michael's room. She got up and lightly closed the plastic door.

As she sat on the edge of the bunk, she found herself wanting to be next door, in bed alone with Michael. She shook off the feeling and threw herself back on the bunk and shut her eyes tight hoping sleep would take her in its selfless bosom soon.

Jacke huddled over the crackling fire, its orange glow dancing across her dark features. Lizzy sat cross legged on the opposite side watching her intently, her face streaked in shadow, her eyes two points of orange light.

The only sound was the fire, hissing and spitting.

Jacke was hungry, the berries and the banana like plants failing to quell her rumbling belly, no matter how much she ate.

They were inside the cave and the lush Jurassic park outside was bathing in the fiery red dusk.

The encroaching darkness was bringing with it a deep chill that settled like a whisper in the ear. Neither Jacke nor Lizzy had spoken since their spat in the jungle clearing.

The little girl had kept her distance from Jacke for the remainder of the day. Jacke's face had been hard; her expression one Lizzy knew meant stay away. Sighing, Lizzy cocked her head and glanced at nothing in particular.

"Are you going to speak?" she challenged haughtily. Jacke's almond eyes flicked up like knives at her. She was looking at her as if she had made a new discovery but couldn't quite decide what to do about it.

"Bored are we?"

"No," replied Lizzy. Jacke's eyes flashed.

"Sure?"

"Sure." Jacke nodded slowly. Her voice was cool, thoughtful.

"This doesn't make sense," she said quietly. A puzzled expression flitted across Lizzy's face. Jacke looked at her almost expectantly making the little girl shift uneasily.

"Why would you bring up what happened?"

"What do you mean?"

"If you really have lived in my head all this time, you would know what has happened since and how I've dealt with it." Her tone was pointed, harsh. "And am I that stupid to sit and justify it to a figment of my imagination, here, in no man's land? I don't think so."

"I am more than a figment. I am part of your psyche, I am part of your personality, I was created by you; in effect, you are my mother." Breaking into a wide grin, Jacke chuckled, shaking her head disbelievingly.

"Somehow, I don't think I've ever wished myself white and certainly not a blond."

A cold anger crept over Lizzy, the words like a slap in the face.

"You brought it up to get a reaction from me," continued Jacke, "and that you did. I haven't stopped thinking about it all day." She held her gaze. "And it's put me in a very bad mood."

"I didn't mean to," croaked Lizzy in that perfect little girl lost voice.

"Yes you did. Question is why. Who are you?" Her face was impassive but the eyes betrayed a panic. Jacke could see it, she had trained to recognise body language as part of her course but it was something she had been able to read in people over the years, call it a gift or an instinct but she could pick up on the slightest change in stance. Lizzy was lying, she knew it but why?

"Who are you?" she repeated frostily. Lizzy remained tight lipped, eyes locked on Jacke as her thoughts raced.

But she said nothing.

Nodding resignedly to herself, Jacke stood up and walked round to the little girl, the fire twinkling in her baby blue eyes.

With a twisted sneer, Jacke grabbed the pony tailed hair and jerked Lizzy's head right back, ignoring the screams of pain as she tightened her grip and pulled her head slowly back.

"I know I'm not going mad and I also know you couldn't possibly exist," hissed Jacke darkly, "so you'd better tell me what is going on before I kick the crap out of you."

A sharp shriek ripped the air, echoing in the night air and down across the valley.

It was the sound of twenty screams all mixed in together, retching from a tortured soul as it peaked and died. The scream made Jacke's skin creep with a million goose pimples and she slowly turned to face the hollow black maw of the cave mouth, silhouetted amid the foliage.

It was as if a giant creature was opening up to roar at her and the screech seemed to fade in the cave entrance. Jacke loosened her grip on Lizzy's hair and stared cautiously at the darkness.

"Well, I wasn't expecting that," curled the little girl slowly.

Tyran woke from a confused dream of money spiders and old faces.

She stretched and lay quietly as she remembered where she was. Her mouth was sticky and in need of a clean but she realised she had no toothbrush. Worse still, she had no deodorant.

She stared at the cracked stone ceiling, her stomach aching to be filled. Forcing herself up, she wandered out into the corridor, passing Michael's quarters and noticed the unmade bed was empty.

Hope he showered, she thought wryly. God, the little pleasures go a long way, she realised. A shower in the morning or a nice relaxing bath filled with her favourite oils and scents, followed by the feel of clean clothes and a nice cooling cup of tea with raspberry jam on toast.

Right now that would be heaven to her.

She met Ruba on the way, carrying a small tool kit, her hair scraped back in a greasy bob and looking redder in the face than yesterday.

Tyran smiled and asked where she could get something to eat or drink. Ruba blushed as if Tyran had asked her to strip.

"I thought Michael would have made sure you were properly looked after before we leave," she mumbled shifting from one foot to the next. Raising her eyebrows, Tyran shook her head.

"No, Michael let things get on top of him last night, literally; probably drained his brain cells," she said innocently. A thought struck her. "What do you mean, leave? Where are you going?" she asked.

With those wide eyes and puffy face, Ruba stared at Tyran as if she had the stupidest question ever.

"Didn't he tell you?" she stumbled awkwardly over the words, "We're going to launch a direct assault on the Supremacy headquarters and take out the members in one go. Canteen's this way."

Michael stepped back as Tyran stormed into the room, her face ablaze with anger. She ignored the others gathered round the holographic map which clearly showed the strategy for today's assault.

"Ten years and you're still a gimp!" she shouted. "What's going on, Michael? I'm here one day and you're suddenly Luke Skywalker. Why are you attacking today? Why after ten years have you suddenly realised today's the day and you can set right the evils the Supremacy have created?"

Michael gave her a stern look before sweeping his gaze around the crowded room, hopeful faces locked on him and his idea. They could almost taste the hope emanating from him.

"It came to me last night," he began.

"Yes, I heard," snapped Tyran, feeling the look from Sela, "you really should get soundproofing."

A smug grin cracked her friend's face; a look that made her want to slap him and one he never would have given her in the past.

Leaning forward, he hissed, "Jealous?"

Taken aback, Tyran went to slap him but he caught her wrist in a tight grip. She glared at him disbelievingly. He snapped her arm to her side and let her go.

"I guess ten years is a long time," she said bitterly. It was a reproach rather than a comment and she fell strangely quiet. Michael ignored it and continued.

"In all this time, we have only been gnats to the Supremacy. We gain the odd skirmish here and there but we don't make a big enough impact." He gazed at Tyran, her face flushed, her blue eyes burning with resentment. "You made me realise what I was missing. The fire to fight hard and straight, that's what you always had, what I always admired about you. When we fought the Numarans, you didn't think twice about fighting their ship in that little Dagger, even though the odds were astronomical. Everything happens for a reason." His face fell slightly, tinged with sadness. "I was too busy making a life here; I didn't think it through properly, what it means to change a system. I lost my way and you have given it back to me, Tyran. An all-out assault until the tyrants are all gone. There is only one way, Tyran. I am going to assassinate the entire Supremacy today and give the people back their freedom." He rounded on the others, their expressions fuelled by his passion and begging him to take them on his journey. Michael stood tall, as he made a fist, his face beaming with passion.

"No one else will die in their slave compounds, children shall run the streets free and feel the sun on their faces without fear of a beating, and families will sit together and know their lives will be plentiful and fruitful. The towers will fall and the Supremacy will be crushed beneath them, and with that fall will come a new dawn of hope and freedom. There will be no more darkness for today life itself will be reborn, full of potential for a better day!"

The rebels cheered, caught up in his enthusiasm. They thumped the tables rhythmically and chanted as Michael soaked it all in. And in the midst of it all, Tyran felt like a daisy before a hurricane.

Breathing through her mouth, Jacke stared into the pale womb of tunnel that snaked away into the distance in an infinity of twilight.

The coarse rock threw up gnarled arches and twists that seemed to coil shadow around it like protection. Mossy walls hang back like broken veils as a strangled glow of the plants gave Jacke little idea what lay ahead.

Having lit one of her home made torches,(the veined leaves of what appeared like a giant weeping willow were perfect of sustained combustion, almost like an everlasting match), and sighed determinedly.

Her heart was pumping, her adrenalin racing. She turned and gave Lizzy a steely glare.

"I would warn you not to follow me but since you already live here, I guess that would be pointless," she said pointedly. Lizzy was still sitting by the fire, her face streaked with tears and rocking back and forth softly with her arms wrapped round her pulled up knees.

"I swear, Jacke, I don't know what you're talking about!" she wailed pleadingly.

Jacke's dark face held fast, ignoring the frightened little girl. Her eyes shone with coldness as she stared at her old friend.

"I don't know what's going on and maybe I am cracking up a bit; I would love a Cajun Chicken Panini, but whatever you are, you are not my imaginary friend. Four days ago, I was the only living thing in this place and suddenly we have noises from a cave that was previously unoccupied." She narrowed her eyes suspiciously. "Question is, is it in my head?"

She turned her back and bearing the torch in front of her like a burning sword, she stepped into the shadows, watching them peel back like wary predators as she took one nervous step after another in the direction of the wail.

Her eyes darted over every patch of light, expecting something to leap out and grab her. The granite like walls spread out higher above her as Jacke came to a bigger chamber which for some reason reminded her of that scene in Aliens when the marines entered the alien hive.

Darkness coned above her into a shadowed ceiling and her boots crunched on brown gravel, different from the outer passage's floors.

The walls veered into a wider convex shape and seemed bulkier and thicker than before.

Jacke paused, listening to the sound of her feet on the ground. She stamped the gravel a couple of times, focusing on the reverberation. This chamber was bigger certainly but she pulled a yellow leaf from her pocket and laid it at the edge of the passage.

"Better than bread crumbs," she murmured, speaking just to break the silence. There had been no more noises so could it be I imagined it, she wondered worriedly.

She hadn't been walking for more than five minutes so she pressed on. She kept an ear out for the echo of her foot falls as she continued.

Her shirt stuck to her, licked with sweat in that uncomfortable way. It was either getting warmer or more claustrophobic.

Humming "We're off to see the wizard" inwardly to herself, Jacke looked to the light before her. Oh God, what if I have died and stuck in purgatory, she panicked, Am I literally following the light? Get a grip, she told herself, there's something else going on, has to be.

It watched the figure surrounded in a cocoon of fire as it stalked the passageway. It stayed silent as Jacke passed and waited, shivering as she became a silhouette in the half light and faded.

It tensed, listening. Detaching itself from the ceiling, it attached itself to the granite walls and followed.

Tyran was crouched in the converted Dagger behind the pilot's seat. Michael was at the controls, emanating an air of steely resolve. Gingerly, she looked about the crowded ship at the other rebels packed in like sardines.

They were armed with pistols and sleek rifle like weapons which delivered a lethal charge of energy. She recognised some of the faces as engineers, cooks and general maintenance.

Ruba was sweating like a chubby horse while Sela seemed to be coiled like a snake shading itself beneath a rock. She caught Tyran's eye but looked away expressionlessly. Her only movement was a slight tightening of her grip on her rifle.

Jentos was crouched away at the back, his face lined with fear. He had a shoulder strap lined with grenades and a squatter version of the rifle weapon. The smell of unwashed bodies and bad breath made Tyran nauseous and she was aware of a young man's arousal as he squashed against her too close for comfort.

Nudging him away with a dig in the ribs, Tyran rolled her aching shoulder blades. The Dagger held forty of them, much more than it was designed for but Michael flew steadily and confidently.

Squeezing up behind him, Tyran grabbed the head rest for support, her hands sweaty on the leathery material.

"So what's the plan?" Michael never turned his head as he spoke, instead frowning as he concentrated on the readings on the mini holoscreen before him.

"The Supremacy has a council meeting every day at noon. They will all be gathered in the tower complex on the 29th floor. We are going to fly right in and take control."

He spoke as if it was the easiest thing in the world and nothing would go wrong. To Tyran, it sounded like he was rhyming off a shopping list; problem was, you could forget to add something to a list and come back short in your shopping.

"As easy as that?" she asked; the doubt heavy in her tone.

"As easy as that," Michael replied cheerily, "they won't be expecting it." A dread crept over Tyran as she studied her friend.

His voice was so steeped in self-confidence, his manner so steadfast, she understood why the others believed in him, and despite all her barbs at him, she had come to realise he was the type of man who would do exactly what he said he would and if he had told these people that this was their day of deliverance, then he just might pull it off.

It was his method that concerned Tyran.

He intended to effectively murder the government body of this world and end years of terror.

Varran would never have approved but as Michael showed her, they had no way off this world and to face this life forever was too much.

Nothing had changed in 10 years and it wasn't likely to. And something else struck her, ever since she had arrived; they had worn a depressed air like a suit, a down trodden drudgery like someone pissed off with their job after realising it was the same thing day in, day out. If that was what Michael had live with and looked at all this time, no wonder he was so focused on taking control. Tyran heard her mother's voice telling her never to judge someone until you'd walked in their shoes. She cast her gaze around the people pressed together with her. Everyone's story lay in their faces.

Ruba caught Tyran's eye; she was pretty if a little over weight but she seemed like she was constantly on the verge of tears, her face lined with repression, as if to smile would bring the wrath of God down upon her.

Jentos too had that sense of keeping your chin up and his blue eyes were glazed, haunted by thoughts known only to him.

What had these people seen over the years? Families slaughtered, put to slavery, poor hygiene and medical conditions; how many children had died because of this Supremacy, mothers and fathers watching helplessly as their babies wailed themselves to death from starvation.

Her eyes filling up at the thought, Tyran realised Michael was right, there was no other way.

She leaned forward and put her slender hand on his shoulder. She noticed how dirty her finger nails were as she put her mouth to his ear, catching a faint scent of cologne before whispering, "Let's do it." He turned and looked at her, a broad smile carving his face.

"Sure?" She nodded.

"This can't go on." A monitor chirped before him on the concentric controls. The mood changed, tensed.

The citadel rose up before them. Engaging the cloak, Michael veered upward before levelling out above the vista of buildings. It was basically a vast city encased by a huge stone wall that surrounded it in a tight circle. And today that wall was going to come crumbling down.

Beyond spread the ripples of fields and workhouses, with factories pumping morbid grey smog into the air.

The slave pens realised Tyran as she brought her attention to the tall squat building that reared before them like an ancient Mayan temple. It was made from sand stone with was laced with green stained glass windows and she could swear it glittered as if embedded with diamonds and gold.

"Built from the blood of the helpless," cursed Tyran bitterly.

Michael passed her a rifle without looking round and she took it without a second thought.

"The council meet on the 29th floor," explained Michael, "the top of the building so they can look out over their domain."

Tyran pulled a face. "Unlucky for some," she grimaced, tightening her grip. "And the plan is..." she prompted, faltering for a second. There was that scent again, like a half remembered dream.

"I'm reading 26 life signs in the main chamber and 12 in the outer corridors," Michael read off the monitor. Sela leaned over to see.

"Only 12 guards; they are careless. All the Supremacy leaders are gathered; it's been at least 6 minutes since the meeting started. They've just made it a tomb," she grinned, stroking Michael's shoulder. Something niggled at the back of Tyran's thoughts but she couldn't bring it into focus.

"What do you mean?" she asked, slightly puzzled at their apparent glee. Adjusting the converted Dagger's flight path and speed, Michael explained that the council held all their meetings in a sealed room with 12 guards at each entrance.

No one came in or out unless the council allowed it. The chamber was airtight and only those inside controlled the building.

"Once inside and the council are dead, we will release this," added Sela, her green eyes alive with hatred. She held a red canister up for Tyran to look at. It was about the size of a rugby ball, made from a non-reflective material with a nozzle attachment on the end.

Staring at it in horrified recognition, she looked at Michael with a shocked expression.

"Where did you get that?"

"It was aboard the Dagger when I came here, hidden in a magnetic compartment beneath the lower level strut."

"Varran couldn't have known or he would have destroyed it!" she almost shouted. "You are going to gas the building."

Michael's face darkened and he roared, "Tyran! We control the building and this gas will be released only to kill the guards, that building houses most of them and with them dead…"

"The people will rise up and take revenge on the rest, leaving us free!" cried Ruba, earning a cheer from the others. Tyran was wavering.

"What if some of the guards come over to our side? What if they are doing the Supremacy's work just to keep themselves or their families alive? Have you thought of that?" she persisted, "Cut off the council and maybe you will have a willing army, think about it! That gas is lethal, Michael, you can't afford to screw about with it."

"Sit down and shut up, Tyran. If you don't like it, stay here while we save the world."

Tyran glared at him. She had to stay close. "Bring it on." she said coldly, eyeing Sela curiously. The image of a vulture came to mind.

The top level came into focus in the Dagger's front cockpit window, its red and greens glittering with golden droplets of sunlight, its sandy curved walls a beautiful coral colour in the noon day haze. They could see figures inside, faint and indistinct.

"A hive of tyranny," hissed Michael as he moved his hands to the weapon controls and opened the laser cannon ports. They heard the wheeze of machinery as the cannons dropped out of the under carriage and aimed at the windows.

With a chatter of orange fire, the armoured glass windows shattered into a million screaming shards under the barrage.

The rebels were almost bouncing with anticipation as the ship's cloak fell and it swooped forward like a great bat with a roar of thrusters. It banked sharply and landed in the centre of the room, smashing the large oval marble table beneath its bulk.

With a collective yell, the side hatch slid open and the rebels poured out, weapons blazing. Michael watched, beaming with delight as Sela leaned across and kissed him. Tyran faltered, remembering the scent she smelt. She lowered her gun and stared at Michael.

"You're wearing aftershave," she said. Michael looked at her blankly. "It's the one you always wear but that's not possible. Unless this place has a Superdrug store, you couldn't be wearing any. Everyone else stinks except you."

"I wash every day," he replied. Tyran shook her head.

"No, you were wearing it the day we fought the alien ship in the vortex." She looked at him challengingly, levelling her rifle at him. "Who are you?"

They were interrupted by cries from outside, calling them. Gruffly, Michael and Sela shoved Tyran aside and ran outside.

The rebels were standing about, looking at each other blankly.

Tyran hovered in the hatch and realised the room was empty bar the rebels.

"I thought you said they were in session here," she challenged. Her question was echoed by some of the others. Michael ignored their questions as he moved to the door and pressed an intercom set into the wall.

"We're here."

The 12 entrances hissed open and a swarm of black and red clad guards stormed in, lethal looking blasters at the ready. In seconds, the rebels were outnumbered with Michael raising his hands and ordering them to lay down their weapons.

A sick feeling gripped Tyran as she watched helplessly. She ran down and slapped Michael in the face.

"You bastard! Why?" Sela leapt forward and punched Tyran, knocking her to the floor.

"For a better life, you stupid bitch! I am sick of living like a rat and this is our way out." Michael looked smug as he regarded his fallen friend.

"The rebellion is a lost cause, there is no win. Ten years for what? Skulking in the shadows living like rodents; that's no life for anyone."

Shaking with anger, Tyran got to her feet, wiping her jaw where Sela had cut her. She held his stare hatefully fully aware of the watching guards.

"Well, you and Cruella were shagging like rabbits, so rodents does fit." Smirking, Michael leaned closer, his breath hot and stale.

"And you wanted to be in her place; you know you did."

"Not in your life time," she spat. "You are not Michael."

"No, I'm the Michael you left behind, the one you all walked away from but then again, that pretty much sums up my life. I'm looking out for me." Anything further was cut short as someone grabbed his shoulder and yanked him back. Ruba's sweaty face was trembling with loathing.

"You betrayed us on her say so," she said indicating Sela.

"It'll be better this way," soothed Michael but Ruba shoved him back, knocking him into the nearest guard and raised her weapon, aimed at his head and pulled the trigger.

Nothing happened.

Ruba fired again and again but Michael burst out laughing. Tyran was staring at the guard Michael had knocked against. His helmet had fallen off and he got to his feet.

His eyes were glazed; unfocused and protruding from the top of his swollen skull was a scaly crust that heaved like a sleeper's chest. It was as if someone had sliced his head open and left it, the hair clotted round the edges with congealed blood.

Her jaw dropped as Michael turned. He looked unsurprised at the guard as if he knew what to expect.

"These are the monkeys Tyran; we're here to meet the organ grinders," smiled Michael. He turned to the open door. "I said we're here!" he shouted.

A strange noise bounced across the room, like the clip of horse's hooves on marble. It grew louder as if a hundred horses were filling the room.

The guards parted respectfully as a shape filled the door.

The creature bowed as it ducked to get through the door. Tyran caught a glimpse of powerful broad jointed legs, covered in thick bristled hair as the figure straightened up and surveyed the room.

Tyran gasped and took an involuntary step back as the creature strode into the chamber.

It was six and a half feet tall with a humanoid torso covered in the same thick hair, dark in colour with stripes of red and brown.

The body was attached to a bulbous orb like body straddled on each side by six multi jointed legs, ending in sharp claw like spikes.

The great ovoid head swung about, four amber eyes reflecting the horrified faces before them as two razor- like mandibles clacked hungrily, relishing the moment. It flexed its powerful muscled arms, two on each side as others like it marched into the shattered chamber.

The leader strode up to a waiting Michael. It towered above him, watching him expectantly.

"As promised, your new livestock!" he boomed, bowing slightly.

Tyran stared incredulously as the huge creature flicked its leg and speared one of Michael's people, a thin scraggly man in his thirties with sandy hair, the shocked white face imprinted on

Tyran's mind, as his bulging eyes stared at the bloodied spear like leg sticking in his chest as he was lifted into the air.

The creature pulled its leg free as it took the man in its thick hairy claw like hands.

A sharp appendage flicked from its mouth and pierced the man's forehead. Tyran gagged as a sick sucking noise accompanied the head shuddering before it fell back, his mane of hair dangling with blood.

Tyran stared disbelievingly at Michael as tears welled in her eyes.

The creature made a gurgling sound, one of deep satisfaction, as it threw back its head, licked its blood stained jaws and laughed.

Jacke was breathing heavily as she came to a large opening which led to a wider, cooler tunnel. Sweat soaked her back, chilling beneath the calming breath of air that sailed down the cavern from the gloom beyond.

There must be an air vent leading to the surface, she thought, grateful for the relief from the stifling heat.

She glanced behind her, checking her flower trail was intact.

There had been no sign of Lizzy but equally no sign of whatever made that howling. This part was littered with large rocks and boulders and for some reason one put her in mind of a mushroom.

Taking a breather, Jacke sat on it and wiggled her burning toes.

When she got back she would take a dip in the rock pool and give herself a thorough scrub. The flame from her torch was down to its last so she carefully wrapped a fresh strip round it and with a tiny fizz, the flame grew brighter, making the dank walls jump in idiotic shadow.

The ceiling was higher here and studded with black veins of some sort of mineral.

Rubbing her aching neck, Jacke straightened up. There's nothing here, she decided, maybe it was my imagination.

She froze as a large shadow fell across the entrance.

For a second, she thought it was the torch going out.

She heard the sound of horse's hooves on marble as she watched the figure surge through the entrance and stepped back in horror.

It was over six and a half feet tall, a torso covered in sharp black bristled hair mounted on an orb like body suspended by eight spear-like legs. It straightened up and let out a piercing screech as it saw Jacke.

It reared above her, its jaws snapping, its amber eyes focusing on her, screaming like a banshee.

For a second the world froze.

Jacke stared helplessly at it. It shuddered and bore down on her.

With a scream, Jacke fell back over the boulder, swinging the torch before her, scraping her elbow sending a sharp pain along her arm.

She winced as the creature fell over her, one of its long legs scraping her fore arm on its bristles as the torch scorched its under belly. Its legs caught amid the boulders and it toppled with a roar, landing on its back.

It kicked and screeched, finding no purchase.

Jacke rolled forward and scrambled to find her feet in the dirt as the creature braced its right legs against the passage wall and heaved itself onto its feet, making a noise like fluid filled lungs.

It swung its head round searching for Jacke.

It lashed out at her with its fore legs and the wall by her head cracked as it pierced the rock in a shower of shrapnel. She ducked as it struggled with the space, lashing blindly out at her.

Using the phosphorescent glow from the lichen, Jacke ran as fast as she could back the way she came, watching for the flower trail in the gloom.

The creature's shrieks shredded the air like lightning as it lurched after her. The passage narrowed giving her the advantage but the tough bristles on the creature's body seemed to cut into the rock, allowing it to follow, its great legs bending and contracting to compensate for the loss of space.

Blind panic gripped Jacke as she lost the trail, those tiny yellow beacons of hope suddenly gone. She dropped to the ground and felt quickly about but to no avail.

Suddenly she felt something; a shoe; a small white shoe with a buckle up front.

On her knees, she looked up and saw Lizzy staring down at her, her angelic face seething with anger. It betrayed a malevolence that chilled the Irish girl.

"That rather spoiled things, don't you think?"

Her voice had lost the child like quality and seemed more adult, more powerful. She positively radiated anger as she glared at the creature which let out an ear piercing shriek as it reared up over them, slashing the rocks away with its scuttling legs.

It paused, watching them as it stalked forward, eyes gleaming in the light. Lizzy stepped forward and ordered it to stop with her palm upraised.

"Stupid creature!" she spat. "You had to ruin it but then she was cleverer than you, not as primitive as we thought."

With a sigh, she clenched her fist and a beam of green fire lashed forward and struck the creature on the chest. It howled in agony as it spread across its form before dissolving in a cascade of flame. Jacke leapt to her feet as Lizzy swung round on her, eyes blazing.

"Your turn," she purred as she raised her fist at Jacke.

Tyran and the others had been rounded up and herded out of the senate chamber and down a jade corridor towards an escalator which had proved awkward for the giant spider creatures who stood back and allowed their guards to escort the prisoners down the stairs and out into a courtyard dominated by a huge fountain, the cascading water glistening in the burning sun. Tyran's mind was whirling with confusion.

Could isolation here with no hope of escape really turn Michael to betray the people he had inspired for so long? Was this a ploy to rescue them all at the last minute? she wondered but her sinking heart knew that was a false hope as the guards whipped anyone who dared break the line or look the wrong way.

A noise made her look up squinting against the sun.

The familiar clip clop of powerful legs made her heart race as she saw the creatures scaling down the side of the senate tower as easily as she walked to the bathroom.

Their shadows slimed across the limestone surface in their wake as they descended, heads swivelling to survey the crowd.

Tyran started as she felt the man beside her recoil, tensing to run. She quickly grabbed his arm and met his shocked stare. She shook her head slowly, squeezing his arm reassuringly.

With surprising speed, the monsters circled them ordering the guards to continue to the pens.

As if of one mind, the guards took crystal tipped rods from their tunics and held them aloft. They blazed with a flash of energy and an orange energy field spread all around them engulfing the entire area.

Tyran's guts wrenched as she felt the power surge through her body as if hailstones were raining down on her. Her sight blurred and swam before resolving into a shadowed complex of iron bars. The walls were thick with slime and pocked by dark patches. The prisoners shared momentary disorientation as the orange field faded.

A sick feeling knotted Tyran's stomach.

"Where are we?" she demanded, turning on the nearest guard, a thick set man with bad skin and pale grey eyes. He stared impassively at her, his eyes empty of any feeling or compassion for the people before him. Swallowing, Tyran straightened up and faced him.

"If the creature inside this man would like to explain where we are and what you're doing, I'd very much appreciate it." Her mind raced, half remembering old movies and television shows. "Don't you have any prisoner of war treaties or Geneva conventions?" Of course, Geneva was very far away and she hadn't a clue what a Geneva Convention was but it was still worth a try.

Her scalp crawled as the guard's lips peeled back in a knowing grin but there was nothing behind the smile, no emotion, no spark, no life.

He was dead, the corpse merely a vehicle for whatever was nesting inside the brain.

With a skin crawling screech, a heavy worn iron gate heaved up and the guards shoved the crowd toward the opening. The floor was covered in large thick black slabs of stone and little else. When the last of the prisoners were in, the gate smashed down with a resounding clang.

With a sigh, Tyran gripped the bars and wearily let her head fall forward until her forehead rested on the gritty bars.

What the hell was happening? Could being trapped here for all these years have tipped Michael's mind, unbalanced him?

She couldn't picture it but she had only known him for a while and they did say you never really knew anyone. She let her gaze drift around her. She saw the disbelief and anger on the other's faces; the despair at their leader's treachery. Fair play to them for lasting all this time but now they were defeated, their fates unknown.

Tyran knew those creatures had a taste for human flesh and it made her skin crawl. And how the hell was she going to stop them and free the others? I'm eighteen and sure as hell not going to end up the main course for alien spiders, she resolved. Maybe this was some sort of plan on Michael's behalf, maybe he knew that the rebels couldn't sustain an ongoing battle so delivered them all to one point, the enemy stronghold where they could do most damage, strike from within.

Maybe.

But the look on his face dismissed such hopeful thoughts. The rough bars scraped her palms as she gripped them and gave them a hopeful rattle.

The air of helplessness was almost palpable. Dammit, there has to be a way out, has to be.

"Listen to me!" Tyran shouted. She drew herself up and paused while the rebels slowly looked in her direction, eyes vacantly expecting nothing.

Her heart pounding, Tyran moved towards the middle of the crowd, the shadows of the bars across them like tattoos. "I know you don't know me very well, well not at all really but I am not going to end up dying here. I refuse! Don't give up, wait and watch for an opportunity! You've lasted this long, fought these things all this time. We're still alive so there's still a chance."

A scruffy looking man sighed wearily, his grey eyes heavy beneath the thickest eye brows Tyran had ever seen.

"Big words, girl but you forget our glorious leader has betrayed us and we're now fruit in a basket for those monsters. They have their guards and weapons and an army of creatures, so where exactly do you see any hope?"

Flustered, Tyran's eyes darted across their faces, Jesus they were a tough crowd!

"There!" She pointed at a woman in her thirties, her long auburn hair scraped back in a ponytail. "There!" This time a middle aged man, squatting in a corner, a millipede like insect scuttling beneath his shadow. He seemed surprised to be singled out. "There!" Tyran continued, helping a stocky man with a balding head to his feet. "As long as we're alive, so is hope. You're fighters, so what if your boss has screwed you over? You adjust, adapt. Find another way!" She paused. "Or has Michael been leading sheep all this time?"

Good point, she prided herself, should consider a career in politics. The air of pessimism was melting in their cautious glances towards each other. A stocky man with long black grey hair tied back in a ponytail stood up, his face alive with defiance.

"She's right!" he shouted. "We've fought too long to die in this bloody cage!" A wave of agreeing murmurs rippled among them, making Tyran smirk triumphantly.

Then it all went black.

She awoke with a buzzing in her head and a taste of metal in her mouth. Tyran groggily blinked against the bright light and realised she was pinned by the arms, the smell of body odour making her head snap up. She saw the uniforms and struggled against the guards' grip, her arms aching from their hold. A familiar voice made her grimace, ordering her the guards to release her.

"You ok?" asked Michael, his voice full of concern. She rubbed her arms and glared at his beautifully ironed clothes and musk of aftershave, Sela beside him, dolled up to the nines and looking like a gangster's moll.

With a brief glance, Tyran realised they were outside the cage. Most of the other rebels were gone, leaving only ten frightened men in the cage. Her stomach began to knot as she saw two creatures rear up behind them and about twenty guards at various points around them.

The one closest the cage held a grey metal box in his hands, watching Michael closely.

"Well, if it isn't asshole and his slut bitch from hell. Scrub all you want, love, you're still a dog." Sela smirked amusedly, slinking alongside Michael and curling her arm around his waist.

He watched Tyran for a reaction and was disappointed when she stared expressionlessly at them.

"Tyran," Michael said, his features melting with mock sincerity. "Is that any way to talk to the man that saved you from a fate worse than death?"

"If that man sold out his friends to giant man eating spiders, then yes!" she smiled icily, the gnawing in her stomach increasing. "Where are the others?" Michael glanced at the creatures, clicking their mandibles, watching the humans.

"The Mentara needed them elsewhere," explained Michael, "by the way, great speech, very inspiring, almost made me switch sides." He made a gesture with his hands, holding his thumb and finger close together, "almost." The lead Mentara stomped forward, prodding Michael with its pincer. "Have the humans been moved to the appropriate designated areas?"

Turning to face it, Michael nodded.

"As per your instructions, the younger females and younger males have been transported to the breeding farms and the others have been placed in the stasis larders. And as you can see your personal guards' numbers have been swelled." He paused narrowing his eyes. "That was what you wanted was it not?" The Mentara shifted on its great trunk legs, clicking contentedly.

"Everything is as we specified. These new breeding farms will produce excellent stock."

"I'm glad to be of service," bowed Michael. "When can we leave? I think I have spent too much time here already." He glanced around, eyeing the citadel with disgust. His eyes lighted on Tyran's shocked face. He grabbed her hands tightly so she couldn't pull away. "I did this for you, Tyran. The Mentara have a way out of here and we have a ticket booked."

"In exchange for what?" she asked pointedly, "Finger licking rebel for the spider horse freaks." She watched him smile sneakily, with a slight shake of his head.

"I always loved that about you; say what you think and damn the rest. It stood you well against the Collector on Ether as I remember." She pulled her hands away, ignoring Sela's jealous glare, rubbing them on her trousers to take his sweat away.

"Oh come on!" he yelled angrily, shoving her. "It's the only way home for us. It's alright for you, you've only just arrived, and I've been stuck here for ten years, everything I had gone! I don't even know if my gran's alive or if she died alone. I will do anything to go home, anything and I'm sorry if you think this is too much for you to take but these people will die out here, locked in this bubble with nowhere to go. We were so noble, let's fight the good fight, kill the monsters, and let the people sleep in their beds at night and for what?"

"That was our choice," answered Tyran quietly. "We were caught up in the adventure and loved it. Who else gets to see the things we saw, experience the galaxy and time travel and discover that life is more than getting up to work and eating greasy kebabs on a Saturday night after a skinful?" Her eyes misted for a second before regaining her composure. Tyran stared Michael in the eye. "We didn't know the risks, not fully but it didn't matter. We still chose to do this and if you have even a bit of your old self left; you'd know that and help these people. Imagine these Mentara reaching home and destroying everyone we know, your whole family."

A harsh coldness gripped Michael's manner. "I have no family."

Tyran sighed sadly, her eyes flicking to the ground before placing a hand on his chest and looking directly into his eyes.

"You had a family. They were with you in the ship before the accident."

For a split second, Michael faltered, his brow curling as if something long buried had been dug up. The Mentara scuttled behind them as they sensed something. Michael looked up again, every hardship etched in his face.

"Guard, release the Tir." His voice was stone, eyes cold and furious. Tyran watched the guard near the cage nod and turned to his cohort. He set the box inside the cage and peeled back the lid. The rebels backed away, including the man with the pony tail who had backed Tyran.

Ten red eel like creatures spewed forth from the box and paused as if to sniff the air. Their ribbed bodies shivered as they launched themselves across the concrete floor and straight at the men.

They scattered but the Tir followed, fast and determined. Two reached their prey and shot up their trouser legs. The men desperately tried to catch them, beating their trouser legs but to no avail. The creatures were too lithe and agile for them and in seconds had entered their mouths.

With gargled screams they fell to the ground as the Tir burrowed into their brains.

Tyran stifled a cry of horror as their skulls swelled; the backs of the Tir poking out as their tendrils entered the brain and took over the nervous systems of their hosts.

A trickle of blood sidled from their mouths as their eyes snapped open and they stood rigidly to attention.

The Mentara made a clicking sound and the men moved obediently out of the cage.

"Perfect soldiers, their minds are gone, replaced by the intelligence of the Tir, the young of the Mentara," nodded Sela approvingly. Tyran lunged at her and managed to grab her long blond hair and give her a yank hard enough to cause whiplash. Michael grabbed her and dragged her away still kicking.

"I'll kill you bitch!" Tyran spat. She shoved Michael away, sending him stumbling to the ground.

Guards rushed forward, weapons raised towards her.

Eyes wild and wide, Tyran stared at her former friend, spittle bristling her lips. Her fury shifted as she turned to face Sela. "It's you!" She breathed deeply. "She's doing this to you but how?" Tyran looked at Michael disbelievingly, her mind racing. Something wasn't right, something didn't quite click.

She whirled round, the Mentara watching her, bodies bristling with confusion at the scene.

The rebels turned slaves with those slug things feeding their brains with alien thoughts, the already converted guards surrounding her weapons ready to fire and Sela calm and assured like a cobra round Michael.

Her mind was a blur, like trying to think through a drunken haze. Something was blanking her like a half hidden memory.

"Mentara, how long have you lived here?" she demanded. The centaur like spider rocked slightly at the question, its features confused.

"I don't know," it slurred uncertainly, "a long time, I think." It seemed taken aback by her question and looked to its companion for support but it seemed equally uncertain. Sela's face crumpled with anger.

"Restrain her!" she screamed, gesturing to the guards. Tyran dodged and yelled.

"Restrain me? Why not kill me? It'd be easier wouldn't it? No, you need me alive." She punched a guard as he lunged at her.

Grabbing the end of his weapon, she swung him around, the momentum carrying him into three of his fellows. Tyran wielded the rifle at Sela.

"Want to tell me what's really going on?" challenged the blond girl. She shook her head disbelievingly.

Sela stared like a cougar about to pounce. Michael said her name and made to move towards her but she pointed the rifle at him menacingly.

"What's the aftershave Michael? Funny, because as I don't recall you having

a backup supply on the Dagger or is there a Boots handy here?" He stood rigid.

"It's not like that."

"Then what is it?" she asked. "Remember when you showed me the night sky, big black void with no stars; you told me there was nowhere to go, this place was sealed off from the rest of the universe." She paused, watching for his reaction. She stepped forward, gun aimed at his face. "So where does the sun come from? By your reckoning this place should be in darkness all the time, so how come I'm getting a tan?" Tyran didn't expect an answer; his face was impassive, eyes glazed like he was spaced out.

Michael swayed slightly like a crack splitting ice. He faltered, his eyes flickering.

"How could you condemn your friends like that?" pushed Tyran, "The Michael I know would sooner die than do something like that. It's just not in him. Unless someone put it there, twisted his perception, made him act like the thing he abhors."

He put his hand to his head, his face contorted in anguish. "That's what's been going on, twisting us, forcing situations to break us; my faith in you, my hope these good people would rise up having been betrayed, seeing them broken and infected with those creatures."

"Oh please, always the drama queen, Tyran. Doesn't it get boring, trying to be centre of attention?" spat Sela. "Does it bother you I'm the centre of Michael's attention and you're not? That I share his bed and you don't. Isn't that what this is really about?" She stood right in front of her, glaring down at Tyran, the sun making her flowing locks sparkle, the epitome of beauty. "Aren't I what you want to be?"

Tyran smirked giving her a pitying look. Michael staggered, his face covered in sweat.

"Michael, she doesn't want you, she never did, she's controlling you!" yelled Tyran. "Come on you soppy big lump, remember!" Michael convulsed, crying out as he shimmered. His beard contracted and he began to grow younger. His head snapped up and his eyes focused on Tyran.

He looked at Sela who seemed to be simmering with rage.

"Oh my god!" he cried disbelievingly. "I'm a slut! Good times!" he whooped.

Sela roared; a sound so alien that it made Tyran's skin crawl. Michael leapt to her side in a second.

"She broke it, we failed!" screamed Sela at the very air.

A shrieking filled the compound as a wind brewed. The guards were staggering uncertainly like puppets with their strings being cut one at a time. The Tir squealed and fell from the open skulls of the rebels who collapsed and faded away, like ghosts.

A wind like the doors of hell opening blasted them and in a swirl of red light, Jacke tumbled to the ground beside them, her head covering her arms.

"About time you showed up!" mocked Tyran, barely standing in the blasting winds. A small girl appeared out of nowhere beside Sela who grabbed her roughly.

"You failed!" she screamed furiously. Lizzy slapped her hands away.

"We failed, but I was so close, so close. I found her weakness but you had to bring two of them together, you should have separated them and worked on them alone. We would finally have been free!"

The air filled with streaks of black light which swirled like a tornado overhead. Tyran tossed the gun to Michael and ran forward and punched Sela square on the nose. She fell back, Lizzy scuttling aside only to be grabbed by Jacke, her face a mask of hate.

"You tried to use my pain, break me, break us; for what?" she yelled into her face.

Tyran had Sela flat on her back, hands round her throat. It struck Michael she was enjoying it a little too much. He noticed the Mentara rearing up behind them and swung the rifle at them, warning them not to move.

"You were the aliens on the other ship!" he realised. "They trapped you too." The creatures glanced at each other. "How the hell were you going to break them?" he asked Lizzy. Her face was twisted, seething with hate.

"Starvation." With a grimace, Michael muttered, "Lovely, Alice in psychopath land."

"We needed to break your minds," hissed Lizzy. "Isolate you, wear you down, relive your greatest pains and commit acts that would tear your very souls. Michael is your weak link, using him to break you was the obvious way to go. For Jacke you both died, her friends both dead before their time, left alone, lost in time. Once we broke your minds, we would have been able to take your bodies as our own and escape this endless torment, end the loneliness, lead our brethren to the real world and take revenge on those that trapped us here!"

Tyran glared at the helpless Sela. "Didn't we pick the wrong victims?" she gloated. "Send us back, now!"

With a guttural shriek the Mentara reared up and galloped across the courtyard.

Jacke startled as Lizzy began to wail. "We've lost, we can't control them!" The buildings began to warp and shatter as they dissolved into mist in a billion sparkles of energy. Tyran got up and stood with the others. The sky was cracking like an egg as thunder deafened them. Lizzy knelt defeated by Sela and took her hand.

"Pray we never meet again," hissed Sela as the world around them compressed into a black void. "Next time, next time…."

Jacke snapped awake first and realised she was in the Dagger and it was tumbling end over end in a crescendo of explosive light as the ship fell back into the time vortex. Tyran gripped the edge of her console as Michael slipped from his chair.

Wrestling with the sheer forces buffeting the craft, Jacke wedged herself back into her seat, bracing her feet against the base. Her hands deftly moved across the controls and turned the ship into the hurricane as Michael reworked more power to the engines.

"We're levelling out!" shouted Tyran, as the cockpit window dulled down as the whirlwind of lights began to fade.

In seconds they welcomed silence and allowed a brief sigh of relief. They looked at each other, uncertain yet bonded.

"We never left the ship," breathed Jacke. "They made all that happen in our heads. Those things must live in the vortex, somehow our battle with the Mentara ship created the right conditions for them to latch onto our minds and make us believe all those things."

"You should have seen what they found in his head," Tyran smiled at her, giving Michael a knowing look. His face fell as he remembered his ten years as a rebel leader. "Ten years with super slut and you're still a virgin; that's depressing."

"One night with me and you'd see who the virgin is," he retorted grinning. He hugged her long and hard. "Thank you; not so dumb for a junior." She smiled back, then blushed breaking the hug. He embraced Jacke who seemed exhausted.

"Are you ok?" he asked anxiously, looking into her tired face. She nodded but something in her eyes said there was more to it. "Let's just say if I ever say I want to be alone, smack me."

"Crap!" Tyran leapt to the window searching outside. "Where's the Mentara ship?" Michael checked the scanner but there was nothing.

"They're gone."

"If they escaped," offered Jacke. "Maybe we were the only ones to make it out because we broke their hold on us." The comms system bleeped and Varran's anxious voice came through.

"Jacke, Michael, Tyran, respond please, this is the Juggernaught, please come in! If you can hear me, I'm coming in!" Jacke hit the button.

"It's ok, we're coming home." They heard a relieved sigh.

"I'll be waiting." The relief in his voice was not lost on them.

"Home," mused Michael, "I suppose it is, maybe it always will be." He sighed, recalling what had been said about him. Am I really that weak? he wondered. He tried to ignore the twisting in his chest. Maybe this isn't for me after all. Maybe I really am the twat people think I am.

Silence fell over them as Jacke punched up the engines and guided the Dagger back into normal space, following the reassuring shape of the Juggernaught. The Mentara were gone for now but they would be back, they all knew it. But whatever those things were masquerading as Lizzy and Sela….They all exchanged glances; none of them spoke, they didn't need to.

No one dared look up at the imposing form of the auburn haired woman as she strode angrily towards her office.

She slammed the door shut behind her, her face a mask of fury as she took her seat. The operation had been a disaster, their presence almost exposed to Varran and his friends.

"I am surrounded by morons!" she yelled, taking a deep breath to calm herself. She had waited so long, nothing could jeopardise her plans now.

She leaned forward to a communications panel set into the glass desk.

"Any word from our friends yet?" she asked.

A male voice came over the system in answer.

"Everything is proceeding as planned and I will have solid data for you shortly, Madame. The data from Farron was most helpful."

"Thank you Mister Ling. I can always rely on you."

"Always," he answered.

She leaned back in her chair and stared into space. A sly smile carved her face as she thought to herself.

"Soon Varran, very soon, you will bow before me. That I promise you!"

LEGACY

It was a sweltering July day and Jason Cairns stood by his open patio doors with an iced tea in his hand, relaxing in the comfort of the cooling shade.

He stared out at his long rectangular garden, lost in thought. The trimmed lawn housed carefully arranged flower beds awash with flowers of every size and colour.

His rambling roses snaked along his lattice archway in a trail of pink and white at the head of the straight crazy paving path that that led to a dark wood veranda that stood sentinel at the bottom of the garden, positioned so the sun always hit there.

Sunflowers stood flanking it along with crocuses, fox gloves, begonias and a whole host of fauna protected by the laptop fencing that boxed the whole garden in. It was Jason's sanctuary. He watched bees dance from flower to flower spreading pollen as they went, resolute and determined in their work.

He stepped outside with a sigh onto the coral stone patio and settled on the bench of his patio furniture, setting his drink on the table. He started as a ladybird flitted onto his hand.

He let it explore the hairs on the back of his hand before it shot upwards out of sight. His face was already sunburnt, his ginger hair making him susceptible to the rays. He was hitting 45 and his stomach was forming a little mound against his green polo shirt.

A sure sign of getting older, he thought, so he pulled it over his head and threw it on the table, sitting bare-chested.

He closed his eyes and let his head loll back. The lines on his face were deepening and his hairline was slipping away like a thief in the night.

He didn't feel old, you're as young as who you feel, he consoled himself but he had had trouble sleeping recently. It was a case of the mind was willing, thinking you're still eighteen, but the body wasn't, as seen by his expanding waist.

He smiled wryly as he made a mental note to buy new trousers with a slightly bigger waist size. Thank God for elasticised shorts.

A shadow fell over him. He didn't see the figure approach but the sudden loss of sunlight on his face made him look up, hand shielding his eyes.

"Alright love." The woman nodded and slipped onto the bench beside him. Angela looked at him with those baby blue eyes he'd fell in love with all those years ago.

She had maintained her figure even after three kids and her mousy bobbed hair was always neat and shiny. His eyes fell to her tight shoulder less top she was wearing, marine blue to match her shorts. The first time they'd slept together suddenly flashed in his mind. He slipped his fingers between hers and frowned at her teasingly.

"It's not funny, I'm worried." The shadows in her eyes echoed his own anxiety which he'd kept locked inside; no need for Angela to see it, he'd always been her rock; the one that stayed positive in every crisis for he knew everything would turn out alright in the end.

There's a reason for everything he'd always chip up and she always seemed to take comfort in his optimism.

"There's no need to worry, it's only natural, she's turning eighteen tomorrow. Once that happens, everything will be back to normal," he assured her. She stared at him, eyes darting all over his face as if to catch out the lie behind the impassive confidence. Seeing none, she sighed squeezing his hand gently.

"I don't know, she seems different than from when we went through it."

"It's a new generation; it'll be a breeze for her." Angela nodded.

"I suppose, I'm probably over reacting." He leant forward and kissed her lightly on the lips. Her eyes fell to his stomach. "Thank God for elasticised waistlines," she smiled.

"Relaxed muscle, that's all, besides you've never complained before," he teased stroking her back. She grinned, the worry falling way from her face.

"There's always a first time." He smirked as her fingers trailed down his chest and plucked at his shorts. "The kids won't be back until after six. Does the old man still have it?"

"We haven't done that in ages," he smiled, his hand sliding round her waist as he nuzzled her neck.

"That's the joys of kids, by the time they move out, we'll be too knackered to do anything," she moaned.

"Then seize the moment," he challenged getting her up and trailing her inside the house, smacking her behind, laughing like teenagers.

Pulling her close to him, Jason kissed her long and hard pressing his body into hers until she was against the table. It scraped the tiled floor in protest. She grinned naughtily as she realized what he was planning.

"Here?" He nodded. "Dirty old man." She pulled his shorts down as his hands worked at hers.

"Oh my God!" The cry made them jump as they saw their seventeen year old daughter Suzie had come home earlier than expected and was gawping at them from the doorway.

"You're not supposed to be back yet!" was all Jason could say, uselessly hiding his bare behind by wrapping Angela's legs round him. Angela buried her face in his chest.

"You're too old for that!" she yelled as if she'd seen a murder. With a snort of disgust she glared at them.

A wall mounted glass fronted cabinet exploded outwards, showering them with glass.

Jason pushed Angela backwards on the table covering her from the explosion. He winced feeling it cut his back.

With a scornful glare, Suzie stormed upstairs. The husband and wife looked at each other despairingly as they heard the bedroom door slam.

Pulling his shorts up, Jason turned to let Angela brush powder fragments from his back.

"That girl always was the best contraceptive we ever had," he said wryly, trying to lighten the mood. Angela's eyes were welling up.

"I need to clean those cuts," she answered. He held her tightly, feeling her hot tears on his chest. Angela was right; Suzie needed to be sorted now before tomorrow came. He shuddered as the consequences flashed tauntingly through his mind.

"I have to make a call."

"So much for Live Aid," complained Michael as Jacke parked her Ford Focus. Rolling his eyes, Varran looked at him in the rear view mirror.

"And we will, once I take care of a little business," he assured him. Michael made a disbelieving face.

"I really wanted to see Freddy Mercury, he's a bloody legend!" added Tyran. "I take it you blagged us free tickets?" she ventured.

Varran threw her a reproachful look.

"Certainly not! I bought the tickets like everyone else. How amazing that one man can change the world's perception and rally them behind one good cause. That Geldolf man is amazing. I admire him a lot."

"Where exactly is here?" asked Michael, as they got out of the car.

"We're in Leeds. I got a call for help and the clock is ticking," explained Varran. Jacke shivered, her bare arms breaking out in goose bumps.

Tyran frowned concerned. "Are you cold?"

"In this weather? It's roasting!" Michael pointed out.

He looked up and down the street, kids playing, minimal traffic, a typical suburbia scene.

"It looks normal enough to me," Michael remarked, shoving in hands in his pockets.

Jacke stood staring at the house, a strange look on her face.

Varran stared at the dark skinned girl knowingly.

"What do you feel?" he said quietly.

"A coldness; something's not right here." Her face grew concerned. The house was a normal semidetached with Tudor trimmings. The front garden was small but tidy with blooming pot plants by the white PVC door. A knee high red bricked wall lined with black wrought iron railings gave way to a gate that squeaked as Varran pushed it open. He saw the living room blinds twitch as someone inside peeked out.

Michael was exasperated." Who called you? Why are we here? What's the big crisis?"

Pausing, Varran gave him a curious stare.

"A birthday."

They felt the disturbed atmosphere as the balding ginger haired man opened the door and ushered them inside to the spacious living room. A slender woman sat on a dark brown leather armchair her face a masque of worry.

Varran gave her a warm smile as he sat opposite her. Jacke stood as Michael and Tyran sat on the couch.

Making the customary introductions, Varran paused while Jason perched on the arm of the chair Angela occupied, putting his arm round her shoulders.

"Tell me what happened," he said.

Wringing her hands, Angela looked to her husband.

"Thanks for coming so quickly," said Jason. "It's our daughter Suzie. It's her eighteenth tomorrow but she's started having strange abilities."

"Is the kitchen cabinet her doing?" asked Jacke from the doorway. Jason nodded.

"Yeah that happened this afternoon."

"Why?" Michael asked.

Angela blushed and looked down. Jason tripped over his words but Varran held up a calming hand.

"It doesn't matter. I take it she was angry."

"Yeah, she blew a gasket and the cabinet just exploded. That's not normal for this is it?"

Sighing, Varran thought about other eighteen year olds. He couldn't recall a case like this ever.

Michael was slightly lost. "I'm sorry but what is wrong exactly?" Settling back in the armchair, Varran explained.

"Well as you know, when every Xereban child turns eighteen, a race memory is unlocked and they remember everything about our history including what happened from the accident that destroyed Xereba until our arrival on Earth. They know their heritage and what we are about and they know we're here to help whenever they need it."

"One thing I never understood," interrupted Tyran," why don't we remember anything until we're eighteen?"

"Genetics. When the decision was made to live here, myself and others decided to alter the racial gene to activate only when a person turned eighteen. Can you imagine children remembering that and telling their friends or teachers about monsters and aliens. They'd be sectioned or scrutinized by all sorts of people, people that don't need to know." He paused. "At eighteen, you are virtually an adult; you are on the cusp of what to do with your life. Your decisions are more reasoned and as you know teenagers are secretive at the best of times."

"You can say that again," muttered Jason. "We barely know where Suzie is day to day." Angela looked up.

"She's a good girl, never brought trouble to the door but these powers have manifested out of nowhere."

"I know when my memory happened, I was relieved," Michael offered. "When I woke up, it was a case of, so that's what it's all about!"

Jason nodded in agreement. "Me too; I knew that there were other things out there and have always been aware of it but it made me more protective of this world and the people around me." He glanced at the ceiling towards Suzie's room. "But this is different, she's really changed."

"Has she been anywhere or been in different company recently; anything out of the ordinary?" Jacke enquired. Jason and Angela looked at each other exasperatedly.

"Nothing; she goes clubbing, is part of the local drama group, doesn't have a boyfriend that we know about, spends too much time on her computer and watches too much of those American shows. She's a typical teenager."

"Apart from turning into Carrie," Tyran said drolly, earning a dark glare from Varran.

She uttered an apology sheepishly.

"What do you think, Varran?" Angela asked pleadingly. Raising his eyebrows, Varran shook his head.

"Jacke is an expert in this field." He looked at the porcelain clock on the Mexican pine fireplace; five o'clock; only a few hours before Suzie's eighteenth. When she went to sleep her race memory would come into play, in the form of the most vivid dream she would ever experience and maybe her powers would fade with the memory but he had to find out. "Where are your other children?"

"They're staying at my brother's place," Angela said. "I thought it was for the best."

"Rightly so," assured Varran. "May we go talk to her?"

Tyran sat up. "What are you going to tell her? She'll think we're part of a cult or the Stepford nut jobs or something!"

"What would you have us do? Drug her and hope the memory cures all? No, if Suzie has unusual mental abilities then we need to help her cope and understand them."

"As long as the knives don't start flying across the room," Tyran put in. Michael told her to shut her mouth.

"There's a time and a place," he chastised.

"Tyran, if you can't be helpful then leave," growled Varran warningly. She blushed, feeling very small. She couldn't believe Michael had spoken to her like that.

"I'm sorry," she said to Jason and Angela. They shrugged it off. She stood up abruptly and flicked open her hand unit, activating the teleport sequence. She threw Michael a filthy glare as the blue light carried her away.

He stared incredulously at the empty space. What the hell's got into her? he wondered. Varran's face was impassive. Getting to his feet, he signalled to Jacke.

"It'll be better if Jacke and I go up alone," he said. "Michael, why don't you make tea and sandwiches, give Angela and Jason a break. Watch Deal or no Deal, they might have the next quarter of a millionaire." Biting back a smart remark, Michael smiled disarmingly and headed towards the kitchen.

Varran opened the door for Jacke and quietly closed it behind them.

They padded up the oatmeal carpeted stairs almost subconsciously quieter than normal. The four panelled white door with its brass handle loomed before them against sand coloured walls.

Family pictures adorned the walls along with a couple of artworks. Angela and Jason obviously had good taste, mused Jacke as she approached the door, Varran behind her.

Tentatively she knocked the door lightly, hearing a bed creaking as someone moved inside. She glanced at Varran.

"Teenagers," she grinned. "It's okay Suzie, we're here to help." She whispered to Varran. "Who are we supposed to be?" He frowned for a second.

"Noise control?" he suggested hopefully. She gave him a wry look. "Okay, physic investigators."

"That'll scare her off," said Jacke. The door opened suddenly startling them. Suzie stood defiantly in the doorway staring at them with her dark brown eyes from beneath a raggedy fringe. She had good skin, swarthy and acne free and was dressed in grey sweat pants and white muscle vest with a huge pink tongue on the front.

"Where did my parents pick you two up?" she asked, looking them up and down disbelievingly. She stared at Varran's white hair then back at the beautiful Jacke.

"Isn't he a bit old for you?" Blushing, Varran cleared his throat embarrassed, lost for words.

"Older than you think," smiled Jacke. Well that broke the ice already, she thought happily. "Can we talk?" Suzie smiled dutifully and slammed the door in their faces.

Bitch! Jacke thought. She shoved open the door and strode into the room, Varran hanging back slightly. It was cleaner than she'd expected with dirty clothes neatly in a basket, the curtains held back by ties, the bed crisply made.

A dresser was covered in make up in little baskets, pictures of the family and friends, brushes, little knick knacks alongside which a cd player stood atop a false pine stand with discs alphabetically place in a CD tower.

An mp3 player and earphones lay on the bed and a laptop sat on a slim desk in the far right corner of the room. Suzie spread herself uncaringly on the bed.

"Ever hear of knocking?" she spat sarcastically. Jacke stood over her hands on hips, face livid.

"Do you know what it is Suzie? I haven't got time for the cotton wool approach. You can do things with your mind that aren't normal and we need to find out why." A trace of fear flickered across the girl's face.

"You're not taking me anywhere!" she cried. "I've heard about those places. Is that why my parents called you? Turn eighteen and sell me out as your guinea pig, well screw that!" Her face clouded and the bedroom door slammed shut, narrowly avoiding catching Varran's fingers in the process. Jacke tensed nervously; maybe the cotton wool would have been better.

"See what I mean?" Jacke said pointedly, quaking inside but still outwardly defiant. Suzie glared unrepentantly. "That's only a taste of what I can do," she grinned chillingly.

"And I'm supposed to be scared? Listen, Suzie, I've seen things you couldn't even imagine that can do more than slam a door. We're not here to take you away, we only want to help." Jacke sat next to her on the bed. "Why are you so angry?"

"You're here because I caught my parents shagging on the kitchen table and now you want to take me away," she growled "You try to take me away and I'll show you exactly what I can do."

Jacke held her gaze, refusing to back down. "If you'd shut up and listen, we're not here to take anyone away! And your mum and dad….well, it happens to everyone."

"Not in the kitchen, they have a room for that."

"Spice of life," commented Varran; "apparently."

"Haven't you ever done it anywhere strange?" Pulling a face, Suzie shuddered.

"I haven't done it yet," she admitted.

"That's good, nothing wrong with that. Too many teenagers rush into it, sex should be with someone special," Jacke praised. "When did these powers start manifesting themselves?" Suzie shrugged, looking down to the pine wooden floor.

"Dunno," she muttered. Taking a deep breath, Jacke pushed the point.

"Let me guess. You've always had dreams that have come true, strong intuition in certain situations, a gut reaction that you knew was right even when others didn't." She paused. "I'm right, aren't I? I'm the same but nothing like you can do. How do you do it?" Suzie looked at her relieved.

"It's like my right ear burns and I know something bad is going to happen," she blurted out. "Or I sense something almost like a vibration and I'm ready for anything to happen. But, this moving things just by thinking about it only began a week ago. Is something wrong with me? Am I mental?" Putting a reassuring hand on her shoulder, Jacke smiled warmly.

"I can assure you, you are not mental, if anything when you wake up tomorrow you'll feel a lot better, a lot of things will make sense."

"What do you mean? Are you going to drug me or something?" she recoiled slightly. Rolling her eyes, Jacke shook her head.

"Would you stop with the men in black paranoia? It's hard to explain but everything seems to start making sense when you turn eighteen." She nudged her conspiratorially. "And you can get drunk in front of your parents without hiding down the park with your mates and puking in the bushes. Trust me, Suzie." She paused, choosing her next words very carefully.

"My friend here is called Varran. He's the most remarkable man I know, except for my dad of course, and he would like to know if it's alright to do some scans on you."

Uncertain, Suzie narrowed her eyes and began to bite her bottom lip.

"I'm not going anywhere." Fearing she could lose trust here, Jacke quickly reassured her.

"No, believe me, he can do them here but your case is the first he's met. Your parents can be present and you'll be wide awake for it." Relaxing slightly, Suzie looked at her sideways.

"Will it show what's wrong with me or is it that we only use 10% of our brain thing you always read about?" she asked. Jacke breathed lightly.

"To be honest, he can compare your brain to mine and see what areas you're using that I don't but," she continued, "you have a great gift Suzie. Once you learn to use it properly, you could do amazing things, things you never even dreamed of. Will you trust me?" she probed, taking her hand. "Will you let me help you?" She could sense a certain resistance from the teenager. "Your mum and dad are worried sick about you and a little afraid so you'd be doing them a favour too."

Alarm flashed in Suzie's face. "They're afraid of me?" she asked incredulously as if the very idea of her parents running from her was like cutting a life line.

Suppressing a chuckle, Jacke said, "I think it's more a case of keeping their kitchen intact," Suzie blushed ruefully. "And maybe have a bit of fun without someone walking in on them." Suzie grimaced again.

"I still say they're too old," she smiled. "Okay, let's see what's going on in my head."

Varran stepped forward as Jacke motioned to him to come over. He brushed off Suzie's apology for nearly severing his fingers with a smile and knelt down before them. He took out a medial scanner and switched it on.

"What do we do?" She went to lie back on the bed but Jacke stopped her.

"No need for that, this will map your brain and give us all we need to know," Jacke explained. "Believe me, it's totally painless."

"That's one fancy brain scanner," breathed Suzie eyeing the device. "Where'd you get it?"

"I have a whole cupboard full of them," Varran replied with a glint in his eye. He explained he would simple stand over her and move the scanner above her head. "You'll feel a slight tingling sensation but that's all, I promise. Tomorrow, we can discuss it further." Holding up her hand, Suzie stopped him.

"Wait, I'd rather do this downstairs, let mum and dad be in on it, so they know I'm not a freak." Varran shook his head understandingly and offered her his hand gallantly to get off the bed. She took it gracefully.

"They don't think you're a freak," he assured her. She nodded understandingly.

"By the way," she paused, "seriously think about hair dye, it'll take years off you."

"It has been mentioned," he replied wryly, ignoring Jacke's laugh.

Suzie sat straight in the kitchen chair, a Mexican pine one, and looked straight ahead. Michael, Jason and Angela stood back as Varran gently moved the scanner about her scalp. It flickered softly, an orange funnel beam playing about her.

Features crunched with concentration, Varran watched the readings as they played on the screen before him. Jacke stood arms folded watching intently.

"You ok Suzie?" she asked, more to let her know she was still there than anything else. The girl nodded nervously, eyes straight ahead.

"Well Varran, am I crazy?"

"No," he answered slowly. "This is interesting, very interesting." His eyes clouded as he saw something that disturbed him. It was a slight change in expression but one Jacke knew well. She moved slowly beside him and peered at the screen. The scanner was beeping, soft tones at first then rushing into an alarmed screech.

Suzie snapped to her feet and she whirled round to face them. The relaxed features were hard and determined; the eyes like ice. Angela cried out her name. Varran stepped back as Michael got to his feet.

It was as if Suzie was possessed. Her face was hard, without emotion. Her head jerked as if processing the situation. Jason moved towards her but she raised her hand and forced him to his knees, locking him there, his face contorted in agony.

Angela fell to her husband's side crying out for Suzie to stop but her daughter looked at her like an insect. Michael slipped his hand into the back of his jeans and whipped out a laser pistol.

With a jerk of her head, Suzie tore it out of his hands and pinned him to the ceiling. Varran was thrown outside where he crashed to the patio unconscious, the scanner flying out of his hand.

"Suzie, stop! What are you doing?" yelled Jacke, edging away from her around the table. Suzie leered at her coldly.

"I told you I can do things," she chuckled. "Looks like mummy and daddy have more to worry about than their nice new kitchen, don't you think?" Jacke made a bolt for the door and managed to get the front door open as an urn flew at her.

She tumbled outside, scraping her knee as she fell over one of the plant pots. Suzie moved slowly, stalking her as she emerged from the open door, her face a mask of power.

"Trust me Suzie, relax Suzie, did you really think I believed that crap? You're using me for some sick plan, a human freak for you to study. It's my birthday Jacke did you know? I'm an adult and I can do anything I want, literally."

She looked at the tree by the side of the road and frowned as she concentrated. The great oak, lush with foliage, trembled, the branches quivering like chattering bones as it began to tear itself from the pavement.

The concrete cracked as its roots heaved free, birds fleeing the scene. It rose into the air and hung there quaking. Suzie strode down the path and raised her hands. The other trees began to shake and rise from the ground. She looked back at Jacke who sat helpless.

"So you think you're like me Jacke? I understand Suzie, I'm just like you," she mocked evilly. "Shall we see how fast you can deflect these trees?"

"I don't have your abilities Suzie! You know that!"

Jacke watched as her car rocked into the air beside the tree, held fast like giant puppets. "You tried to interfere in things you don't understand and there's no way you can match me. I will crush this house and everyone in it to dust and there's nothing you can do!" She sneered darkly as she moved to bring the trees down on the helpless woman.

"I wouldn't say that!" chipped a voice from the side of the house. Tyran was crouched by the side gate aiming a pulse rifle. She fired, catching Suzie in the chest, fired again, this time in the neck.

With a scream of rage, Suzie staggered, the car crashed to the road, the trees hovering uncertainly as she tried to hurl them at the two girls. Sinking to her knees, she was able to hit Jacke with a fallen plant holder before slumping on her face. She fought the tranquiliser every inch of the way, snarling hatefully at them before passing out.

The trees fell like broken puppets; Jacke's car crushed in a shower of shattered glass and twisted metal.

"You couldn't have shot her before she lifted the trees?" Jacke shouted at Tyran as she helped her to her feet. Tyran looked hurt.

"Excuse me, I had to play the bitch to give you breathing space and I know I did nothing for my reputation. My mother would have a fit if she thought I was rude in someone else's house." Brushing herself off, Jacke hurried to Suzie's side.

"Help me get her inside," she grunted, lifting the dead weight. "Before the neighbours see us."

"How the hell do we explain that?" Tyran asked gesturing to the uprooted trees.

Jacke shrugged. "Global warming," she grinned.

Jason grabbed his daughter off them as they carried her unconscious body into the living room. Angel scurried to plump a couple of cushions to rest her head on as he lay her gently down.

"What did you do?" cried Angela, her daughter's prone body scaring her. Tyran shuffled guiltily.

"I'm afraid that was me but don't worry, it's only a sleeping drug of sorts." Varran knelt by her side checking her vitals, his hands a blur. He tossed Michael his hand unit.

"Michael, hook this into the television while I explain." He got to his feet and winced, aching from his fall. He turned to Jason and Angela. "I'm sorry but we had to put her out. I wasn't sure how extensive her abilities were so I sent Tyran back to the Juggernaught under the pretence of ill manners just in case." Angela stared at him wide eyed.

"But how did you know?"

"I didn't," he admitted sheepishly. "It was just a feeling." Michael smirked.

"You watched Carrie, didn't you? It scared the crap out of you."

"It most certainly didn't!" snapped Varran indignantly. "I've never come across this before so I simply took precautions; and I was right."

He clicked on the 44 inch plasma TV and switched on the medical scanner. It had been scraped in the attack but was otherwise unscathed.

An image formed on the screen of Suzie's brain, the view rotating amid cross hairs and highlighted sections. It swung round to the base of her brain and zoomed in on the bottom. They leaned forward puzzled by what they were seeing.

"It's an implant," said Varran. "Wired specifically to a part of the brain that focuses her mental powers."

"But how did it get there?" asked Jason. "Has she been abducted by aliens? You read about it all the time and there are all those witnesses."

"Well if they are being abducted, I haven't been able to track them and the Juggernaught is very well armed," replied Varran.

"Is it Xereban technology?" Jacke wondered.

"No but there are a few minor similarities; I think it was activated when I did the medical scan." Angela put her hands in her face, scarcely able to believe what was happening.

"Hang on, are you telling us someone took my daughter and put something in her head to control her? How? When?"

"Has she been missing for any unusual length of time recently or been with people you don't know?" asked Tyran.

Shaking his head, Jason could barely contain his frustration. Someone had hurt his daughter and he'd never even known it.

"Now she's just someone's puppet ready to jump at the push of their button!" he cried alarmed. Jacke wheeled on Varran.

"Can we remove it?" He frowned, glancing at the TV. A plethora of notions ran through his mind as he tried to answer her question.

"I honestly don't know."

"I thought you were a genius, you haven't been around for the last one hundred years without learning something. Surely you know some brain surgeons who can help her," pleaded Jacke.

He turned angrily on her. "That's not the point. I have no idea what it's for. How many others have been implanted? Is someone building an army of super powered teenagers? I don't know what to do with this thing in her head, if I touch it, it may kill her."

"And if you don't, she will kill us," reminded Michael. Jason's face widened as a thought occurred to him.

"What if your scan alerted whoever did this and they're on their way here?" he said.

Varran expression was hard. "It had occurred to me."

"Then we need to go now," Tyran pointed out, "back to the Juggernaught."

Opening his hand unit, Varran activated the teleport command sequence. A curtain of blue shimmering light played over them all and faded. They were still in the living room.

"What happened?" cried Angela. The others looked at each other alarmed.

"Someone's blocking us," said Varran darkly.

"Remind anyone of anything?" quipped Michael.

"What do you mean?" Jason demanded. Michael gave him a weary look.

"Well, to put it mildly, jellyfish monsters and black ops are a bad combination."

"Are you sure this isn't Xereban technology?" urged Tyran. Varran looked flustered, uncertain. Someone had the ability to interfere with their technology and he hadn't the faintest idea how.

"I told you not to rely on technology too much," he said wryly. He scanned the room suddenly, realizing something. He picked up a signal and began moving out into the hall and out the front door. He paused, checking the signal strength and walked slowly to the black lantern like light at the side of the door. He reached into it and pulled out a small metal disc. He held it up to the light, studying it cautiously.

"I don't recognise it but it's an alarm system of some kind, very sophisticated." He glanced round the street, pulling a face when he saw Jacke's car. He muttered an apology as Jason and Angela gawped at the fallen trees.

"I can't believe my daughter did this," he said disbelievingly.

"She didn't intentionally, she was being controlled," assured Jacke. "I wonder is that thing amplifying her natural ability or harnessing it."

"I'd say from the scans it's an amplifier, fine tuning her latent ability via the implant," reasoned Varran. "It's undoubtedly the same technology as this."

"But that sort of engineering doesn't exist yet," Michael added moving in for a closer look. "Wait a minute," he thought, "is there one in Jacke's head?"

Jacke looked panicked, she hadn't even thought of herself being implanted like that. Putting a comforting hand on her shoulder, Varran shook his head.

"I already checked; you're clear," he said with a smile. He cried out in pain as the bug suddenly sparked and melted in his hand, burning it. He jumped back letting it fall to the ground where it melted to scrap.

"Someone doesn't want us to find anything do they?" Tyran said. She caught the expression on Jason's face. "What if that happens to the implant in Suzie's head?" They rushed back inside; fortunately, Suzie was still lying quietly sleeping.

Any sense of relief was short lived as Jacke noticed the wall lights beginning to bend on their brackets, slowly unerringly heaving themselves free. The chrome chandelier was curving to the left as if trying to bite its way through the ceiling. There was the rattle of ornaments against wood as the Belleek China began trembling as it rose into the air. The patio doors slammed shut, the lock sealing tight. The kitchen table began shaking as if trying to jump into the air as both the living room door and the kitchen one slammed shut, the glass shattering freezing in mid-air in a cloud of lethal shards.

The room temperature dropped, their breaths steaming in the chill. They stood where they were as Suzie snapped upright on the sofa, eyes wide open, blazing with dark intent. She smirked as her head turned to the others in the room.

"Bloody hell, it's the Exorcist!" breathed Michael, his heart pounding at her hateful expression. She moved with slow deliberation, unblinking as she surveyed the group before her.

Varran's unit began beeping, the signal pulsing faster with every second passing. The readings are off the scale.

"Suzie?" cried her mother, afraid as she looked at the girl wearing her daughter's face but not recognizing the creature staring at them like a tiger in a field of cows.

Jason instinctively pulled her back as Varran stood in front of them facing the teenage head on, holding up his hands fingers spread.

"Suzie, listen to me!" he said, voice calming. "This is not you; the implant has been turned up to full volume making you do this. It's opened your brain and harnessed your abilities." She stared at him, same curious expression on her face.

A chill ran along his spine as he saw the fire in her eyes. It was soulless, an emotionless intent that knew no bounds or morals. It recognized only its own needs, its own avarices; there was no love, no family, and no feelings. It was a primeval entity locked away deep in the human brain slumbering until the implant had opened the door and allowed it to surge through every fibre of Suzie's body.

For a second, Varran recalled his vision while trapped in the temporal accident that had destroyed Xereba; felt the essence of the darkness he had seen consume the universe.

It was almost personified here in the body of a teenage girl about to enter adulthood, about to know there was more to the universe than she had ever seen on the telly and she was about to kill them all. She threw both arms into the air above her head, bringing them slowly down.

Jacke, Tyran, Jason, Angela and Michael were forced to their knees, faces contorted in pain as Suzie's mind overwhelmed theirs. Only Varran remained standing, helpless, uncertain what to do as the others were held down by thought alone. Suzie had to be in there, there had to be something left of her and if there was one thing teenagers were, it was strong willed.

"Suzie, stop this!" he bellowed. "Listen to me, fight what they're doing! They took you, put a machine in your head and are about to use you to kill your parents. Remember them? Remember catching them today having sex, remember how angry it made you? They're too old for that sort of thing, embarrassing you like that. They should know better but no they didn't care about you catching them. Come on Suzie; tell me how that made you feel!" Her face changed slightly, a ghost of memory crossing her mind. Her eyes flickered as she looked at Varran, studying him with those black eyes.

"You have no idea," she said simply approaching him. "Do you know the power of the brain when you find the right people and augment them? Imagine, just one thought and you could do anything, command anyone. No one could stand against you and you had power absolute."

"A sniper's bullet would do the trick," Varran bit as she brushed against him, watching him carefully as if she was recording every reaction.

On hearing his reply, she sniggered arrogantly, her breath hot on his cheek, trailing across his exposed neck.

"You think?" She stood behind him. He heard her take a deep breath and sigh. "A thrush is chirping ten miles away as it drops a worm into its nest, the younglings squabbling over the meat. Nearby a wasp is bouncing against glass, confused because it doesn't know what glass is, why its world is blocked by this invisible barrier. Oh," she gasped, "it didn't see that newspaper coming; too bad, so sad." She rounded to his left side, mouth close to his ear. "A man is drowning off the coast, not his fault, he got a cramp and there's no one to hear his cries except me; pointless really, he's 150 miles away. Oh that's disgusting," she grimaced, "a woman is being violently ill on a plane except she's missed the bag and it's all over the seat in front and she still has 9 hours to go." She flicked her eyes skyward without moving her head. "Do you know how many germs people are breathing in from her sick? That's not healthy. All these things are in my head, I see them as plainly as my helpless parents and you think a bullet will stop us?"

"Us?" picked up Varran sharply.

"Well, I can't be the only one, can I? Stands to reason," she droned balefully.

"It's not natural, someone is controlling you and it can be for no good reason!" he shouted. "Where's big mouth Suzie, so all knowing, so sure the world owes her a favour, where is she?" She seemed to appear before him in a flash, her face curled with anger.

"I am here, better than before," she hissed venomously. "Now let's see, Daddy likes to bare all in the kitchen so let's see how he copes in the living room." With a flick of her head, she threw Jason in the air, every bit of clothing dissolving from his body, leaving him stark naked. He fell in a heap of helpless embarrassment before the others. Suzie grinned as she swung round and focused on Jacke. The dark skinned girl held her gaze defiantly refusing to show fear. Kneeling before her, Suzie regarded her with false compassion and gently stroked her face.

"My dear Jacke; my Good Samaritan. So eager to help; so full of good intentions. Yet it was all for nothing. I believe your heart is in the right place, I truly do but your true place is at our side so why don't I reach inside your mind and show you the way? The best birthday present we could ever have."

"Stay out of my mind!" Jacke warned. Suzie held up her hand, palm out and concentrated. The air shimmered and an implant formed against her skin. She smiled. Jacke's eyes widened fearfully a she realized what she was going to do.

"Amazing, aren't I?" she smirked. "I know how to implant this in your brain and I've never had a minute's training. But in a moment, you'll be just like me. Won't that be great? Two peas in a pod. They'll come for us soon and we'll be with the Family."

"Leave her!" Varran roared. Suzie lifted her fist and his knees buckled as he fell to the floor, catching Jason's pleading stare. Suzie snarled scornfully as she eyed the frozen group.

"You have no place here," she purred thoughtfully. Her gaze fell on Michael coldly. "You," she said smoothly, "dispose of the others, then yourself."

Fighting every step of the way, Michael's face twisted agonisingly as he stood and took step after reluctant step towards the kitchen, his face pleading Varran to help him. The door opened courteously for him.

He knew what he had to do, knew it was the only way but he screamed silently as he slid the steak knife from the wooden stand on the kitchen sideboard, holding it upward catching the light as he stiffly moved back to the living room.

Nodding approvingly, Suzie grinned. "A bit messy but a single cut should do it. Funny, mother was always so house-proud." She noticed Angela's terrified expression and it amused her. "Cut their throats then put it through your heart. Do Varran last; let him see what he has done." Fearful wonder flashed through his mind.

"What do you mean? What I have done?" He clicked suddenly. "You're not Suzie, she's still unconscious. You're using her to speak? Who are you? Take us alive and we may be able to work together. Or are you afraid of us beating you again like we did on Farron?" he goaded, hoping their encounter with the genetically engineered jellyfish monsters would peak their interest, giving them a chance.

Suzie stalled as did Michael. Her face shifted as confusion washed over her as she processed the information.

"You're very smart but I'm afraid not quite smart enough. Yes, Suzie is just the beginning, a new era but she's the tip of the iceberg as they say. But thanks to you, we have another to take us to the next step. Your friend will kill you all and the police will think he did it, case closed. Just another bizarre freak out murder lost to human rhyme and reason."

Eyes filling with tears, Michael held the knife tightly as he stepped towards the cowering Jason. He was face down on the wooden floor, his cheeks burning with fear and embarrassment. He could just see Michael's feet slowly coming closer. He closed his eyes fearfully, waiting for the blade to fall.

"Please, Suzie, fight back! Just like I told you!" he gasped but his daughter ignored him as she watched Varran in amusement.

"What's wrong Varran? Confused, not sure what's going on?" He glared at her angrily. How did they know him and to block his technology? His mind raced desperately, trying to figure a way out.

They couldn't move, could only wait for the blade to slice their throats. Michael determinedly raised the blade, his face a mask of sorrow and apology.

Jacke tried to move but couldn't, every fibre of her being straining to get away from Suzie. She caught Varran's helpless expression, a face drained of all hope.

Suddenly the world exploded in darkness as Suzie's fingers sliced bloodlessly into the back of her skull locking Jacke's scream in her throat.

There was a chiming.

What a strange thing to hear with someone's hands in your head, Jacke thought. I'm surprisingly calm, that's odd. It feels like sitting in a doctor's waiting room with no magazine to read.

Those chimes again.

Where was Suzie? Had she already put the implant into her brain?

There! There she was, just on the edge of her consciousness, hovering like an angel of death waiting for God to fall. But Jacke could feel uncertainty, someone pulling her away from the task in hand. She couldn't make it out but something was interfering with her operation.

Something flashed across her mind like pollen on a breeze. She couldn't believe what she saw in Suzie's mind.

Michael had frozen mere inches from a sweating Jason's bare neck. Suzie's face was contorted with anger as she stared in frustration at the living room door beyond which was the locked front door.

"Bloody Jehovah's witnesses!" she cursed, almost trembling with anticipation. Michael tried to yell out but his jaw just flapped uselessly. The door chime sounded again. "They never give up!"

Relieved, Varran's mind raced desperate for an escape plan. She whirled on her mother.

"Go to the door, tell them to go away and slam the door in their faces!" she barked. Suddenly composed and looking as if nothing was wrong, Angela stood up, smoothed down her clothes, ran her fingers through her hair and put on a sweet expression.

Suzie watched through the crack in the living room door as her mother did exactly what she had been ordered. Varran closed his eyes, concentrating on Jacke, urging her to break free. She jerked, feeling him in her thoughts as the front door slammed shut. Her eyes shot opened and she looked at him eyes wide and alive. It was as if she were drawing power from him.

"How are you…?"

"I'm using my mind to draw on Suzie's implant and project my thoughts to you," he thought. "She's distracted for the moment but we don't have long. Focus on the implant and nothing else, that's how they're controlling her, focus on its circuits, its innards and imagine it burning in a fire."

"But what will that do to Suzie?" she returned worriedly. "She's only a kid."

"I don't know, it's all we have." He groaned. "I just need a second to distract her."

Angela returned to the room and knelt by her husband smilingly. She glanced sideways at the knife near his throat and nodded reassuringly.

"This is turning out to be one hell of a birthday," mused Jason helplessly to himself. He would never see his kids again; they would be orphans, maybe the next victims of whoever had taken Suzie and done this to her.

He'd promised them a rabbit and now it would never happen. He'd never be able tell Angela he loved her or make love to her again. If they got out of this he'd kill them, somehow, someday.

"Back to business," crowed Suzie as she reached into Jacke's head again. The Irish girl focused on the implant seeing it twist and burn in flame, the metal twisting and charring as the flames grew into an inferno.

She gasped as she felt Suzie's fingers reach into her flesh and begin attaching the implant. She shivered as it felt like the device was alive, tiny tendrils reaching for her brain eagerly.

"What are you doing?" wondered Suzie as she felt her mind. She laughed. "That won't do any good," she chuckled. Ignoring her as much as possible, Jacke imagined the sun reaching up to ensnare the implant and sucking it into its fiery throes. She felt Suzie jerk with pain as searing pain gripped her head. Jacke pressed forward a hand of fire, grasping the implant and squeezing it into ash over and over again.

"No," gasped Suzie, "you aren't powerful enough. You will be like me. The Family demands it!"

"I have a family!" retorted Jacke, mentally punching the teenager's hands away from her. "And I would never do anything to hurt them. You will not destroy this family or any other! Let her go now!" Suzie hissed tormentedly as she writhed against Jacke's attack.

"The Family is all!" cried Suzie pressing the implant against the base of Jacke's brain, tiny spikes reaching out to sink into the flesh. Jacke roared in pain and the flames grew higher. She gasped as a symbol formed in the flame, leering over her, gnashing hatefully, eager to tear the flesh from her bones.

She screamed as the living room snapped back into focus. Suzie was shaking like she was having a fit, eyes wide, mouth locked in a grimace. The coldness in her eyes gave way to uncertainty as Michael pressed the knife to Jason's throat. Her head jerked back and she let out a pitiful gasp. Her eyes rolled in her head as she fell backwards into Varran's arms.

He held her in one arm, the other he was pressing a length of cable against the base of her neck. It was fizzing with power, minute tendrils of electrical power ripping through the exposed wires. Jacke fell sideways, exhausted, seeing the broken lamp on the floor.

Varran slumped back, gently cradling the unconscious girl as Michael dropped the knife and jumped back in disgust. He could not hide his resentment of Suzie even though he knew it was not her fault. Angela cried out in fear as she leapt to her daughter's side. Varran demanded a hand unit and scanned her head with it. He sighed with relief.

"The implant has dissolved, she's free. It must have a self-destruct built in." He grinned at the sweating Jacke. "Good job."

Pulling on his boxers, Jason took his daughter from the Xereban scientist and laid her on the sofa.

"I never thought I'd be glad to see Jehovahs," Tyran said lightly. She helped pull Jacke upright and sat her on the armchair. "You alright?" she asked. Nodding, Jacke looked for the implant but it was a charred lump on the wooden floor.

"We won't be able to find anything out from that," she said. Varran glanced down, looking disappointed. He pocketed it anyway. He looked down at the sleeping Suzie. Angela was stroking her forehead, stifling worried tears. He rested his hand on her shoulder, squatting beside them.

"She'll be fine now." With a smile he looked at the clock on the fireplace. "It's almost midnight," he smiled; "Happy birthday, Suzie."

It was 3 o'clock the next afternoon. It was another glorious day and Jason had opened up the patio to his guests. Varran and the others had returned to the Juggernaught and rested and changed before returning to the celebration.

Jacke's car had been teleported to the junk yard while she contacted her insurance company and now they were here back at Jason and Angela's house where hours before they had almost died.

Suzie was beaming with the vigour of youth and chatting with some of her friends. Jason smiled acknowledging the Time Warriors' arrival, raising a glass. Angela came forward and hugged them all, ushering them onto the patio for food and drinks. Jason poured his daughter out a glass of wine and handed it to her proudly.

"Now you don't have to go for a sneaky one in Julie's," he teased, making her blush.

"But Dad, you know I'm a good girl!" she declared in mock shock.

"Just don't make me a grandfather just yet," he pleaded. Suzie pulled a disgusted face.

"As if!"

"I want to introduce you to some people," he said, herding her over to Varran and the others.

Jacke wore a plain white summer dress, accentuating her dark skin. Michael couldn't help but notice, painfully aware of his slight bulge in his T shirt where his stomach was. Jacke could wear sack cloth and ashes and still look great, he decided. Tyran, in shorts and blue off the shoulder top, was raiding the food table with Angela as she poured them drinks.

"This is Varran, Michael and Jacke. Tyran's the one hoarding the vol-au-vents." Jason said. Varran beamed broadly as he handed Suzie a large box wrapped in silver shiny paper. He wished her a happy birthday. She thanked him and gave him a big hug.

Next was Jacke leaving Michael awkwardly hugless.

"Thank you," she said.

"Our pleasure," he replied simply. "How do you feel?"

"So my grandparents were aliens, how cool is that? It's like everything makes sense now." She looked at Varran strangely. "You look good for an old man."

"Told you, you should dye your hair," teased Michael.

"I'm not that old!" Varran protested, "relatively speaking."

Angela and Tyran joined them with a tray of food and beer. Gratefully taking one each, Jason looked over his shoulder, lowering his voice.

"The news put the trees down to a freak tornado, global warming," he whispered.

Jacke smugly looked at Tyran. "Told you." Tyran made a face back while Jason continued.

"No one heard or saw a thing at our house," he revealed. Sipping his beer, Varran shook his head slightly.

"The blind fist of suburbia, although the news said a minor earthquake caused the damage with the trees," he commented ruefully. "Probably for the best," he mused.

Angela set the tray down on the table, slipping her arm round her husband's waist.

"She remembers nothing about being controlled," she said. Glancing at the girl laughing with her friends, Varran took a small breath.

"That's definitely for the best. Birthdays are happy days, especially an eighteenth."

"Thanks to you all," Jason acknowledged. "If there is ever any way we can help you please tell us."

"Have you discovered anything at all about who did this?" Mournfully, Varran shook his head.

"There was very little left of the implants so we know as much as you. If this Family is trying to harness mental abilities, who knows how many they've implanted or where they are." His eyes glazed over as events played in his mind. Jacke took his arm. She had told him about the image of the wolf but believed it had been a manifestation of their combined fears.

"Or the other way to look at it is, Suzie could have been the first and since we beat them, maybe she'll be the last. We may have nipped this in the bud before it got too far," she reasoned.

"Maybe, maybe not," he answered. "But someone out there knows about us and our technology and they call themselves the Family. They know who I am, knew Suzie's heritage and can affect our teleport system. They engage in genetic experiments and they don't give a damn who gets hurt in the process. I doubt we've seen the last of them."

Angela grasped Jacke's hand gratefully.

"And thanks to you, we have our daughter back. Your abilities must be as great as hers." Blushing, Jacke gave a flick of her eyes.

"It was only with Varran's mind, we stopped her. Besides, Suzie's natural abilities were magnified tenfold by that implant."

Jason clapped him on the shoulder with a grin.

"And that's what we're here for, family, the only thing that matters. Come on, let's party." Jason gathered everyone together and proposed a toast. He looked at his family, their friends, his daughter and the Time Warriors, each bonded by the past and the future, each standing by each other in the face of adversity. Jason raised his glass.

"To family!"

The auburn haired woman stood gun in hand, legs astride as she stared down at the technician's body. The bloody hole in his forehead spoke volumes to the stunned crowd.

Her face was a mask of pure hatred.

Her dark eyes flickered round the group and she could see she had made her point.

The dead man had activated the implant early, in some misguided act to curry favour from her but it had exposed them to Varran. How she had enjoyed imagining the scientist trying to figure out who on Earth could possibly cut his lifeline to the Juggernaught off so efficiently. But now he knew the silent enemy had a face, knew someone was watching him.

And for that she had put a bullet in the technicians head. Mister Ling, her faithful servant, stood sentinel behind her, the rock she relied on these so many years. He was the epitome of loyalty and would be depended on to clean up this mess, once the message had sunk in to any other disillusioned employee. The plan had been put in jeopardy and she would not allow it to fail now, not after all this time. She would have to contact her allies and explain but first, time to ram the lesson home.

"Let that be a warning to all of you. I haven't waited all this time for someone to interfere." She paused, seething with anger. "Let me make it clear. The same will happen to anyone that steps over the mark. Varran is mine to deal with and mine alone!"

OWEN QUINN

TO BE CONTINUED IN
THE TIME WARRIORS BOOK 2

THE VOALOX HORROR

Made in the USA
Charleston, SC
30 July 2013